LOVE ON A SUMMER NIGHT

A PINE HARBOUR NOVEL

ZOE YORK

WWW.ZOEYORK.COM

Never say never. Especially not to a determined bad boy.

Zander Minelli is exactly the wrong kind of man. He's dark, dangerous, and knows far too much about sawed-off shotguns.

Faith Davidson finds him irresistible. The widowed single mother knows she should dip her toe back in the dating pool with someone solid and dependable. Definitely no tattoos. But every time she looks up, the brooding soldier is watching her, and she can't help but wonder what it would be like to let herself have a taste...

Small town summer nights have never been hotter—and one transplanted city-girl's heart has never been more fragile.

to the life-altering, deeply rewarding,
immensely challenging reality that is motherhood

For Kat Townsend, a reader and mother and military wife

— —

Kat's also living with a terminal diagnosis of metastatic breast
cancer, so let me take this opportunity to say a couple of things
that have nothing to do with the book you're about to read, but
important nonetheless:

My mother died in 2001, two years after her breast cancer
diagnosis. I'm now ten years younger than she was when she
was diagnosed. For all the advances we've made in treating early
breast cancer, I'm still terrified. So:

~ Never, ever ignore a lump or bump or rash or puckering or
new dimple in your breasts: any change in the skin or tissue
inside, go to the doctor
~ Learn about metastatic breast cancer, and how few research
dollars are spent on improving treatment for the women who are
living with the disease that will kill them

CHAPTER ONE

FAITH WOULD KILL to have a Japanese katana in her hands right now.

Or Barbie dolls that moved like real people and could wield a juice box straw like a sword.

Even a decent YouTube video that somehow magically gave her the vocabulary to describe the visceral feel of hefting a sword high above her head, ready for the kill.

But this was the side-effect of hiding away at the tip of an isolated peninsula, surrounded by glittering water and soaring pine trees and not much else. Research had to be done remotely—and when she got writer's block, figuring out the logistics of a specific action sequence was that much harder. It all felt mechanical, when she wanted to really *get* the visceral feel of the movements.

With a strangled cry, she shoved away from her desk and prowled around her office, looking for something that would provide the right weight in her hands so she could properly describe the curved sword being ripped from her heroine's grasp by a soul-sucking demon.

The imaginary lives she crafted were the only excitement she'd allowed herself in the four years since Greg had died, so she had to make them spectacular.

As she lifted a golf club—never used for actual golfing —and gave it a tentative downward slash, she heard the front door swing open.

"Mommy!" Eric called out, his voice full of breathless enthusiasm and the tell-tale edge of a sugar high.

"Up here," she hollered back, tucking the club away and leaning over her desk to save her book. She'd figure out the katana problem after his bedtime. "Did you have a good time—ooof!"

She twisted her body and looked down at her almost five-year-old son, now hanging on her right leg like a spider monkey. She ran her hand over his wavy dark-blond hair and as she had been for months now, silently mourned the loss of his paler, softer, straighter baby hair. It had happened one night when she wasn't looking, another vestige of toddlerhood falling away. He was small for his age, though, and sometimes it was hard for her to believe he was going back to school in a few short weeks for kindergarten.

"Got you." He gave her an angelic smile complete with a glint in his eye he'd inherited from his father. She loved that Eric looked so much like Greg, that she'd always have the best of her husband right in front of her. And he was so cute it almost excused the fact that he'd barged into her office—a no-go space for many reasons, including the fact that she often precariously balanced stacks of paper on all available surfaces, manuscript chunks so she could grab a chapter and read on the fly.

Plus the regular weapons testing that happened, even if it was just with makeshift stand-in props.

"You've got me good." She winked. "But you remember the rule…"

"Out?" He made a face.

"I'm coming with you. Work time is over for now. Tell me about the ferry ride."

He slid his hand into hers as they left her office overlooking the front garden and the harbour in the distance and headed down the stairs. From the kitchen, she heard pots clanging a little too loudly. She winced.

"Did I forget to take the chicken out of the freezer?" she asked gingerly as they stepped into the large sunny room at the back of the main floor. It overlooked a terraced back yard, shaded and sunny in all the right spots. This kitchen and the backyard were the reasons she'd bought the house. Their life was far from perfect, and she couldn't do anything about the jagged parts of their hearts that would never mend, but with her first big royalty check she'd been able to put a down payment on a gorgeous house on a safe street, and she'd never regretted the impulsive decision.

That it had a granny suite for her mother to live in and her mother happily cooked for them were nice bonuses.

Except Faith had forgotten to take out the chicken, so dinner would be something other than the plan stuck to the fridge.

Her mother really liked the meal plan.

They all coped differently with how their lives had gone sideways, and Faith tried to remember that Miriam needed order and routine.

Lists were king.

"It's fine," her mother sighed, clearly not believing herself. She kept chopping as she talked, efficient as always. "I can use tomorrow's steak that I started marinating last night."

"I'm sure whatever you make will be awesome," Faith said brightly. Her mother was ninety-nine percent awesome. The one percent that drifted toward melodrama when things like meal plans got flubbed...that was best ignored. And maybe fed some chocolate from the good-stuff stash after dinner.

"Did you get a lot of writing done?"

"Some." Faith opened the upper cupboards and got down three plates. In the last two years, they'd fallen into a comfortable routine, and forgetful-writer's syndrome aside, they were all as happy as they could be with their adopted roles.

Miriam was the nurturer. She cooked and tidied and listened proudly to Eric's endless stream of imagined stories.

Faith was the provider. She worked her ass off to put a roof over their heads—and keep it there. And, slowly but surely, she was putting the broken pieces of her soul mostly back together.

Eric was their inspiration. Only one when he lost his father and barely two when he lost his grandfather, he was their little man, and they'd do anything to protect him from the ravages of the world.

Together they were a small but mighty family, and Faith never wanted to take her mother or her son for granted. After setting the plates on the table, she went back to the counter and gave her mom a tight, bone-crushing hug from behind. They were the same height and size, and other than a bit of grey sprinkled in Miriam's hair and some adorable laugh lines and delicate crinkles at the corners of her eyes, they looked like two peas in a pod.

"I'm sorry about the chicken," she whispered.

"That's okay, dear," Miriam said, setting down her

chef's knife to pat Faith's arm. "I don't expect you to remember."

"No, I should have. I could've set a reminder on my computer or something."

Her mother shook her head. "You're just like your father. He'd disappear into his office for hours, working on one equation or another. I'd bring him tea at midnight and he'd look at me, surprised that the night had slipped by."

"Are you saying I'm the husband in this dynamic?" Faith scrunched up her face, but her mother just laughed.

"Exactly. One of these days we'll find you a nice wife and I can retire to the Caribbean."

"I don't need a wife," she grumbled. "I just take advantage of your generosity because I can. *One of these days* you'll grow a backbone and fly south like all of your friends. And I'll find a way to feed my son just fine." A pang stabbed through her chest at the thought of her mother leaving them, but Faith knew she couldn't selfishly cling forever.

"I know you will. You're not as hopeless as your father —you're not hopeless at all. You're strong and capable, it's just…" Miriam trailed off.

She didn't need to finish that thought. Faith knew that she was leaning too much on her mother. In the last few months, that had changed, bit by bit, though. She was working on sliding back into the world, building connections beyond blood, but it was challenging. "I can only do one thing at a time."

"Honey, you do more than you think. Give yourself credit."

She didn't want to. If she thought she had this all under control, then it would be time to address all that she *didn't* have a handle on. All that she'd cut out of her life four years earlier. "I'm happy with my life just the way it is now, Mom."

And any time she thought otherwise, she quashed the doubt like a bug. No room for loneliness or self-pity in a widow's life. There was too much at stake. She had to embrace what she had and make the best of it.

"I'm just saying, one of these days you're going to want to do something just for yourself. And you should do it."

"Stop. I don't need a social life." She sighed and rubbed her thumb against the lines forming between her eyebrows. "I *have* a social life. I have friends." Well, she had three best friends, all other writers who lived a plane ride away in different directions. And she had a number of solid acquaintances on the peninsula.

Okay, now she was sounding defensive, even in her own head.

"I wasn't talking about that, exactly, but since you brought it up…don't you want someone who will rub your shoulders and ask you how your writing went?"

Unbidden, the memory of firm hands and a rough, low voice rattled through her mind. The unsettling reminder that her life was missing a certain masculine presence wasn't easily pushed away, either.

She sighed.

Her mother lowered her voice. "I'm not saying reconnect with your inner wild child or anything."

Sometimes being the daughter of hippies was a challenge. Faith cleared her throat and gave Miriam a bland look. They never talked about how she used to be in front of Eric and they weren't about to start. Not that she tried to hide her personality, but she'd matured beyond that young woman who wanted the next thrill to be bigger and brighter than the one before.

"I'm just saying it's been a long time," her mother whispered. Eric was lost in a bin of Lego at the far end of the room, but his little ears still managed to hear everything. "Don't worry. One day soon, Mr. Tall, Dark, and Handsome is going to zoom into your life and you're not going to know what hit you."

"Oh no," Faith said quickly. "Stop. I don't need or want anyone to zoom anywhere. Right now, I just want your stir fry in my belly, a bedtime story with my kid, then I'm going to the bakery to get some extra words in for the night."

"Don't go crazy," Miriam mocked lovingly.

Faith snorted. There were barely a thousand people in their tiny little town at the tip of the Bruce Peninsula. Wilderness and water surrounded them on all sides, and other than a few restaurants that mostly catered to tourists getting on and off the ferry and the hoity-toity cottagers that briefly visited the area in the summer, there was absolutely no trouble to get into.

They didn't even have a Starbucks. The bakery on the edge of town was the only place that served coffee and had decent WiFi service, so she went there to write when she needed a change of pace.

Banana nut muffins were as crazy as Faith Davidson got these days.

And most of the time, that was just how she liked it.

— —

DUSK WAS FALLING as Zander Minelli rolled his Harley

off the last ferry of the day from Manitoulin Island to Tobermory.

Thirty minutes from home. Twenty if he didn't care about his best friend Dean or his brother Rafe, both local police officers, maybe giving him a ticket.

Even though this wasn't his official homecoming—he wouldn't retire from the army for another six months—it was the first time since transferring out West that he'd ridden his bike back for a visit. Since he'd be moving at the ass-end of winter with all his earthly possessions, riding out now and leaving the bike behind in his brother Tom's garage made the most sense.

It even checked off the cross-country bike ride from his *That Would Be Awesome* list.

So why did he feel so weary?

It was good to be home…he guessed. It wasn't *bad*.

Good to have some leads lined up for potential security clients.

In theory, his post-retirement plan was great.

In reality, something didn't feel quite right—something he couldn't get a firm grasp on. Maybe because forty was just around the corner.

He didn't want to be one of those guys who moaned about a milestone birthday or getting old. He was able-bodied, fit as fuck, and his smile still worked when he felt like making a female friend.

He had nothing to complain about.

Nothing to really celebrate, either.

He was definitely melancholy about leaving behind his career in the military. But re-upping for another contract didn't feel like the right call, either. At his age and rank, he'd be working a desk job anyway.

If he got out, he could do anything he wanted. The problem was, he still didn't know what exactly that was.

As he climbed out of the small town and headed down the two-lane highway toward Pine Harbour, the wind in his face and the familiar landscape all around him, he knew he was on the right track. Once he got settled here, the restless feeling would go away. Or he'd act on it and do something else.

The possibilities were endless, and maybe that was his issue. He'd been bound by orders for two decades.

Maybe he needed to focus on his other reasons for moving back to Pine Harbour. Family. The year before, Rafe had been shot in the line of duty. Thankfully he survived, and now had a baby on the way with his beautiful wife Olivia. Zander's only sister, Dani—the baby of the family—was set to get married in a month, on the last weekend of the summer. He'd fly home for that, because he'd only have a few days off.

He'd be home at Christmas as well.

He was going to spend a lot of time in Pine Harbour because of his family over the next few years, so why not set up a home base there?

If wanderlust struck, he could take off.

Not if. When.

It wasn't in his nature to stick to one place.

It wasn't even in his nature to set down roots. In all his time in the army, he'd never bought a house, always preferring to live in base housing or rent a room from another guy who could use the cash.

Maybe that was it. Just down the road lay a permanence he'd never let himself sink into before. Renting in Pine Harbour would be foolish, and there was no way in hell he'd live with his parents or mooch off one of his siblings.

He was a grown-ass man, and he'd buy a damn house, even if it killed him a little inside.

Ahead of him, a hatchback with a dizzying array of geek and feminist bumper stickers slowed and signalled a right turn into Greta's Bakery, the last bit of civilization before the road out of town faded to wilderness, provincial parks and remote cottages. Someone had a craving for something sweet, he thought idly.

Actually, pie didn't seem like such a bad idea for himself.

He ignored the small stab of guilt. His mother would have pie. And cookies. And squares and lasagna and salad and everything else he might ever want. He could already feel the smothering.

It's not like she'd ever know. And this might be the last opportunity to be alone with his thoughts for the next week. He needed to sort his shit out and put on his accept-able-for-public-consumption face before he hit his home town.

He parked his bike at the side of the gravel lot and set his helmet on the seat, then rubbed his hands through his hair as he slowly walked toward the glass-fronted build-ing. A warm yellow light spilled out, beckoning him inside. He'd only been here a few times--Greta was a friend of his mother's, but a competitor as well. Things were complicated in the restaurant game on the peninsula.

The hatchback he'd followed in had parked closer to the building, and as he approached, the driver's side door swung open. Zander watched with lazy appreciation as a curvy leg emerged first, followed by the rest of an attrac-tive woman with a swinging ponytail and a giant backpack. She wore a faded Star Wars t-shirt and jean shorts that hugged her hips in a way that made his mouth water. Her feet were shoved into flip flops, and her gaze was intently focused on the inside of the bakery.

He hung back, letting her go in first. If she noticed him, she didn't give any indication, but when she pulled the door open, she held it with her arm extended behind her until he grabbed it.

Which was both polite, and convenient, because it brought him to within a few feet of her.

Maybe it was time to put his smile to good use.

"Thank you," he said, but she didn't turn around. Polite, but not social. Okay, noted. Maybe the smile wouldn't get a chance to come out and play.

At the counter, she ordered a coffee and a cheese Danish, then darted to the corner booth right after paying, before her food was even set onto the self-serve counter. Zander ordered himself a coffee and a slice of apple pie, with ice cream, but his attention was only half on the cashier.

He watched, fascinated, as Ponytail Girl unpacked her bag. A small laptop. A giant textbook. A notepad, pen, highlighter, headphones. Bottle of water.

There was some serious plotting of world domination about to go down in the corner.

He should leave her to it. He would.

But then her order was filled and the cashier called out her name. *Faith.*

And as Faith looked over at him—well, not him, exactly, but her coffee and Danish, which were right next to his head—Zander felt like he'd been hit by lightning.

It was a complete cliché, and he didn't care.

She was gorgeous. *Pretty* wouldn't do her justice. It

wasn't an interesting enough descriptor, because her mouth was unusually full and her eyes extra piercing. She had a beauty mark to the right of her lips that made him wonder if it would disappear in a dimple if she smiled, and her wavy hair had strands slipping out of her ponytail all over the place, like she'd been busy all day and not noticed her hair-do slowly coming undone.

And she had a youthful glow to her that had nothing to do with her actual age, which he pegged in her thirties, maybe just a few years younger than himself. Whatever it was, it took his breath away.

"Here," he said, lifting his voice as soon as he could find it. He grabbed her cup and plate before she slid out of the booth. "I'll bring these over."

She just stared at him, a strange man with his hands all over her snack, and he tried his making friends smile again.

It didn't seem to work.

That was unfortunate, because he'd never wanted it to work more than in this moment.

"Don't worry," he said after crossing the small eatery section of the bakery and setting her order in front of her. "I grew up waiting on tables. I know better than to bother a customer clearly in the middle of work."

"Thank you." She flashed him a quick smile before her mouth twisted back into the concentrating pout from before.

"If you need anything else..." He took two slow steps backward, then glanced over his shoulder. His own order was up. "I'll be over there, eating apple pie."

Her lips quirked up, just a hair. It felt good to make her smile, but he didn't want to distract her, so he turned away.

"Hey, do you know anything about swords?" The sound of her voice behind him did weird, warm, funny things to his insides.

He glanced back at her. "I'm sorry?"

"You look..." she trailed off and waved her hands in the air. Something sparkly glinted in the middle of her face. She had a tiny nose piercing. He tried hard not to stare. "You know. Tough. Like you might know what it's like to have a sword ripped out of your hands."

He grinned and flexed his arms, his hands curling into fists. It might be an unconventional way to get a girl to talk to him, but as far as conversation openers went, one that pointed out he looked badass was pretty good—although he'd rather like to think he'd be the one knocking a blade from his opponent's hands. Of course, he couldn't say that. *Play it cool, man.* "Sure. Why do you ask?"

She gave him a wincing look that was halfway between *I-don't-want-to-tell-you* and *I-can't-explain-it-in-less-than-a-minute.* "Research?"

That was interestingly vague. He liked it. "I'll just grab my coffee, and then... can I sit?"

His chest tightened as she stared at him for a beat. Two beats. And when she nodded, a stuttering little jerk of her head that suggested maybe she was as surprised as he was, his heart jumped back to life, giving his ribs a fist bump of the likes he'd never felt before.

CHAPTER TWO

THE BIKER WAS...WELL, he was a biker, to start.

So that should also be the end of it. Except she couldn't stop looking at him and listening to him. He'd not only answered her question about the katana, but also given her a very patient lesson in sawed-off shotguns.

She was *fascinated*. And if he hadn't said he was just passing through, she'd have run screaming in the other direction, because this kind of bad boy wasn't allowed in her life now.

Not anymore.

Fifteen years ago, she'd have been the one to spot him, the one to wink and compliment his ride, his tattoos, or the dirty gleam in his eye, real or imagined. Her younger, more foolish self would have leapt at the first invitation to hop on the back of his bike and take off on an adventure.

Maybe she'd still be like that, if life hadn't made her a mother at thirty and a widow at thirty-one. The one-two punch of good fortune and tragedy sent her life into a tail-spin, and in the four years since, she'd made a set of rules for herself.

No risk-taking.

No adventure-seeking.

No men who…

The last rule was a bit nebulous. No men, basically, just to stay smart and safe. She'd barely dipped her toe into dating before yanking it back out again, not quite sure she wasn't looking for the exact wrong reasons. And over time, that proved true: she'd stopped yearning for physical connection.

But this guy made her wish that, if just for a night, she was looking for a sexy stranger.

He even had a sexy as sin name. *Zander*. That one corner of his mouth twisted a little higher as he said it, and his voice got a little huskier, like he knew his name alone was a turn on…

It was sexy enough a girl might just accidentally take off her panties.

Luckily there was zero risk of that happening. For one thing, Faith was wearing utilitarian day-before-the-period-might-arrive safety underwear. And for another, they were in the middle of Greta's Bakery, where nudity would surely be frowned upon.

She blamed the heat rioting through her body on her mother, for bringing up the idea of Mr. Tall, Dark and Handsome. Of course, Miriam wouldn't have meant a tattooed weapons expert.

And there was no blaming the way she was hanging on his every word, furiously scribbling notes about ammunition size and wound descriptions, on her mother or anyone else. This was Faith being a greedy girl, absolutely. She couldn't help herself. Zander knew everything she needed to know about weaponry and more. And he wasn't bad on the eyes, either.

Eyes, ears, brain…he was far too good for far too many of her body parts.

He's an expert. This is a research interview. And he kept talking, making the lie plausible.

"What kind of mess do you want the blast to make?" he asked, leaning back in the booth.

She snuck a hungry little look at the edge of a tattoo peeking out from the collar of his low-slung t-shirt before re-focusing on the scene, further in her book, where she needed to leave obvious evidence of a shotgun death. "What would happen if he was killed in the middle of the warehouse? Just a massive pile of blood?"

He rocked his jaw from left to right, thinking completely unsqueamishly about her poor character's guts being blown apart. It turned her on in an unhealthy way. "Better if it was near a wall; that might get a better spray pattern and contain the shell. In the middle of a warehouse it could go skittering anywhere."

"I can do that." She tapped her pencil against her forehead. "But they'd probably take the shell with them, right?"

"Yeah, if they were smart. But there's a lot of adrenaline pumping, and shit happens. Or maybe they pick it up and it leaves an outline. That's not going to be easily ID'd, but you can play with that a bit, right? Beauty of fiction?"

Beauty of something. She nodded like a freakin' bobble head and he grinned, all white teeth and deep laugh lines.

But most of the time as he talked he was dark and brooding, heavy eyebrows pulled tight as he described a dozen ways to kill a man. He paused from time to time, tilting his head a bit to the side as if asking, *are you sure you want to hear all of this?*

She did. She gobbled it up, because she'd been stuck for days, thinking she didn't quite get the mechanics of the fight scenes, when really, she hadn't sunk far enough into the mind of a killer.

Not that she thought this guy was a *killer*, exactly. But he certainly spoke with a certain legitimacy that made her wonder.

How twisted was it that she still wanted to pump him for information, regardless of where his knowledge came from? Because it was a heck of a lot better than watching YouTube videos on repeat, that was for sure.

"Hey, you want more coffee?" he suddenly asked, interrupting himself.

"Sure." She passed her cup across the table before she could talk herself into saying no.

He got up and stretched, his arms reaching practically to the ceiling. She tried and failed not to notice how his t-shirt rode up, revealing a tanned, muscular stretch of skin above the waistband of his jeans. Her gaze lingered on the narrow line of dark, curly hair that ran south from his flat belly button and disappeared behind his heavy leather belt.

So much for utilitarian underwear protecting her. She was pretty sure they'd just spontaneously combusted.

He might be a hardened criminal, she chastised herself as he grabbed their mugs and sauntered across the eatery. He leaned against the counter, crossing one leg behind the other as he smiled at the cashier, then waved at someone in the back.

Faith sat up a little straighter. She narrowed her eyes. He was laughing at something someone said.

A nervous tremor rippled through her belly.

He leaned back from the counter, his body twisting

fluidly. Why did he have to be so beautiful? And dangerous? And obviously, since he knew Greta, *not just passing through*.

Did it matter?

Part of her wanted to run screaming from the restaurant. She'd shown her hand, and he had to know she was interested—but it wasn't an interest she could follow up on. This only worked if he would disappear into the night, never to be seen from again.

Disappointment zinged through her gut, and that in turn lit a tiny spark of anxiety.

Because it wasn't in Faith's nature to want just a *little* taste of adventure. She wrote about epic battles between good and evil, about larger than life heroes and kick-ass heroines, for a reason.

Once upon a time, Faith had lived life to its absolute fullest.

So had Greg.

Neither of them ever imagined the price they would pay for that choice.

And here she was again, getting swept away in the imagined romance of a dark, brooding bad boy with an endless capacity to thrill her.

Faith didn't deserve thrills. More to the point, she had a responsibility to avoid them now.

But she couldn't bring herself to leave the booth.

Not just yet.

Soon, though…and with that thought, she pulled her gaze away from Zander just as he turned back toward her, coffees in hand.

Ignoring the way his broad shoulders bunched and rolled like a slow-motion Levis commercial—because he didn't just look like a biker, he looked like a movie star playing a biker, an extra-hot cliché of snug denim and leather-clad masculinity—she looked down at her notes. She hadn't written any new words tonight, but in the margins she'd sketched another scene. Where her heroine, Vera, duelled it out with a shotgun-carrying mystery man with two days of stubble covering his square jaw and black aviator sunglasses covering his hooded gaze.

Even with her little trio of question marks next to that note—because how could she know his gaze was hooded behind the sunglasses?—she still knew it would be wicked hot. When she got home, she'd write like the wind.

And then probably delete it all, because it was mostly fantasy fodder and not actually something that would further Vera's search for her missing father, which was the plot she'd outlined.

Sigh. Faith drew a sad face below the shorthand scene notes. Maybe she'd fit it in.

Now she just needed to find a way to say thank you and goodbye, and get the hell out of there.

"Tell me more about this urban fantasy stuff you write," he said as he set the coffees down, at the same time as she planted her hands on the table and took a deep breath. He paused, his lower lip caught between his teeth as he gave her the exact same hooded glare she imagined Deacon giving Vera.

Deacon? What the...? No. This guy wasn't inserting himself into her novel with a character name and everything.

"You're heading out?" he asked after a beat.

She nodded. "I should."

He didn't say anything else, just gave her a slow, understanding half-smile and took up a lot of space.

"Thank you for your help," she started, then stopped.

"My pleasure." God, his voice. Rough and low, but kind and interested and…sigh. She didn't want to stop listening to it.

She reached for her mug. She should at least drink the coffee since he'd gone to the effort of re-filling it.

And then she'd leave.

"Do you come here a lot?"

Her resolve to run away from him fell apart as she jerked her eyes up, meeting his gaze again. "Uh… yeah. A few times a week. For a change of pace. I usually write at home, but when I've been trying to do that all day and nothing is clicking, a change of scenery sometimes helps. Occasionally I'll even write outside…"

She was babbling. She bit her lip.

He laughed. The corners of his eyes tugged into very pleasing lines, and she blushed.

"Yes. The short answer is yes."

"I liked the long answer." He kept his attention on her as he lifted his own mug, taking a slow sip. "And this book that you're writing…you said it's in a series?"

She nodded, not trusting herself to not flood him with a TMI answer again.

He didn't let her off the hook that easily. "So this would be… book two?"

"Four." The look he gave her made her all warm and fuzzy inside. *Danger, danger, danger.* "And I had another trilogy before this series."

"Oh yeah?" He tapped his thumb on the table. "And your author name…"

Oh God. She swallowed, hard, and made herself cough.

"Is it a secret?"

She shook her head. It would be easier to tell him if it

was a secret pen name. "Faith Davidson. On the covers it just says F. Davidson, you know, for the cross-over appeal to male readers, but you can search for me by my name. Not that you should search for me. You shouldn't."

"I shouldn't?" Another tap of his thumb, another amused twist of his lips. "Okay."

"We should talk about something else." She was all off-kilter now.

"Like throwing stars?"

She breathed a sigh of relief. "Yes please."

— —

IN THE TIME it had taken Zander to get refills on their coffee, Faith had gone from interested to wary. Both under-statements, really. They'd both dove headfirst into the conversation, and when was the last time that had happened to him? But now she had a new, nervous look in her eye, and she'd pulled back.

But she wasn't sprinting out the door, so he supposed that was something.

"The thing to know about *shuriken* is that they're not killing weapons—at least not by design. You want your characters to use them when they're still in hiding, or as they storm in. Aim for exposed skin. Weaker opponents will be distracted by the sting of a surface wound."

"And stronger opponents?" She double-blinked at him, her hand furiously writing again.

Zander bit back the urge to show off and tell her about his own hand-to-hand combat experience. But real life

wasn't like a novel, and he wasn't much of a hero. He was
just a guy who did a job. He did it well, but it would be
wrong to use that to make those stars in her eyes any
bigger. Not when she didn't want them there, either. "You
learn to ignore it. The guys who don't stop coming at her
—those are the ones she'll have the sword fight with."

In his pocket, his phone vibrated. Probably his brother,
wondering where the hell he was, since he'd messaged
more than an hour ago that he was getting off the ferry,
and it was only a thirty minute drive to Pine Harbour.

It was time for him to go. Not because of his family, but
because he wanted to see Faith again, and he didn't want
to overstay his welcome—she was skittish and he didn't
want to spook her. He pulled his wallet out of his back
pocket and thumbed through it, looking for the business
card he'd stuck in there a year earlier. He never had any
use for them, so he only carried the one and...

Shit. He was nervous to give it to her. The idea she
might not want to meet up again bothered him. Or even
just stay in touch.

"Listen," he said, finally sliding his card across the table.
"I'm not exactly local, but I'll be in the area for the rest of
the week. If you need any other questions answered."

He wanted her to take it from his hand. Wanted her
fingers to slide against his. Instead, she just looked at the
card as he slowly drew back across the centre line of the
table. Then up at his face.

Then back at the card.

She was killing him.

"All right, humour me," he said gruffly. "This might be
the most interesting conversation I've ever had."

"Says the guy who seems to have firsthand knowledge

of a disturbing array of weaponry." She curved one eyebrow high on her forehead, doubt written all over her face, and he laughed as he pointed at the card. She picked it up, upside down at first, but once she turned it the right side up her mouth fell open. "Oh."

"Did you think I was a hired gun or something?"

Her cheeks turned pink again. He found that rush of nerves adorable every time. "Um...maybe."

"Sorry to disappoint."

She laughed at that, a slow, rolling sound that wormed straight into his chest. Sighing, she read the rest of the card between glances across the table, each one more relaxed than the last. "Canadian Forces Base Wainwright. So you live in Alberta?"

For the next six months. "Yep."

"But you know Greta."

Why did he feel like he'd just been busted in a lie? His pulse thumped heavy in his neck. "Yes."

She nodded slowly, then tucked his card into a paper pocket on the inside cover of her notebook. "I really do need to go."

Had he just made it worse? Honesty was the best policy, but damn, he wish he hadn't talked to Greta up at the counter. He wanted every chance he could grab to get to know Faith better, and he had the sneaking suspicion there were already a lot of barriers to that. Him being local apparently one of them. "Same. It's been a long day of riding."

She glanced out the window at his bike. "So you're not the president of a motorcycle club, eh? I guess this means I can't cross off *coffee with an assassin* from my bucket list, then."

The unexpected tease made him laugh. "I'm going to take that as a compliment."

"You should." She gave him a slow, warm look that made his breath catch in his throat, then they shared a nervous laugh as neither moved. Nervous wasn't quite the right word, though, because the feeling wasn't bad. Skittish, yes. Possibly fleeting—there was a solid chance he'd never see her again.

He'd hate that, but sometimes life dealt bum hands. If all he had was one night of coffee and conversation with Faith, he'd be grateful for it.

She finally looked away and slowly started packing up her bag.

"Thank you," she said, glancing at him through lowered eyelashes. "For your help tonight."

"My pleasure." He meant it. He'd never wanted a conversation to continue quite as strongly in his entire life. "Good luck with your writing."

He stood first, but waited for her to slide out and hook her backpack over her shoulder. He wanted to press his hand to the small of her back, but what would that touch look like to the curious observers behind them? If she came here often, they'd know her. They definitely knew him. The black sheep of the Minelli family in some ways. The one who ran away, who didn't love living on the peninsula.

Walking next to her was a reasonable compromise, and when they got to the door, he reached past her to open it. At her car, he shoved his hands in his pockets to keep from touching her. By the time she pulled out of the lot, his knuckles were stiff and white, and he needed to flex his hands to get the blood flowing again.

He walked slowly to his bike, and even after he pulled

out his phone to text his family and reassure them he hadn't hit a wild animal and skidded off the road or something, he just stood there.

Meeting a pretty woman—an interesting, smart, funny woman—had never felt like this before. He was a little dazed.

And he was pretty sure he was in a lot of trouble.

Ponytail Girl had him all a-flutter.

It didn't feel half bad.

CHAPTER THREE

THE NEXT MORNING, Zander stared at his baby sister across her breakfast bar and shook his head. "What part of *I came to your house to hide from people* don't you understand?"

Dani stared right back, completely unaffected by his bluster. "You don't mean people, you mean Mom. And if you hadn't taken two hours to drive from Tobermory to home last night, she wouldn't be all up in your grill like that."

He just blinked at her.

"I can't pull that off, can I?"

"No. Leave the cool lingo to the kids and accept that you're an old lady now." He sighed. "Why can't I stay here while you go to this barbeque?"

"Because Hope Creswell could be a good customer for your new business."

"I already have client interviews lined up this week, and I'm not even opening shop for another six months. I don't need new customers."

"Of course you do. And *good* ones. You have the farm

implement store and a bunch of Jake's reno customers. Hope is a *celebrity*. She knows people who need bodyguards."

"I'm not going to be a bodyguard. I'm starting a security firm to do something a bit better —"

"Than the basic install and monitoring package offered by the national chains. Blah blah blah. That sounds boring. You know what sounds fun? Being a bodyguard to a movie star. Also sounds like it might pay better and let you travel to more interesting places than the other side of Highway 6."

He got off the bar stool and peered toward the stove. "Are you making me an omelette or lecturing me on my career choices?"

"Both?" She shrieked as he rounded the kitchen island. Grabbing her spatula, she waved it in his direction. "I'm warning you…"

He laughed. It was good to be home, especially hanging out with Dani like this. She'd been a kid when he left, and to see her as a grown woman, in her own home… even if she was a nosy Parker, he didn't care.

Grabbing another spatula from the crock on the counter, he just shrugged. "I'll finish it myself, then. Pass me the cheese."

She narrowed her eyes at him. "Don't change the subject. You should come with us to the party."

"You should get me some cheddar," he said blandly, not rising to the challenge. "And I'll think about it."

"Think about what?" Dani's fiancé, Jake Foster, wandered in and poured himself a cup of coffee before offering Zander his hand. "Hey, man."

They shook while Dani filled Jake in on her crazy plans

to introduce Zander to the new local celebrity. Jake just shrugged at him, like, "what are you going to do?"

Whipped. The man was whipped.

"I'm just going to eat this without cheese," Zander muttered, edging the spatula under the almost-done eggs.

"Oh, shut up and stop whining about cheese when I'm just trying to help you," Dani snapped, tossing the block of cheddar at his head with enough force to be concerning.

"Okay…thank you for your loving and gentle support?"

She stuck her tongue out at him.

He turned his attention back to Jake. "Are you seriously marrying this brat?"

Jake just grinned.

So whipped.

Zander turned back to making himself breakfast.

— —

NO BIGGIE, Faith told herself. She was just going to hang out with one of Hollywood's most talented actresses. Hope Creswell was the peninsula's newest resident, because she'd fallen in love with a local man, Ryan Howard, and his three young children.

Ryan's family had been through an awful, traumatic year, and it felt like a miracle they'd found someone like Hope—who was known by her real name, Holly, to Ryan and the kids, because that's how she'd first met them. When she'd arrived early to film a movie, Ryan had mistaken her for an intern, and she'd let him carry on with that assumption. She'd given him her real name instead of her stage name, although Faith still thought of her as Hope.

Faith didn't know much more of the story than that. She was friendly with Ryan, who she'd met through her bereavement group, but as her mother had pointed out, she hadn't gone out of her way to forge real friendships in the last four years.

Maybe she'd change that soon. That's one of the reasons she'd torn herself away from the computer to come to this party, after all.

She took one last look at the driveway, lined with pickup trucks. Ryan had told her that Hope wanted to have his friends over for a casual barbeque, and it seemed like they'd all turned out. So, there you go. Lots of friend potential.

She was such a dork to be worried. She'd already met Hope once, had fangirled hard, and they'd still invited her.

Maybe it was the weird week getting to her. The stress of a deadline approaching, and she'd stayed up late the night before writing. Woken up early to do more of the same, too. It was a minor miracle she'd gotten showered and dressed and made her way to Pine Harbour on time.

But she hadn't had time to talk herself through being *normal*.

She wasn't prepared for this, and kind of wanted to go back home and keep writing about Zander.

You mean Deacon.

She shook her head. Really, she meant neither of them, but that wasn't what kept spilling out of her fingers.

So she'd made a deal with herself. She'd indulge the flight of fancy inspired by the stranger at Greta's Bakery, and then get back to the actual work of writing her series. The one that paid the bills and made her fans happy.

The front door of the house swung open, and Ryan almost stepped into her before he realized she was standing there.

"Faith!" He gave her a surprised smile. "Did you knock? We didn't hear it."

She shook her head. "Not yet."

"Everything okay?"

"Would you believe I was composing myself?"

He laughed. "Yes. Will it make you feel better if I tell you that Holly was stressed out about messing up the taco dip?"

"No!" Faith laughed.

"Come on in, I'll introduce you to everyone." He glanced around. "You didn't bring Eric?"

Their kids had met twice at play dates over the summer, and Eric liked Maya and her brothers well enough. But when she'd asked her son if he'd wanted to come to the barbeque—where lots of people would be—he'd given her an alarmed look and insisted he had a Lego fortress to finish instead. The apple didn't fall far from the tree with that one. "Not tonight," she said without elaborating.

"Ah, okay." He stepped back, swinging the door wider so she could join him in the spacious, modern foyer.

Technically a cottage, the year-round house was more than big enough for Ryan and his kids to move in with Hope, but Faith knew they hadn't officially made that step yet—their relationship was still new and Ryan, a widower who'd met Faith through the bereavement group she coordinated, was very protective of his children.

All in good time, he'd said. But the way that he and

Hope loved each other, fiercely and just as protectively as they did the kids, she figured it would be sooner than later that they'd make their new family dynamic official.

Not for the first time, Faith reflected on the curious fact that she could see and support a new relationship as being best for Ryan, but not be ready for it yet herself.

She heard it every day from her mother, as well. She wasn't sure what was holding her back, but she'd learned early in the days after Greg's death to trust her gut, and right now, her instincts were telling her to wait.

Wait for the right guy, because life was too fragile to take risks.

"You remember Faith, sweetheart?" Ryan lifted his arm and his beautiful girlfriend folded herself into his side.

"Hi Faith," Hope said with a twinkling grin. "Did Ryan tell you I bought one of your books?"

"No!" She didn't care if her squeal was weird or high-pitched. "Wow, thank you!"

Hope winked. "I think you should brace yourself for this fangirling to becoming a mutual thing. It was awesome. I've packed the next two in the series for my next trip. I'm trying to pace myself, because I know it'll be a while until book four comes out."

Faith blushed. "I'm working on that right now, actually."

Hope pressed her lips together in delight. "Seriously, I love Vera. She's so kickass."

They talked for another minute about Faith's series, then their conversation turned to another popular urban fantasy series that they both had read, and how Faith's series was similar (and different) to it.

Ryan waited until they were done, then gave them a bemused look. "Can I continue the introductions?"

"Yes, of course." Hope lifted her hands. "Faith can come back another day when we don't need to be social. Right?"

Was the Pope Catholic? Or Edward a vampire? Heck yeah, Faith would come back.

"Everyone else here is either Foster or a Minelli, and then there's Dani, who's going to be both in another month or so. She was my partner when I was a paramedic, and all of her brothers and the Foster guys have been..." Ryan shrugged. "They're like a second family to me. There's Rafe and Olivia, Jake and Dani..."

Faith was nodding, and trying to remember names as people around the room waved at her, but something that Ryan said was niggling at the back of her mind.

Then they turned toward the staircase and her gaze collided with a newly familiar set of dark eyes looking at her over the rim of a beer bottle. Zander tipped the bottle up an inch in a private greeting, his eyebrows lifting just enough to tell her he was surprised to see her here, too.

Deep inside her belly, her lady parts started doing a burlesque dance.

Her brain, though, had a completely different reaction. That niggle in her mind turned into unexpected panic.

This is why you've got a no men rule, she told herself. Because the second you let yourself have a safe, secret night of flirting, Mr. Tall, Dark, and Handsome turns out to be the complete opposite of a stranger, just driving through.

Which she'd realized the night before, but not to this extent.

Zander Minelli wasn't just visiting family in Pine Harbour. Her brain whirred through the connections. She knew of the Fosters, everyone did. You couldn't drive through a local festival without seeing something sponsored by Foster Construction.

The dark eyes burning a hole through the space between them belonged to a man deeply connected to her safe space—this peninsula where she'd built a sphere of solitude around herself and her son.

Not under any circumstances could her lady parts dictate what happened with him. No, her brain was in charge, and her brain wasn't interested.

Much.

Except for all the ways he fascinated her, of course.

Sigh. This would require a double-dose of serious denial.

"...and this is Tom Minelli," Ryan continued. Faith didn't blink until her view of Zander was obstructed by someone else. A man.

"Tom," she repeated, smiling belatedly when she realized she was acting like a space cadet. "Nice to meet you."

"Likewise," the handsome, younger, less-tattooed version of Zander said. He pointed to the large, open kitchen. "Can I get you a drink?"

"Sure," she murmured, still hopelessly distracted by his brother's gaze. "Coke or water would be great. I'm driving, and not staying too long."

Tom stepped a hair closer. Not too close. But...flirting close. "That's a shame," he said, and when she blinked and really looked at him, his eyes were warm and dancing. "I'll be right back with something cold for you."

As Tom shifted out of the way, Ryan finally started the introduction she'd been bracing herself for the last ninety seconds. "And visiting from out west, our returning soldier. Zander, this is Faith Davidson."

He stood, stretching himself to his full height and

impressive breadth. He didn't say anything at first, just looked at her. His eyelids slid to half-mast, covering his glittering dark eyes but she could still feel the full weight of his appraisal. Then he slowly hitched his shoulders and reached out, offering her his right hand.

"Nice to meet you, Faith."

Her breath caught in her throat as she slid her fingers against his, hyper-aware of every muscle in his hand as their palms lined up and his grip closed around hers.

These were hands that could strip a rifle in the dark and dig endless trenches. Probably climb tall buildings, too. And still he held her fingers with gentle ease.

The lines on his face deepened as he smiled slightly, and as her breath rushed out of her body, she realized he'd let go of her hand.

She missed the feel of his skin—rough in places and warm all over.

No, shrieked her brain.

Wow, said everything else.

"Shit," Faith muttered under her breath before catching herself. Zander laughed quietly as she pursed her lips and narrowed her eyes up at him. "Soldier you say? Interesting. Nice to meet you, too."

"Interesting. I'm going to take that as a compliment." His voice had a very distracting rub of amusement to it and she ducked her head to hide a blush.

"Here's a Coke," Tom said at her elbow, appearing out of nowhere. Zander reached out and took the glass from his brother and handed it to Faith.

She couldn't hold back a laugh.

Really?

Tom apparently had the same question, but he said it out loud.

Making a murmured excuse as her heart skipped trai-
torously, she left the siblings to their stare-down and
escaped to the kitchen. She found the previously
mentioned taco dip—delicious—and soon fell into a
conversation between Jake Foster and one of his brothers
about some of the renovations Holly wanted done on the
place.

The whole time, she felt Zander's gaze on her. Warmth
wrapped around her and her cheeks stayed permanently
flushed as she moved through the party.

What had she fallen into?

And how long until the tall, dark, handsome not-so-
much-a-stranger left the peninsula and life returned to
normal?

After making a round of the room, surprised at how
many people recognized her, she found herself standing
with Hope again. They were talking to Olivia Minelli,
who'd recently started working with the movie star as her
assistant. Listening to them talk about work was fascinating and not that different from her own writing world,
although on a very different scale.

A soccer balled zinged out of nowhere and bounced off
Hope's leg. She grabbed it and gave Gavin, Ryan's middle
kid, a gently scolding look.

"Sorry Holly," he said, and she pulled him in for a
quick hug.

It was a sweet moment that made Faith's chest ache.

"Come on, outside with this," Hope said, guiding him
to the back door.

Olivia snorted as soon as her boss was out of hearing
range. "No way will I be that chill about a ball inside the
house."

"I've got a little boy," Faith said, shrugging her shoulders. "Sometimes you lose your mind. Sometimes it's not a big deal."

"How old is he?"

"He'll be five in October." Faith glanced at Olivia's obviously pregnant belly, rounding out the middle of a ruched maternity shirt. But you still didn't ask *that* question. "Do you have kids?"

Olivia patted her bump. "First one. A girl, due in November."

They talked more about pregnancy and midwives, sleep and sciatica pain and cravings, but Faith's attention kept drifting out the window to watch Hope, who'd joined Ryan and the kids in a game of pick-up soccer.

"They're so happy, eh?"

Olivia sighed. "Disgustingly so. It feels like she's been here forever, not just a couple months. But she's so good for all of them."

"And you like working for Hope—I mean, Holly?"

"I call her Hope, too, it's okay. I think it's easier for her, you know? To be Hope all the time with most people."

Faith suddenly felt awkward. She'd been a fan of Hope's for years online, and had participated in many conversations about the private star. Theories about her personal life, etcetera. Nothing like seeing the celebrity play soccer with her boyfriend's children to be reminded that her private life was just that—private, and her own. "It makes sense," she said so quietly it was probably a whisper. "They're her safe harbour. The rest of the world always requires her to be *on*, right?"

"Yeah." Olivia caught her gaze and smiled. "Do you have anything like that as an author?"

Faith shook her head. "Not really. The only expectation

my fans have from me is that I don't kill their favourite characters."

Olivia giggled. "Which is fine if you don't have homicidal tendencies."

"Right?" Faith sighed dramatically. "The challenge is real."

As they dissolved into laughter, Faith felt Zander's gaze turn toward her again, like her laugh had grabbed him from across the room. She took a deep breath and steadied herself. She needed some air.

"Will you excuse me?" She smiled at Olivia. "I'm going to check out the soccer game."

"Of course." The other woman gave her a look. It said, *brace yourself*. "We should do this again. Without people around."

"That's what Hope said."

"She's smart."

"I'm on deadline right now, but as soon as this book is done, I'm all over a tea party."

"Awesome." Olivia winked at her as Faith moved toward the back door.

On the deck, she found Ryan refilling the coolers with bags of ice. "Having fun?" he called to her.

"Actually, yes."

He laughed. "Don't sound so surprised."

"Ahhh." She waved her hand. "It's just that I'm in writing mode right now, so conversation is a challenge. I'm always drifting away. I'm going to head home soon, but I wanted to thank you for the invite. It was great to meet some of your friends."

"You and Eric are welcome any time. Either here or at my place. He could play road hockey with my boys and we could talk."

She snorted. She didn't know what was funnier—the idea of her serious little boy playing road hockey or Ryan willingly talking about anything.

"Talk about you, I mean," he added, reading her mind.

"Oh. Me." She wrapped her arms around her middle and looked out over the lovely, long expanse of lawn behind the house. "This is a great place."

"Smooth change of subject," he said wryly.

"Sorry, I left my social savvy at home, clearly." She sighed. "Go play soccer. Maybe I just need some fresh air."

"I think you're savvier than you give yourself credit for." He patted her on the shoulder and jogged down the stairs from the deck to the grass, catching up to his kids and his girlfriend.

She couldn't even really blame her current mood on writing, which did make her a bit absent-minded, maybe.

Crazy-sexy soldiers who looked like sin and rode motorcycles without a care in the world...they messed her up. Big time.

Especially when one in particular was under her skin and all around her—literally.

Zander's boot steps on the deck behind her were the first clue she wasn't alone.

The butterflies taking flight in her stomach were the second.

She turned to look at him and smiled, which she told herself was being polite but she really knew was because she couldn't help herself. "Hi."

"Fancy meeting you here."

"Yeah. The peninsula is a small world sometimes."

"I've forgotten that over the years."

"How long have you been gone?"

"Almost twenty years. I come back a fair bit to visit, but it's not the same."

She nodded.

"How about you? I don't remember you growing up, but you might be younger than me."

Ha. "Might be."

He winked. "I'm not asking."

"I'm thirty-five. But no, I'm not from around here. I grew up outside of Toronto. Moved here seven years ago for the outdoor lifestyle and never looked back."

"It's been a while since I've gone hiking around here. Maybe you could show me your favourite trail?"

She resisted a glance to his mid-section, where her suddenly hormone-addled brain remembered a glimpse of a trail of dark curls that led right from his navel to his belt, and below.

What was wrong with her?

This needed to stop. Dragging a deep, shaky breath into her lungs, she held it for a minute before exhaling and crossing her arms. "You seem like a great guy, Zander."

He laughed and rubbed his jaw and up onto his cheek, then stopped and looked at her over his hand. "Huh."

"What?"

"I'd always wondered what the nice-guy brush-off felt like."

"I'm not…" No, that's exactly what she was doing. She blushed. "Well, you do seem like a great guy."

"But you're not interested in grabbing a coffee or something."

"I like coffee. It's the *or something* I can't do. And even if I could, I don't think I can handle what that would entail with someone like you."

A faint muscle twitched in his cheek and his eyes

widened just a touch. Just enough to tell her he wanted to say something—that he had a snappy comeback and was fighting back the urge to let it fly.

Deep inside, a part of her moaned at the loss of whatever dirty/funny/snappy thing was on the tip of his tongue. She kicked that fickle woman in the shins and crossed her arms. "I'm just one of those annoying people who has standards."

This time he couldn't fight the eyebrow lift. Maybe he didn't even try. "Standards? And I don't meet them?"

Shit, shit, sugar tits. "That didn't come out the right way."

He grinned. "No, I don't think so."

"Why aren't you offended?"

"Oldest of four, nineteen years in the infantry. Being told I'm not good enough yet is par for the course."

"Yet? I didn't say yet."

His grin just got wider. "Sure."

"And I didn't say you weren't good enough. I said I have standards. Maybe you've never gotten the nice-guy brush-off because you're not a nice guy." She narrowed her eyes to deliver the next line, but her words didn't carry much heat and they both knew it. "I've heard they take no for an answer."

"Are you telling me no, Faith?"

Her chest tightened. Sure she was. Definitely. She'd just open her mouth and that simple, single syllable would spill right out. "I'm telling you my life is complicated."

"That's not no."

She couldn't do this. She shook her head and took a step back. "I should get back inside. And then home."

Understanding flickered in his dark eyes and he rocked back on his heels, his lower lip pulling tight between his teeth as he nodded at her. "You've got someone waiting for you there?"

It wasn't right to let him think that, but the truth was, she did. Her little man might be a hundred and fifty pounds lighter than Zander and three feet shorter, but he still owned her entire heart.

What about the rest of you? She shoved that question out of her mind. The rest of her didn't need what Zander was offering, either.

"I do." She gave him a regretful smile. "I'm sorry."

"That makes two of us," he said gruffly. If he was upset with her, she'd understand, but he just gave her a look that was way more complicated than single injured pride. "See you around, Faith."

— —

ZANDER WATCHED as Faith ducked back into the house, then grabbed another beer for himself and one for his host from the cooler and wandered out across the back lawn to where Ryan was playing soccer with his kids.

He hadn't seen Faith's admission coming. She didn't wear a wedding band, although that didn't mean anything. But the night before she'd definitely been interested. Not in a hook-up kind of way—he wasn't deluded enough to think she'd be game for something like that—but in a simpler way.

He'd recognized in her the same loneliness he felt inside. No way did she have someone treating her right.

It wasn't his problem, but fuck, he wanted it to be.

"Hey man," Ryan gave him a fist bump as he handed over the bottle. "Did I see you talking to Faith there?"

"Yeah." Zander took a long pull of beer.

Ryan frowned and looked down at the ground. "Look, I'm the last person to give relationship advice, because I never want any myself, but...tread gently."

"It's okay. She already told me she's off-limits."

"I wouldn't say that. But hey, maybe I misread her interest in you."

"You didn't misread anything. We met last night...it's a long story. How else would you say it if she's not off-limits?"

"Faith?" Ryan gave him a long, hard look. "She's got standards."

Jesus, was he wearing a *Loser* sign? "Yeah, she mentioned that. I'm more interested in the fact that whoever she's got at home isn't doing right by her, because she's a gorgeous, fascinating woman who seems far too lonely."

"Got at home?" Ryan squinted at the house. "Did she say that?"

"Yeah."

"The only guy she's got at home is in kindergarten. Faith and I met through a bereaved parents group. She's a widow, and to the best of my knowledge, she hasn't started dating again."

Shit.

He replayed their conversation in his head as they kicked the ball back and forth with Ryan's kids. He'd given her the excuse that she knew would end the conversation.

He needed to back off. She wasn't interested.

No, she wasn't ready. She was definitely interested—she just wasn't happy about it.

He didn't know what to do about that. Chasing her out to her car wasn't the answer. But he had a week, and aside from work and a few family dinners, nothing else to do.

At some point, he'd find a way to see Faith again, and they'd try that conversation again.

CHAPTER FOUR

ZANDER DIDN'T WANT to admit that his sister was right, but after meeting with Fred at the farm equipment store and some of Jake's contractor clients over the weekend, he was decidedly pessimistic about the prospects of a full-time, full-service security firm surviving in Pine Harbour.

The only immediate answer was to drown his sorrows in a cheeseburger. He headed for the diner on the edge of town.

Mac's was humming with activity, and every booth had at least one person in it. Zander headed for a stool at the counter when he heard his name.

Dean Foster waved from where he sat alone in a booth along the window. When Zander slid onto the opposite bench, Dean shoved the menu across the table. "Good timing. I was just about to order."

Zander didn't need a menu, but he took the world's quickest look before setting it down; the waitress wouldn't come over until he did, and his stomach was growling. To distract himself, he started stacking the little creamers and sugar packets.

"You sure you don't want to go into the house building business with Jake?" Dean finally said, laughing as he pointed at the house Zander had built out of plastic and paper.

"Dani's already got opinions about the business I want to start on my own, can you imagine how bossy she'd get if I went to work for her fiancé?"

"What kind of opinions?"

Zander shrugged. Good ones, apparently. "She thinks there isn't enough security business around here." He cracked his jaw. "Unfortunately, I'm realizing she's not wrong."

"We've talked about this before." Dean was a cop, and familiar with the needy, high-maintenance wealthy cottagers who showed up every summer and called 911 every time a raccoon busted into their attics. "It's gonna be a leap of faith, but once you're here next summer, customers will come out of the woodwork. Besides, I thought you didn't want something full-time?"

"I don't." A vein started to throb in his forehead. "Maybe. I don't know. I'm not old enough to retire, man."

Dean laughed. "Buy yourself a boat and call yourself a fisherman. And shut the fuck up about retiring, okay? I'm still looking at another fifteen years."

Where Zander had joined the army right out of high school, Dean had gone to university, getting two degrees before joining the provincial police force. "Could've gone reg force with me."

Dean snorted. He'd thought about it. Zander could still hear the lap of water against the dock as they sat there in their last year of high school, talking about joining up. But Dean's father had been an officer, and officer's kids didn't enlist. They went to university and became officers. Or went to university and pretended they'd become officers long enough grow a pair of balls and do whatever they wanted.

"How's work going, anyway? Law and order being maintained?"

Dean shrugged. Yeah, Zander knew the feeling. He had six more months of shrugging to do. He couldn't imagine another fifteen years. His friend leaned forward and put his elbows on the table. "It feels like there's more and more politics every year, you know?"

"Yep."

They paused their conversation long enough for the waitress to bring them both coffee and for them to order lunch, then Zander changed the subject. "How's the social life? Still seeing that doctor?"

Dean shook his head. "Nah. It was good while it was good, but then it wasn't. For the best that it ended."

Zander recognized the look on Dean's face—relief that the break-up hadn't been ugly, and maybe some disappointment that the casual relationship hadn't continued with ease. But none of the angst that their brothers Jake and Rafe had felt over not having a better half. Even Tom and Matt and Sean made noises about getting married and having kids someday. Dean and Zander, on the other hand, were both bachelors. For life, Zander would have said a week ago. He'd never thought about settling down. Guys in the forces did it, but he thought they were crazy.

One fascinating night and one frustrating afternoon with a single mother later, and the word bachelor left a sour note in his mouth.

Faith's serious face popped into his mind for the umpteenth time. He'd fallen asleep thinking about her and her kid. Getting involved with a single mother was a terrible idea in general—one who'd been widowed and hauled herself back from that, built herself a career—because he'd looked her up, and holy shit, was F. Davidson doing well—and a new life...that wasn't someone a dedicated bachelor should mess with.

His gut tightened, and he shook his head. He was hungry and needed that cheeseburger. Nothing else.

"How about you?" Dean asked over the rim of his coffee mug. "Leaving anyone behind out West?"

Zander shook his head. "Nope."

"I hear you chatted up a friend of Ryan's yesterday at the barbeque."

Fucking small towns. "Who told you that?"

"Who didn't?" Dean laughed. "Faith Davidson, right? She's pretty. Lives in Tobermory? I've met her a few times through community outreach events."

Zander gave his friend a thousand-yard stare. They weren't talking about Faith. That ache in the pit of his stomach intensified. Where the hell was his cheeseburger?

"Not my type, of course." Dean kept going, because he apparently had a death wish. "Maybe Matt's—"

"Shut up."

Dean stopped for a few seconds, and when he started again, he'd dropped the badgering edge to his words. "Ryan says you met her two nights ago?"

Zander rolled his eyes. "You're a bunch of old gossips."

"Nah, man. I'm not going to report back to anyone. I'm just curious."

He didn't believe that for a hot second, but he had to give the guy something or he wouldn't stop. "She's a writer. I stopped at Greta's on the way in—"

"For pie?"

"Of course." And a last bit of peace and quiet, although

he hadn't minded in the least giving that up for an hour with Faith. "And apparently I looked like a guy who knew his way around weapons."

Dean's eyebrows hit the ceiling. "What?"

"She writes novels. Demon slayer books. Wanted to know about katanas and sawed-off shotguns."

"Huh. Maybe she's my type of girl after all."

"No."

"But she's your type?"

"She deserves so much better than either of our ugly mugs." Zander took a deep breath and pointed at the approaching waitress. "Now eat your damn lunch and leave me alone."

The cheeseburger hit the spot, but it didn't get rid of the twinge inside. The one that said he shouldn't hide the fact that he wanted Faith, even if they couldn't happen for a dozen good reasons.

"Listen, about Faith..." He trailed off and rearranged the now-empty dishes in front of him. "There's something about her. I don't know what it is, but it's enough for me to want to figure it out. So fair warning: any Foster who starts nosing around her is going to get their ass kicked."

Dean just laughed. "Man, you don't think we already knew that? That's why Ryan called me. Not to gossip. To tell me that the north end of the peninsula had been marked by a Minelli."

"Not to gossip?" Zander snorted. "The lot of you can't help yourselves."

Dean just grinned. Then he crossed his arms and changed the subject. "Listen, about the security business—I might have a proposition for you."

"Yeah?"

Dean shifted in his seat, then pulled out his wallet. "Not here. Let's head outside."

They paid and headed out to the gravel parking lot. Zander had parked his bike in one far corner, and now that the lunch crowd was thinning out, he could see Dean's truck backed in to a spot in the opposite corner, military-style.

"What's up? You thinking of a career change?" Zander asked with a chuckle.

Dean wasn't laughing. He gave Zander a hard stare and nodded. "Yeah, I might be."

"Shit." No wonder he didn't want to talk about it in the diner. "I'm not sure this security thing is viable for one person, let alone a partner. I can't promise you anything."

"Not asking for a promise. Tell me more about your sister's ideas."

Zander scrubbed his hand over his face and into his hair. "She thinks I should use the fact that I've met Hope Creswell once and Trojan horse my way into being some kind of celebrity bodyguard."

Dean laughed. "Right. You can't do that."

"Thank God, you get it."

"But you could—we could—start a local firm that sub-contracts to some of the big hitters."

"What?" Zander stared at Dean, who stared right back with a bland, mildly amused smirk on his face.

"That never occurred to you? There are firms all over the place that get accredited with the top international security companies, and when a star lands in the area, the smaller firm is the one that provides the local bodyguard."

No, that hadn't occurred to him. "Huh."

"And as Dani pointed out…that's a need from time to

time around here. Brewsters sent up security from Toronto for the film shoot."

Damn. He owed his sister an apology. "Right." He rolled his shoulders, refusing to let the encroaching tension settle in. "That sounds more complicated than what I originally envisioned."

"Don't want to settle your roots too deep here?" Dean crooked one eyebrow. "When are you going to get that we don't want to let you go, man? That's where I'd come in. If you want to take off for a while, I'd still be here."

"That doesn't sound fair." And it wasn't that he needed to run away, exactly. Not permanently. He was going to buy a God damned house after all. Maybe. "We just need a generous vacation plan."

"Sure." Dean grinned and held out his hand. "We can talk more about this, but give it some thought, yeah?"

"Deal."

"I'm off tomorrow as well. Think you can squeeze me into your schedule? I'd like us to sit down with an accountant I know and talk about a possible business structure."

"You've been giving this more than a bit of thought, eh?"

"Sure have." Dean squinted into the sun, then looked toward the town, and the glittering blue lake in the distance, visible above the low-lying buildings because the town ran down the hillside to the harbour. "I'm getting too old to care about the shit they send us out to do sometimes. I'd keep this town safe...the peninsula, too, but that's not all the job is. There's a lot of political shit, and it ends up with good people dying."

Zander knew about the grow-op raid that had gone sideways, of course. His brother had been shot, and Ryan Howard's wife had died in the crossfire. A lot of folks had strong opinions about what had gone down that day, none aimed at the officers themselves, but the fallout had to still be draining.

Dean kept talking, and Zander let him. He'd learned over nine tours in Bosnia and Afghanistan that talking was the best thing for the demons. Let them out.

"Last week we had to raid a farm for not pasteurizing milk. Nobody got hurt, but a lot of community folk came out, and there were legal, registered weapons on the farm. And the tactical response team was called. Over fucking raw milk. It was a shit show. I don't know...I think if I can't do it with my whole heart, then I need to get out of the way and let some younger, smarter, braver kid have a shot."

"Takes a brave man to admit that." Zander clapped his hand onto Dean's shoulder. "And an even braver one to think about going into business with me. You know I'm a wild kid at heart, right?"

"Hey, this way it won't get awkward if you go speeding past me on that death trap you call a bike."

Zander just laughed. "Where should I meet you tomorrow?"

Dean backed up a few feet, smirking. "I'll text you the address. It's in Tobermory."

Of course it was.

CHAPTER FIVE

FAITH WOKE before dawn and pounded out two chapters. She didn't even blink until Eric politely tapped at her office door and announced it was time to take a break that she realized her family had also gotten up.

"Breakfast time, huh?" She grinned at her son as he tugged her toward the kitchen.

"Yep. Then Grandma says you need some sunshine."

She probably did. "Want to go to the park?"

"Can I ride my scooter there?"

Faith pretended the request didn't make her palms sweaty and nodded. "Sure. We can try out the new knee and elbow pads I ordered."

She wasn't going to let her fear stop her son from living his life and getting outside.

She would, however, buy stock in as much safety equipment as possible. If it didn't have a serious social life downside, she'd happily suit him up in bubble wrap.

In the kitchen, Miriam had coffee brewed and tomatoes sliced. Faith pulled eggs and thick-sliced ham from the fridge, only to have them whisked from her hands a second later.

"Pour yourself a cup, honey. I've got this." Her mother pushed her toward the coffee pot and Faith stifled a protest. If Miriam wanted to make breakfast, who was she to say no?

But sometimes—on a day when her daily word count had been met before anyone else woke up, when the rest of her day would look nearly normal, with a trip to the park and maybe finger painting or Lego building or rock collecting—maybe on a day like that, she could make breakfast for her son.

Even if he had come to get her and if he hadn't, she wouldn't have noticed the morning slipping by.

"Thanks, Mom." Faith sighed. She couldn't have her cake and eat it, too. She was blessed and needed to get over herself.

"What's on your agenda for today?"

"We're going to the park first. Then Eric has that back-to-school prep afternoon thing at the library. My day is wide open, really. Need to do some laundry, and order back-to-school stuff for Eric."

Miriam lowered her voice, careful not to be heard. "Remember he needs elastic waist—"

"Mom!" Faith bit her lower lip and nodded. "I remember. We'll look at the online stores together after I pick him up and he can choose what he likes."

The nearest mall was an hour away, and it wasn't particularly good. Other than groceries, everything she bought was delivered by courier companies. She didn't miss fighting crowds to only find out her size was out of stock, although shopping online required a fair amount of advance notice when she needed something specific.

Miriam cracked three eggs into the frying pan, then threw out the shells before sliding a look back at Faith. "So if I wanted to go out for the afternoon and evening...?"

"You don't need to ask me if you can head out." She could feel worry twisting her mouth down at the corners, but she couldn't fight the frown. "Have I been asking you for too much?"

"No. No! Really not. You and Eric are all I've had, and being able to help has been a gift to me. I'm happy to spend as much time as I can with him." Miriam set down the ham she'd just picked up and turned to face Faith. "With both of you."

"Don't make me cry so early in the day," Faith sniffed, then they both laughed. It had been a standard refrain as they established their new normal. No more tears. They'd cried enough for a lifetime. "Go have a day to yourself. You deserve it."

After breakfast, Eric helped her do the dishes—too much soap, and both tea towels got soaked before anything could be dried, but that's what the dish rack was for—and he went and put on long pants without any complaint.

Faith looked down at her black yoga pants that she might have slept in and her tank top that had seen better days. It was an unseasonably cool morning, but as the sun rose, it would warm up and if she wanted to take off her hoodie at some point...

She laughed at herself. It was clearly mid-book, race-to-the-deadline season if she was bemoaning having to put on clean clothes. She jumped in the shower real quick to wash off the grumpy writer, and came out refreshed and ready to be Mom for the rest of the day.

But she'd just thrown her last pair of yoga pants in the

laundry, so she'd be a mom who was flashing a fair bit of leg in cut off jean shorts, apparently.

This seemed like not a big deal at all until they'd been at the park for an hour and she heard the rumbling growl of a motorcycle slow down, then stop.

Zander's tall, broad form was unmistakable, even from fifty feet away. Even with his helmet on.

Heat snaked across her chest and down her arms, making her fingers tingle. He looked impossibly fine swinging his long leg off his bike. He pulled off his helmet and set it on his seat before running his fingers through his hair.

He was wearing jeans and a dark t-shirt. She was torn between wanting to run her hands over his tan, corded forearms and yell at him for having all that exposed flesh.

Stupid, handsome idiot.

He lifted his hand in greeting and her breath jammed hard in her throat. She swallowed uselessly against it and waved back, nerves still sparking erratically in her arm.

The Zander Effect.

It was real and dangerous.

He strode toward her, and her eyes gobbled up the way his muscled thighs flexed beneath the denim that fit him perfectly. *Look somewhere else*, she told herself, but dragging her gaze up only meant she got to sigh over how good the man looked in soft cotton. All of a sudden, her legs felt doughy and far too pale, and she worried if her own t-shirt clung too tightly to her never-seen-a-gym midsection.

Maybe it was his unexpected intrusion into her day or the aforementioned Zander Effect and how uncomfortable it made her, but either way she was rattled. By the time he stopped in front of her, she was feeling suddenly snappish. Like how dare he look that good and make her ogle him.

So instead of saying hello, or something equally polite and normal, she went with, "What are you doing here?"

He gave her a half-smile and enough of an eyebrow lift to show he saw right through her. "I had a meeting with an accountant. Nearby."

"Ah." That wasn't any of her business, and it wasn't what she'd meant to ask, anyway. "I mean, here, in this park."

He gave her a funny look. "I saw you."

"So?" She was being rude, like a teenager with her nose out of joint, but he threw her off-kilter.

His lips twisted a bit, a hint of a smile that threatened to get a lot bigger, and his eyes crinkled at the corners as he held her gaze. "So when I see you somewhere, Faith, I can't head in the opposite direction without saying hi."

Oh. His words pulled at her insides, once again waking up those parts of her body she'd all but forgotten, at least in a real-life, with-a-real-man kind of way.

"Don't look so surprised," he said on a rough exhale. His smile disappeared and he shoved his hands in his pockets.

"I'm not..." Well, she was a little surprised, but it wasn't her primary reaction. Unexpectedly turned on, yes. Achingly drawn to him, definitely. Painfully aware he was just visiting for a week...yep. He at least deserved the bit of honesty she could safely give him. "It's nice to see you again."

He nodded, his gaze holding hers, boring deep.

"Is that your son?" He changed the subject, and like a world-class spy or your average four-year-old, Eric picked up on the inclusion of himself in the conversation and came running.

He stopped between them, like a tiny guard throwing

himself in front of the queen, and stared up at Zander, equal parts suspicion and curiosity on his face. "Who are you? I don't know you."

She could always count on her son to call a spade a spade. She bit back a grin, but her amusement shifted to a bittersweet ache when Zander dropped into a low squat and held out his hand. "I'm Zander."

"He knows Maya's dad," she interjected.

Eric nodded solemnly, his sunglasses sliding down his nose a bit more with each bob of his head until Faith just reached out and took them. "Okay. I'm Eric. I'm almost five. Do you like spaceships?"

Zander nodded solemnly. "Sure do. You ever been on a spaceship?"

Eric giggled, his dimples popping hard at the silly question. "No."

"I have." Zander lowered his voice and leaned in. "But not in space. Not yet."

"I know," Eric said, equally serious now. "No civilians."

"That's a big word for an almost five-year-old. You know about civilians?"

"I have a spy base I go to. We learn about stuff like that." It was his imaginary playscape, where he disappeared when he needed to retreat from the world. Faith heard about the spy base on a nearly daily basis.

"Ahhh." Zander nodded. "Well, I'm not exactly a civilian."

"Are you a pilot?"

Zander laughed and glanced up at Faith, his eyes crinkling. But the smile got bigger than any she'd seen before, and then she realized, he had dimples, too. Damn, why did he have to have dimples? Although his were less boyishly-cute and more seriously-lethal. But her ovaries weren't just aching because he was cute, but because her son brought it out in him. *Zander likes kids.* Her kid, to be exact. Like, more than adults, more than talking about warfare. *Eric* made him smile like this, up at her. The tip of his tongue darted out between his even white teeth as he laughed, a sound of pure happiness, and she just about had an instant orgasm. "The truth is going to be less cool, isn't it?"

She joined him in his quiet chuckle and nodded by rote, although inside everything was still rioting. "'Fraid so."

She'd underestimated the Zander Effect. The height, the swagger, the incredibly sexy, encyclopaedic knowledge about weaponry...it all paled in comparison to watching this conversation, seeing Zander open up and give Eric little bits of himself without even thinking about it. *Zander Minelli, you're a dangerously kind man.*

He turned his attention back to Eric. "I'm in the army, actually."

Eric tipped his head to the side. "Maybe you can still go in the space shuttle."

"I hope so."

"Me too. I'm small. I'll hide in your suitcase."

As cute as this was, Faith couldn't let her son think for a second that hiding in a stranger's luggage was acceptable. "Eric, you've just Mr. Minelli. Ease up on the spy plans, okay?"

Her son sighed and leaned closer to Zander, echoing the grown man's earlier action, right down to the lowered voice. "She doesn't get it. But she's cool in other ways."

Zander laughed and tried to stop himself at the same time, making himself cough. Eric patiently waited for him to recover. Giant man, tiny boy. Instant friendship the likes of which Eric rarely had a chance to form.

Zander held out his hand again. "Eric, it was really a lot of fun meeting you today. Your mom is right about the escape plan—it's not safe—but I like you, bud."

Faith's heart squeezed so tight she had to actually rub her chest to make the feeling go away...and still it lingered.

Eric shook right back with the fervency of a boy on a mission. *Don't count on this plan being dismissed,* his little pumping arm said. But he knew when to re-group. "I'm going back to the playground."

Zander stood and shoved his hands in his pockets as Faith watched her son scamper to the top of the climber. "He's a great kid."

"He's fragile." The warning tumbled out of her mouth before she realized she said it out loud.

"Okay." His mouth tightened and his dark eyes searched her face. "I was just making conversation."

"I know. And you didn't say anything inappropriate. Actually, that was...really good. And thank you for backing me up on the safety thing. We're edging into the age where he's questioning everything I say."

His lips turned up a bit and he nodded ruefully. "I remember the first time Tom told our mother she was wrong. It didn't go well."

Faith burst out laughing.

He shook his head. "I can still hear the wooden spoon splintering as she whacked it against the kitchen counter to make her point about how just not wrong she was, and just how grounded he was."

That was...extreme. Her reaction couldn't have been

well-masked because Zander rocked forward on his heels and grinned at her.

"It was a different time?" he offered, his dimple making another appearance. "My mom takes the whole Italian passion thing quite literally."

"Ah."

"Your parents were different?"

She shrugged. Yes. A quiet academic father, lost in his thoughts most of the time, and when he blinked and realized he had a precocious child growing right in front of him, he'd just found her fascinating. And her mother had doted on both of them. "A bit, yeah."

"Tell me more."

"Why?"

"Haven't you ever met someone and just wanted to know more about them?"

Yes. Again with that stupid tug deep in her belly. "I'm not that interesting."

"I find that hard to believe." His voice rumbled with barely restrained laughter.

"Mom!"

Saved by the child. She turned toward the climber and raised her voice. "Yes?"

"Will you push me on the swing?"

"Yep!" She started moving in that direction, walking backward so she could say goodbye to Zander. "Sorry, Mom duty calls."

He didn't take the hint. "That's okay. I'll join you. I'm not in any hurry."

"Oh. I…" What? Wanted him to go away? That would be a bald-faced lie. Didn't know how to handle his interest? That was certainly true, but not something she wanted to admit.

She blinked as he sauntered around her, coming close enough that his shoulder brushed hers as he passed. She pivoted on her heel, her breath shallow in her chest as she tried hard not to pant at the view of Zander's ass encased in denim.

Ooooh, this was a mistake.

A beautiful, beautiful mistake.

He looked back at her, and the way the sun backlit him as he stood between her and the swing set made him look like a fallen angel. For a second she pictured him as Deacon. Dark, growly, full of attitude. Perfect.

She told her brain to remember every detail of this moment for when she got back to the computer.

The way her heart was pounding in her chest promised that wouldn't be a problem.

He settled against one of the posts of the swing set as she gave Eric a gentle push.

"Higher, Mommy," her son urged, and she made it so, because he didn't call her that very often anymore. If he ever figured out that she'd give him almost anything when he did, she'd be screwed.

After the second push, she waved her hand in the space between her and her airborne son. "This is everything there is to know about me, Zander. Playgrounds and camps and packing lunches and wiping noses and kissing scraped knees. Bath time and story time and middle of the night cuddles because of nightmares. Nothing interesting."

He just stood there, watching her, until Eric wiggled his feet and announced he was done. She wanted to follow him back to the climbers, wanted to escape Zander's pinning gaze and swing on the monkey bars and sail down the slide.

Instead she just stood there and shared a long, silent,

bittersweet moment with a man who would have been perfect for her a lifetime ago.

— —

ZANDER KNEW he should leave Faith alone.

Chemistry didn't trump practicality, and she'd given him a bunch of reasons why being pursued didn't thrill her—being a mom and dealing with grief, although she didn't name that specifically.

But then they had shared looks like this, where her face was naked with longing and he thought, how is this beautiful woman all alone? *How can I not pursue her?* It was a raw, primal reaction that evaded logic and reason.

Eric's strong little voice cut through their moment. "Mommy! I'm hungry!"

She nodded woodenly. "I've got snacks in my backpack, baby."

Zander watched as she turned and jogged over to a bag sitting on a bench on the other side of the small park.

She had the sweetest legs. Long, curvy calves and soft, creamy thighs. This was the second time he'd seen her in cut-off jean shorts and a faded graphic tee, and that outfit was rapidly climbing his top-ten fantasy list. She made it look *good*. All curves and pale skin that made him wonder if it was even paler under the soft, clingy fabric.

And she had a tattoo on her ankle.

How had he missed that before?

He added it to the growing list of little details that made Faith special—the way her hair tumbled loose from her ponytail, the sparkly stud in her nose, how her blue eyes turned grey when she was thinking.

That she was giggle snorting over a bathroom humour joke with Eric.

"Because it's poo!" the kid yelled, and Zander watched as Faith wiped tears from the corners of her eyes.

He'd missed the setup, but it was still somehow funny.

Slowly he made his way over to them. She'd crossed her legs and the dark ink was now hidden, but he'd figure out what it was soon enough.

"Did I miss a funny joke?" he asked.

Eric giggled. "Knock knock."

"Who's there?"

"Touch mop."

"Touch..." *Touch mop who... Touch mah poo.* Zander grinned. "Touch mop who?"

Eric cackled and Faith turned pink. "I'm sorry," she whispered between hiccupping laughs. "It's really inappropriate."

Zander dropped into a squat so he could be eye-level with Eric. "That's okay. Army guys like crude jokes." He cleared his throat. "Not that I'm going to teach you any."

"Teach me!" Eric bounced on the bench. His granola bar got caught in the excitement somehow and tumbled to the ground. The little boy's face immediately fell, and Zander picked up the bar, but it was covered in dirt. Eric reached out with his fingers and gingerly brushed at the sticky mess. "My snack..."

"We've got more at home," Faith said smoothly, standing up again.

That brought Zander eye-to-eye with her legs. Her knees. Her smooth skin and not far from where his hand was hanging, her ankle with it's gorgeous quill tattoo.

A writer's ink.

The quill curved around her ankle bone before exploding into a flock of birds. All her stories?

He wanted to tug her ankle into his lap and trace the outline of the tattoo, make her shiver and giggle until she told him all about it. When. Where. Why.

With who.

He wanted to know everything about her. More than just the surface details that made her fascinating enough already. He wanted to know what made her tick, what got her excited.

What turned her on.

"Let me buy you lunch," he said abruptly, standing up again. He towered over Faith, and he liked it like that. Liked how she looked up at him with that what-are-you-doing expression on her face, and how she licked her lips.

Especially that part.

He wanted to chase the plump, shiny flesh with his own tongue and find out if she tasted as serious as she looked most of the time, or if she was secret laughter and sighs on the inside, too.

"We couldn't..." she said, but her eyes held his. "I tried to explain Friday night..."

"Ah yes." He gave her a reproachful look. "You led me to believe you were a taken woman."

She laughed. "I'm sorry about that. That wasn't fair."

"Then make it up to me." He grinned down at her. "I did make Eric drop his granola bar, after all."

"I want fish and chips," Eric interjected, standing on the bench beside them. He was almost as tall as his mother that way—an equal part of the conversation. "Please, Mommy?"

And thank God for that, because it was likely the

reason Faith relented. "Fine. We can go and get some lunch." She glanced back at Zander. "And if Mr. Minelli happens to go to Castaway Pete's at the same time, that would be…nice."

They were only a block from the tiny strip of restaurants that did a booming business in the summer, for the tourists getting on and off the ferry and area cottagers, too. Two more weeks, once school started and the summer season officially wrapped up, and Tobermory would be nearly a ghost town.

He'd come back at exactly the right time, because this was easy. Walking together, with Eric in the middle, slowly coasting along on his scooter. Grabbing one of the bright blue picnic tables.

Arguing over who should pay.

Faith got right in his face when he tried to treat them, waving a twenty at him. He nearly grabbed her wrist and pulled her tight against him, and from the spark in her eye, she didn't miss what was on his mind.

Oh yeah, she was interested.

And this time, the confusion over how she felt about that fact seemed less vexing than before.

Progress, he told himself. Significant progress.

CHAPTER SIX

FISH AND CHIPS had never tasted so good.

Zander had disappeared inside with her twenty dollars, and returned with a single tray of food—and her twenty dollars.

"Your change," he said with a wink. Then he turned to Eric before she could say anything. "Hey bud, I need help with the second tray. The pirates inside are holding it hostage. Do you have any gold?"

Eric laughed. "You mean, do *ye* have any gold."

"Argh, me matey, I do indeed." Zander held out a couple of loonies, and Eric took the one-dollar coins and led Zander back inside.

When they returned, Eric crowed about how he'd tipped the pirate behind the counter—the main reason to visit Castaway Pete's—and they all dug into their lunch.

Eric filled the silence with excited chatter about the library program he was going to for the afternoon.

Zander nodded along, asking questions like how long it would be and how many days he'd take it, and Eric sat up taller and beamed brighter with each answer. But Faith felt like with each question, she was being stripped bare. Zander didn't look her way and yet she felt his attention most keenly.

"And how about you, Faith? Working this afternoon?"

He knew she had the afternoon to herself—today and every day this week—thanks to her son, so she'd seen the question coming. But she still wasn't prepared for it. "I'm..." Done writing for the day. "Going to do laundry."

His eyes leapt like amused, glittering chunks of coal. "Fun."

Shrugging, she stole one of his French fries. "I told you, nothing about my life is fun."

He dipped another fry in ketchup and held it out for her. "This is fun."

Yes, it was, and admitting that—to him, to herself— was surprisingly easy. "Once or twice a year, maybe we go wild and have lunch out."

He grinned. "So it is possible for Faith Davidson, serious writer extraordinaire, to have fun."

"Possible, yes. Probable, no." Her phone sounded from the pocket of her backpack. She pulled it out—the alarm reminder that Eric's library program started in thirty minutes. "Finish up your lunch."

"Yes, ma'am," Zander said softly, his lips quirking as he looked down at his tray.

"I meant Eric," she laughed.

"Right." Zander turned to Eric. "You've got a busy afternoon ahead."

Eric stared right back at him. "What are you going to do with my mom this afternoon?"

Faith enjoyed seeing Zander speechless, so she waited a beat before saving him. "I think we'll take you over to the library, then Mr. Minelli might walk me home, where I will wash your soccer uniform so it's shiny and clean for your game tomorrow night."

Eric shrugged. "Boring."

"Excuse me?"

"Thank you."

"That's better." She handed over a napkin, then started to stack their trays.

"I'll get these," Zander said, his fingers brushing hers as they both reached for the pile of ketchup-smeared paper plates, crumpled napkins, and empty tartar sauce cups.

Faith froze.

So did the six-foot-something tattooed biker she couldn't get out of her mind.

She didn't know she'd been missing his touch. Not exactly. But the moment the contact was made, she knew she was in big trouble. Even though it was innocent, it didn't feel innocent at all. Faith forced herself to keep breathing.

"Come on." His voice strained to sound normal—or least that's what she told herself she was hearing. It would be good to not be alone in this craziness. "Eric's got a thing to get to, right bud?"

"That's right!"

Faith blinked and pulled her hand away. She buried her burning face in her backpack, looking for the smaller bag and water bottle that Eric would take with him to the afternoon program.

"And then you're going to walk my mom home?"

Seriously, why was Eric so obsessed with what Zander was going to do to her that afternoon?

With. Not *to.*

She jerked the backpack closed and stood up, her hip banging against the picnic table. "Okay, let's go."

She managed not to look at Zander until they got to the library—damn small towns, everything being only a block apart barely gave her time to de-blush and try to restore her natural defences.

"You have a good time." She kissed Eric on the forehead and smoothed her hand over his hair. "I'll be back in three hours to pick you up."

"With Zander?"

She shook her head. "Nope."

"Awww!"

Zander leaned in and offered his fist to Eric, who solemnly bumped knuckles with his new friend.

Faith cleared her throat. "What do you say?"

"Thank you for laughing at my poop joke."

"Eric!"

"And lunch."

"That's better. I love you."

"I love you too."

She watched as her little boy scampered off, high-fiving the program leader as he took his seat on the carpet alongside a handful of other children. Probably all the kids that would be in his class in two weeks—Tobermory didn't have a huge population at the height of the summer. It dwindled to almost nothing over the winter.

When she turned around, Zander was watching her with a weird look on his face.

"What?"

"Nothing." He stepped out of the way and gestured to the door. "Lead the way, laundry lady."

"See? I'm no fun."

Maybe if she hadn't said that, he'd have let her pass him and step back out into the sunshine.

But she had, and as soon as it was out of her mouth,

she'd known it was a mistake. His hand snapped out in front of her, touching her hip.

Zander's fingers brushing against hers had been distracting. This?

This was mind-altering. His palm curved around her side, his forearm a steel bar across her waist. "I don't believe that for a second," he whispered before releasing her just as quickly as he'd stopped her.

Desire seized her body, making her tremble for the first time in years. If they weren't in the doorway of the library, she would have grabbed his hand and returned it to her side. If she weren't still wrapped around the axle about trust and loss, she'd lead him to the nearest alley and let him do a lot more than just touch her.

But they were in public and she wasn't ready for the kind of adventure that Zander promised.

She'd never be ready for that, truthfully, because she'd dated the bad boy before. Married him, had his baby, and gleefully kissed him before he set off on adventure after adventure.

Until the day he didn't come home to her.

Now her face was burning for a completely different reason.

Not her whole face.

Just her eyes.

Damn it.

Just as quickly as she'd burned hot, now she was shivering from the nearness of Zander's large form.

Ducking her head, she started walking again.

Blink.

Blink.

She wouldn't cry.

It wasn't that she was afraid of emotion.

Hell, she was a fan of tears. A big one. They could be cathartic and healing. Freeing and therapeutic. She'd shed them for all of those reasons, and other, sadder reasons. Because she was scared and alone. Depressed and worried and not sure anything would be okay ever again. But they had their time and place, and whatever her flirtations were with Zander, he *wasn't* a confidant.

Over the pounding of her heart, she heard Zander talking to her. Apologizing.

She shook her head, then waved her hand when he didn't stop. "It's not you."

"Hey, slow up." He pulled ahead of her, holding up his hands. "I'm not going to touch you again, just wait a minute."

She jerked her head up. She'd crossed the street and they were halfway down the road to her place.

"What's wrong?"

Faith took a deep breath and shook her head a little to shake the dredged-up feelings loose.

Zander rocked back on his heels and carefully slid his hands into his jeans pockets. She knew what he was doing, backing off and clearly demonstrating he wasn't a threat. But she couldn't find her voice to tell him it really wasn't him, not like that. He hadn't creeped her out. She was just freaked out by all the uncontrollable feelings. *Triggers can be the most unexpected things.* It was a primary lesson in grief counselling and she knew it well. After four years, she thought she'd experienced all the triggers she might encounter.

She'd been wrong.

Zander had sparked the worst kind of reaction by being the best kind of person. By being awesome with her son and teasing with her, coaxing parts of her back to life.

By being gut-achingly perfect in all the most unexpected ways.

"I know I'm a nice guy…" he started, giving her a slow grin that teased her, that promised she'd never live down that brush off. And that teasing eased some of the tension, helped her breathe again. He watched her face, and slowly nodded. "And since nice guys just aren't your type…"

She laughed weakly. "Nice guys are totally my type and I thought we'd agreed you weren't one."

"Is that how that conversation went? Because I assure you, I'm as square as they come."

She frowned. "Let's talk about the fact that you should wear a leather jacket when you're on your bike."

He frowned right back. "I do."

"I watched you get off your bike at the park." She rolled her eyes at the way his eyebrows quirked at her admission that she'd watched him earlier. "Yes, I saw you pull up, and…yes, you are a very distracting sight."

"So the storming away from me at the library was a ninety-minute delayed reaction to that?"

She shook her head, and as he gave her a far-too-gentle, far-too-understanding look, she started to feel silly.

He glanced over his shoulder. "Are we storming to your house, by any chance?"

"*I* am heading home, yes. I think the *we* portion of the day should probably come to a close."

"Even though you found me a *very distracting sight*?"

"Yep." She stepped past him and continued down the street. He loped alongside her, and it didn't matter how fast she trundled, he easily kept up.

She couldn't actually run. That would be weird.

This whole thing was weird, of course, but that would be too much.

So when they got to her driveway, she stopped again.

As did he.

She noted that her mother's car was gone, and ignored the flight of butterflies that started twirling in excitement in her belly.

Being alone with Zander was not a big deal, because he was leaving. She'd go and do laundry and put this whole weird encounter behind her.

Until she fell asleep—then she'd twist it into a bizarre fantasy where they had wild monkey sex at Castaway Pete's, probably.

That would be her cross to bear.

Before he could figure out where her mind had just gone, she returned to their discussion.

"Where were we? Oh yeah. You. Distracting sight. You're also an idiot because you were on your bike in this very thin t-shirt." She tapped her fingers against his chest.

Oh, he felt good. Big, hard, warm... With a slow exhale, she flattened her palm against his *very thin* t-shirt and enjoyed the flex of his pecs against her hand.

She ignored the surprised look on his face.

He'd touched her. Now she'd just touch him. Just for a minute.

"And it would be a shame..." She trailed off, her eyelids drooping a bit as she smoothed her hand across the significant width of his torso. More muscles flexed against her touch. Great.

"You were saying?"

She jerked her hand away and cleared her throat. "Don't be reckless."

"You're right. I do have a jacket—it's in my saddlebag. I didn't wear it from my meeting with the accountant over to the park because I knew I was just going a few blocks."

She knit her brow together. That sounded like he'd deliberately tracked her down. "I thought you said you saw me at the park and that's why you stopped."

He dropped his head, probably to cover up the fact that his cheeks were turning ruddy.

"Zander?"

"Shit, you've got the lecturing mom voice down pat." He shrugged his shoulders. "You'd have to know the Foster brothers to really get it, but they're a bunch of meddling Cupids. Matt's on duty today as a paramedic, and their station backs onto the park. His brother Dean was with me—we went to see the accountant together—and Dean called to see if Matt had time for a coffee. Mentioned me, and Matt pointed out that he'd just seen you and your son at the park."

Faith did know the Foster brothers. Not well, but enough to understand that they were beloved sons of the peninsula, all upstanding members of the community in one way or another. How had they already connected her and Zander? "And what did you say?"

"I said I was heading straight back to Pine Harbour. Then Matt had a call come in and Dean took off as well." He searched her face, his eyes not as dark as before. Endless pools of melted chocolate...a cruel shade of eye colour. Irresistible, really.

"So you came straight to the park."

"I did."

"To see me."

"Yes." He held her gaze for a beat. "I don't need to broadcast what we're doing. I'm not a guy who hides his interest in a good woman, though."

She dropped her gaze to his neck. Solid muscle, tan

skin. A healthy-looking vein she wanted to press her lips against. He thought she was a good woman?

"Is that a problem?" He reached out and stroked his fingers along her jaw, lifting her face. Her mouth went dry at the caress and the look on his face made her knees weak. "If people find out that I like you?"

"You like me?"

He crowded closer, and she took a step back. He stepped forward, she stepped back.

Again and again until they were right up against the side of her house and under the shade of the oak tree that loomed above her driveway and gave a decent amount of privacy.

"I'll ask you again...is that a problem?" The question rolled off his tongue loose and light, but it still made her head swim. He made the simplest words sound infinitely dirty.

"I don't know..." she breathed, bracing her hands against the vinyl siding wall behind her.

"I'm sorry about what happened at the library."

"I've got some issues," she whispered. "About bad boys."

"Ah." His lips thinned and he gave her a steely look. "The jacket."

"All of it. That was just...something I noticed."

"I'm careful. I promise."

"I shouldn't have said anything. Hello, stranger, let me dump my worries on you."

He shifted closer, bracing one arm on the wall above her as he lifted the other hand and brushed some loose hairs off her face. "Dump away. I've got wide shoulders, Faith. I can carry a pretty heavy load. And I don't want to be a stranger to you."

Her heart skidded hard, sending electrical misfires throughout her entire body. She rolled her head to the side, then back again, because hiding from his gaze hadn't worked so far, and really, she didn't want to hide from him. Not right now. "What are we doing?"

"I walked you home so you can do laundry." He grinned. "Now I'm just saying goodbye—for now."

Confusion and disbelief were familiar feelings to Faith. That they were tinged with this bubbling edge of happiness was new and strange and not entirely acceptable.

Nothing was this easy or light.

Everything had a price.

"For now?"

His grin got wider. "I'd like to see you again. I understand if you aren't ready. If you're still mourning…"

"It's not that." She shook her head. She'd always love Greg, and always miss him, but the acute ache had faded. She'd grieved and made peace with losing her husband and, in theory, she was ready to date again.

In reality, she'd never be ready for Zander.

"It's…complicated."

"I'm not asking for much. Just making my interest known, hoping we can maybe see what this is between us."

"I get that. But that's the problem. You're…I have trouble believing that—" She carefully set her hands on his chest—there was that warmth again, making her want to do stupid things—and moved him a foot away from her. She waved her hands up and down between them. "It doesn't make sense that *you* are interested in fish and chip lunches and talking about spaceships and walking me home so I can do laundry."

His jaw clenched and he crossed his arms. Jeez, he had nice forearms. And she had zero focus.

"I mean, not without expecting something."

He lifted one eyebrow. "Something?"

"A booty call or afternoon delight. A one-night stand or an *easy fuck*." She said the words, maybe to shock him—which didn't work—or maybe to make a point that she knew that was something people looked for. She didn't want to think she might be testing him, although as soon as she said them, she held her breath, waiting for his answer.

A scowl darkened his face. "I'm not asking you for an easy fuck."

More's the pity, screamed her lady parts, but the rest of her relaxed.

"Faith, I have four tattoos to your...do you just have one?"

Heat flooded her cheeks. He'd noticed her tattoo? She nodded dumbly.

"To your one. No piercings to your..."

Oh God. The heat inched further down her neck and she was sure her ears were bright red. "Three," she mumbled.

"At some point, I'm going to want a detailed accounting of where all of those are," he said, every inch a modern rake, right down to the dirty twinkle in his eye. "But I don't see those and make any assumptions about you. It feels like you're making some assumptions about me here."

She'd started blushing when he started talking about her piercings, and now the embarrassed warmth sank deeper into her skin. Oh. "It's possible that I'm conflating a few things," she started before pausing to drag in a shaky breath. "And it's definitely possible that I'm making a bigger deal about a lot of this than I need to."

"Hey." He rocked on his feet, bending a bit at the knee to put them more eye-to-eye. "I know I'm not Mr. Right. Never have been, never will be. But the only *something* I want from you is your company. I'm visiting for a week and other than a few family dinners and trying to figure out what the fuck my career is going to be after my current one comes to an end, I have nothing to do. And you are fascinating and kind and beautiful, and I'd love to spend some of this week with you. And Eric, if he's interested and you're willing. Hell, invite the entire town to lunch tomorrow if you want."

"Tomorrow?"

"That was my really bad way of asking you out again."

"Again? When did you ask me out before?"

"I bought you lunch today, didn't I?"

That he had. And now, even though she'd turned pink and lost her tongue, he wanted to do it again. "Oh."

His grin practically sparkled this time. "So. How about you stop worrying about the fact that I'm obviously not Mr. Right, and give me a chance to be Mr. Right Now?"

"Right now?"

"This week. Lunches and whatever else you want."

No... the long list of X-rated *whatever else she wanted* couldn't be on the table. No matter how delicious his forearms were. Or his biceps. Or the chest, the rakish smile, the dark, shining eyes or kind way he disproved all her assumptions about him.

"Okay." She grinned at him, and the answer felt totally right. With one caveat. "I'd love to have lunch with you again. But just as friends."

He gave her a look of pure disbelief. Yeah, she got that.

The chemistry between them was off the charts. She didn't want to just be friends and he knew it.

But it was all she could handle from a guy who was disappearing in a few days.

"Friends…"

She nodded.

He shrugged and his t-shirt bunched up, stretching wide around the top of his biceps. He tugged on the collar, revealing another slice of tattoo. Every time she saw him, his t-shirts were like this, worn and tugged on, like he just couldn't find any that fit his body properly in the store.

Well, that made sense—there was no comparing Zander to the average man that t-shirts were designed for.

This was no khaki-wearing, minivan-driving, rectangular-torsoed man. Lean through the middle, but impossibly broad across his shoulders, she imagined that the only shirts that would properly fit him would need to be custom made. And Zander wasn't the type of guy to be that vain.

Not that she was complaining. The bunching and stretching that should make the t-shirt look ill-fitting did the exact opposite. It highlighted his muscular build. Hugged his strong arms and smoothed proudly across his impressive chest.

And most of all, it said, *this guy doesn't preen.* Zander got up, put his fucking shirt on, and went about his day.

That was obvious and she loved it far too much. Another reason she needed this boundary.

He narrowed his eyes at her. "What are you thinking?"

"Nothing."

He grinned. "You were checking me out."

"I was thinking your t-shirts never fit."

"Sounds like the same thing."

She laughed. "You're incorrigible."

"I hear that's a good trait to have in a friend." He winked. "Okay. Until tomorrow. Fish and chips again?"

She shook her head. "Greta's. After I drop off Eric."

"It's a date. I'll see you in twenty-four hours at our table."

CHAPTER SEVEN

WHEN ZANDER PACKED up for his drive across the country, he didn't have anything other than travelling light on his mind. He'd only brought a few pairs of jeans and a bunch of t-shirts, plus as many pairs of boxer briefs and work socks he could shove in his saddlebags.

This hadn't been a problem until he met Faith and now, after a handful of encounters where she'd given him heated looks and wary side-eye in equal measure, he wanted to look like something other than a rough and tumble biker guy.

After he went for a bruising swim in the lake on Tuesday morning, he called Rafe. "Hey man, I need to borrow some clothes."

"This is about Faith, isn't it?"

Zander hung up. He tried Tom next. "Are you at work today?"

"Yeah. Doing Search and Rescue training all morning. Why?"

"No reason."

He grabbed the spare keys to Tom's cottage from the hook in their parents' kitchen and got on his bike. Soon he was the proud temporary owner of a pilfered pair of cargo pants and a blue buttoned-down shirt. It wasn't a big change, but it was something.

Four hours later he pulled his father's sedan into the parking lot at Greta's Bakery. His old man had been happy to let him borrow it—even more so when he left the house looking like a frat boy.

Well, a frat boy who'd been to war more than a half-dozen times.

He ordered coffee and pie for two and settled into the same booth he and Faith had sat in five days earlier. And then he leaned back and watched out the plate glass window for her car. She'd drop Eric off at the top of the hour. So as the minute hand ticked past that point, his pulse grew sluggish, like more than blood was flowing through his veins.

Shit, he hadn't been this excited-slash-nervous for a date since forever. Maybe high school.

Not a date.

Except she hadn't corrected him when he'd called it that the day before, had she?

Five minutes past one, she pulled into the lot, her little car sending up a billow of dust. Unexpected nerves thudding in his chest and bounding through his veins, he stood up to greet her.

His thighs tensed and his palms burned when she got out of the car wearing a dark blue sundress. *Don't get too excited, she wants nothing to do with you.* That wasn't exactly true. The heated looks she sometimes gave him indicated she wanted all sorts of things, even if she said otherwise. At least she was willing to be his friend.

It was more than nothing.

And given that he was a vagabond currently under contract to the Queen on the other side of the country, he could hardly ask for anything beyond that, anyway.

But watching her straighten her skirt, then step toward the door, her curvy legs even more so in a pair of nude pumps that made him think of sex, he had to warn himself not to go too far. It wouldn't be easy.

What was easy, though, was giving her a welcoming smile—and receiving one right back. Her face lit up as she found him.

That wasn't nothing, either.

"I presumptively ordered apple pie and coffee." He held out his arm and she moved closer. For a second he thought she might lean into his side for a hug, but then she drifted past, leaving a subtle scent of sweet perfume in her wake.

"Good choice, it's my favourite," she murmured, glancing back at him over her delicately curved shoulder. His dick jumped to attention. So the woman liked apple pie. Noted.

He took his time settling back in the booth, because she was taking her time looking him over. Curiosity danced all over her face. Was it that much of a surprise that he'd dress up for her, like she had him?

Friends. Ha.

"How'd work go today?"

She exhaled, blowing one of the loose strands of hair around her face into the air. It settled back in exactly the same spot on her cheek. He leaned across the table and tucked it behind her ear, relishing the zinging in his fingertips as he brushed her skin.

She blushed, but when he kept looking at her, because

yes, he meant that as a serious question, she gave him a real answer. "I've been waking up early—not my usual routine, but it seems to be working for this book. My daily goal is a chapter, and if I get more than that, awesome. I did that today, but it was hard-fought."

A chapter sounded like a lot. "So how long does it take you to write a book?"

She leaned forward, wrapping her fingers around her coffee mug, and told him about first drafts and edits, revisions and world-building. He found every bit of it fascinating, and before long, their mugs were empty, their slices of pie long gone, and still they talked. She asked about his work, too, but he kept steering the conversation back to her and her books because it was infinitely more intriguing.

Talking with Faith was easy and friendly and more than a little arousing. Apparently Zander had a fetish for writers, or one writer in particular.

When her phone alarm sounded, Zander did a double-take. "Pick-up time already?"

No way had they been talking for three hours.

She shook her head after glancing at the screen. "That's my one-hour reminder. I get lost in my work, so I schedule a bunch of alarms."

So they'd been talking for two hours. Still meant the afternoon was slipping by alarmingly fast. "Do you want to go for a walk?"

Her eyebrows hit her hairline, a fair reaction because Greta's sat just off the highway. There weren't any sidewalks in sight.

"Do you not know about the trail that runs behind the bakery down to the lake? Clearly you've never been snowmobiling in the winter and come here for hot chocolate."

She laughed. "Clearly."

He stood up, threw a five dollar tip on the table, and held out his hand. "Come with me."

— —

FRIENDS DIDN'T HOLD HANDS. But today's Zander was clean-cut and kind, and he'd spent the last two hours priming the pump for this moment. Seducing her with excellent listening skills and apple pie.

He might be the devil.

She took his hand, letting herself be breathless and excited for a minute. Two minutes. Maybe five or ten, but soon she'd snap herself out of it.

He led her outside, his hand resting in the small of her back for a split second as he reached past her and opened the door, then he filled the aching silence with chatter about teenage winter exploits. The trail system crawled up the peninsula, he explained, and one of their most popular stops had been Greta's.

Then they'd take their hot chocolate down to the lake and test out just how frozen it was.

"You did not!" She gasped, grabbing his arm. They were halfway down the short, well-groomed trail and all alone.

His muscles bunched under her touch and she wobbled as they turned to face each other. The ground was nice and flat, but it was also soft, and thanks to the stupid heels she'd decided to wear at the last minute, she was a bit unsteady on her feet. He slid his hands to her hips for a second, making sure she was stable before he ghosted his palms up her arms.

Goosebumps skittered across her skin.

He slowly dropped his hands back to his side, then stuffed them in his pockets. Her goosebumps protested.

"Yeah, we did. I was a stupid kid. I also joined the army at seventeen and a half. I didn't have a healthy fear of my own mortality yet."

"Yet?"

His eyes lit up every time he smiled, and he did that a lot. Each flash of white teeth framed by soft lips undid her a little more. She needed to stop asking him questions that made him grin. "I have a lot of reasons to play it safe now."

"Like what?"

It would be *ridiculous* for him to say a pretty single mom he'd just met. And if he did, she'd run screaming. But the pause he took first? That was dangerously addictive.

Fantasy. Hope.

She hadn't allowed herself either in a long time.

"When I was a teenager, I thought forty sounded ancient. That I'd feel like an old man now and nothing would be worth living for, anyway."

There was nothing old about Zander Minelli. She sucked in a breath and held it, not trusting herself to exhale. She might say something stupid like he was the most handsome, virile man she'd ever been pressed up against.

Stop thinking about his virility, she told herself. Or wishing he'd plaster himself against her again. She still hadn't gotten over him pressing her against the side of her house the day before.

He pulled one hand out of his pocket and reached behind him, rubbing the back of his neck. "Now…"

Her alarm sounded again. She'd left her backpack at home, bringing just a small cross-body purse, and she dug the phone out. "Thirty minutes."

His gaze snapped from the phone in her hand to her face. "Now I know that life is for living, and I want to do that for a long time still. I have a bucket list a mile long and I've only seen half of the world. I want to see the rest of it, every inch, and that's going to take decades." He stepped closer. "Doesn't mean I don't still want to seize the moment, though."

She stepped back. Her heart fluttered and her mind blanked. *Do something!* screamed her last vestiges of sensible thought. "Um, I forgot to tell you how nice you look today."

He reached out and gently circled her waist with his hands so she couldn't step back again. And then stepped closer.

"I want to kiss you, Faith." He curved his body over hers, angling his face a bit as he traced the shape of her mouth with his gaze.

"Is this about the chase?"

"Maybe. Do you like being chased?"

Yes. "Not anymore." And he got that, she knew he did. That's why he'd dressed up for coffee. That's why *she'd* dressed up. Trying to prove that she wasn't torn jean shorts and rock-band t-shirts, tattoos and piercings. "I'm not the rebel you think I am."

"I think you're many, many things. A rebel isn't really one of them."

Oh. "Because if you've got some fantasy you've concocted of a wild girl in soccer mom trappings…" She trailed off. It didn't sound right outside of her head. It didn't sound completely wrong, either—and the look on his face admitted as much. But after their lunch the day before, she knew it wasn't really fair to keep thinking of Zander as a reckless bad boy. He was dangerous for a whole other set of reasons, maybe—like the way his glances turned her inside out.

He only looked chagrined for a second, but then . "I'm going to convince you that you really are a fantasy, Faith, exactly as you are."

"Stop it." That would have more weight if she didn't sway against him. He wasn't wearing a t-shirt under the borrowed shirt and she could feel the solid heat of his chest against her breasts.

"I can't. Not until you look me in the eyes and tell me you don't feel the same."

She couldn't do that. "It's not that easy."

"I told you yesterday I'm not asking for much. I just want to talk, to hang out." He lowered his voice, his gaze searing into her. "Let's explore what this is between us."

"There's nothing between us," she whispered the weak, weak lie, almost relieved when his baleful look told her he didn't believe her.

His voice crackled with restraint. "We're two people who want each other."

"I never said I wanted you." That wasn't exactly true. She'd admitted she liked looking at him and shown him that she liked touching him. She'd given him every indication that she wanted him...and then lied about it out of fear.

Zander wasn't afraid. He was bold and brave, and more than a little filthy as he leaned in. "I'm saying it first."

"You could find anyone—"

"I want *you*."

And there it was. The raw, teasing fact that would probably prove irresistible. He wanted her, something that didn't happen very often. And by some strange miracle, given how much she'd closed herself off to this possibility, she wanted him back. But while she could admit that now, she was terrified she'd freak out again. "I'm going to run scared. You know that, right?"

Instead of answering her, he shifted his hands, one up her back, settling between her shoulder blades, the other lower, to the curve of her hip, his fingers moulding to the top of her ass. Zander's idea of tugging her closer was dirty, possessive, and thrilling.

"Zander…"

"You talk too much," he whispered, then covered her mouth with his.

His lips teased against hers, relaxed and coaxing. He smelled like shower gel and sun warmed skin, and his stubbly almost-beard was surprisingly soft against her chin. But the best part of Zander kissing her was that he took his time, and yet still managed to make it abundantly clear that this kiss *was* going to get heated.

More heated. She was already boneless from the first press of his mouth to hers.

When he tasted her lower lip with his tongue, she wiggled closer. *More.* He gave it to her, unlocking the seam of her lips with a single swipe.

And then it got better.

Before he delved deeper, he invited her to taste him, coaxing her own tongue out to play with the tip of his. Lick. Thrust. Parry. And then when she did, that's when he surged forward, filling her mouth. But still it didn't feel like too much—just exploration.

Teasing. Promising.

He was big and bold and demanding...but *nice*. Damn it, the biker dude kissed like a prince. A dirty prince. As they tangled, one of his legs shifted between hers and his fingers inched up her skirt—

Until they stopped.

And he sighed.

No....

Between them, she could feel the press of his arousal against her belly.

Soooo not just friends.

She moved her fingers through his short hair, eliciting a groan and a tighter hug. He tipped her back a bit, moving his mouth across her jaw and down her neck. His nose bumped into her dangly earrings and he muttered something about pretty things getting in the way.

Noted.

His breath warmed her skin before his lips moved across it, and she arched her back, giving him access to more neck. And maybe the cleavage below it.

Maybe.

God, she was a hussy.

When he stood her back up without licking his way into her bra, she was disappointed. Like that made any sense at all.

He'd been totally right. They were the same. Faith wasn't this demure girl in a sundress. She was tattoos and piercings and first kisses that went to second base, at the very least.

Years of solitude hadn't changed that. Hadn't made her

any more sensible when it came to matters of the heart or the body.

"Your alarm is going to go off again any minute, isn't it?" Zander asked roughly, still holding her in his arms.

She sighed and soaked up another moment of the steely warmth before nodding.

He smoothed his hand over her hair and kissed her forehead. "Let's walk back to our cars, then. Before I lose my mind completely."

She ducked her head and smiled at the ground as he laced his fingers into hers. At least she wasn't alone in the crazy feelings department.

At her car, he settled against the door and pulled her close again, sliding her into the space between his solid thighs, spread wide. His dark eyes caught her gaze and held it as he brushed his free fingertips across her cheekbone and down her nose, then over her lips.

Their other hands were still entwined. In her purse, the alarm went off. Ten minutes.

"I'm going to have a hard time not kissing you again," he finally said, breaking the silence.

"I don't think I'll want you to try," she admitted.

"Tomorrow?"

She nodded. "But I have to work more than just a half day." And she had a feeling that she'd get nothing done tonight after Eric was tucked into bed, because she'd just want to crawl under her own covers and relive their kisses, over and over again. "Eric has a soccer game in Pine Harbour tomorrow night. Not a great chance of kissing, but…"

"I'd love to come watch with you. And then if it's not too late, maybe we could go to Mac's for dinner?"

He'd said it the day before. Now it was her turn. "Sounds like a date."

CHAPTER EIGHT

THE NEXT DAY, Faith zipped Eric over to the library in her car to make the most of her writing afternoon. She'd gotten sucked into an online debate for most of the early morning, and then they'd made pancakes...somehow that had taken two hours.

She loved the slower pace of the summer, but there was a part of her that was more than ready for Eric to go back to school. How quickly that had changed—a year earlier, she'd been clinging to him, not ready to send her baby to junior kindergarten.

He'd had other plans. School had been really good for him.

Her, too.

In the last year, she'd finished three novels and if she managed to finish this one in the next two weeks, it would be four in exactly a year, a personal record.

But she really needed to buckle down and focus for the afternoon. No thoughts of Zander, of kissing, or just how much she was looking forward to sitting with him in the late afternoon sun.

Her mother had been gardening in the back all morning, and when she returned, Miriam had moved to the front garden.

"You're a busy worker bee today," Faith called, and her mother sat back from her weeding. Writing could wait a few minutes—just a few—because they'd been like two ships passing in the night for more than a week, seeing each other for rushed dinners and not much else. Sometimes her mother was too good at fading into the background and letting Faith get her work done. She shifted guilty. "I can help more on the weekend."

"You're on deadline, sweetie, it's fine. I'm really just doing it to keep myself moving. With Eric in this afternoon program, all of a sudden my daily exercise seems cut in half. How is the book coming along?"

"Good." Normally Faith would expand on that, but she'd talked about it a lot with Zander the day before, and probably would again tonight while they watched four-year-olds bounce off each other, and the ball, and the field.

"Hey, dinner tonight... there are lots of leftovers. Maybe you and Eric can have your pick?"

"Sure. I meant to tell you; it's soccer night, so I was thinking of treating him to a burger in Pine Harbour after the game. So he really just needs a snack beforehand."

"Oh, good." Miriam picked up a spade and started to dig a hole in the ground.

"Are you going out tonight?" That would be the second time this week and like the fifth time in the last month that Miriam had skipped dinner.

Given that Faith was doing her own secret lust-filled something with Zander, and would never tell her mother about *that*, she hardly had any right to ask, but there was only so much willful ignorance a girl could manage. "Mom?"

"Mmmm?"

"Do you have a date tonight?"

Miriam turned pink and dug her spade a little more forcefully into the ground. "I need to get these hostas into the ground."

Faith sat back on her heels and waited. Three, two, one...

Her mother sighed and looked over at her. Just a peek. "Maybe."

"With who?"

"His name is Bill. He..." She took a deep breath and twisted away, looking out over the harbour. "He captains the ferry. Eric and I met him on one of our rides."

"Wow." She rolled that over in her head. Her mother and someone who wasn't her father. Huh.

"Are you okay?"

"Yeah." She shook her head, then nodded, more vigorously this time. "Yes! Of course. I'm sorry. It's weird when it's your parent. But this is good."

Wow, it was like she wasn't a trained bereavement group facilitator or something. Why was this so weird?

She tried again. "I think this is awesome. I'm just surprised, that's all." A memory of her father—stocky, bearded, happy—slipped into her mind. "So what is he like? Did you find your own Mr. Tall, Dark, and Handsome?"

"Faith Elaine Davidson, you leave this conversation alone." But her mother smiled, and Faith's heart exploded with happiness, because whatever this guy was like, he made Miriam's eyes sparkle like diamonds.

"So he's handsome," Faith teased. "And a *captain!*"

"Of a ferry."

"You know what they say about men with big boats…"

"Go to work."

Faith snickered and leaned forward, kissing her mother's cheek before getting up. "I'm happy that you're happy," she whispered. "And Dad would be, too."

— —

ZANDER WAS BACK in jeans and a t-shirt today, because while he kept the pilfered outfit, he couldn't wear it two days in a row—and really, what kind of douche wore a buttoned-down shirt to a little kids' soccer game when he wasn't coming from work?

And he definitely wasn't *that*. He'd spent the day researching business registration and background checks using a handy checklist provided by a contact at Brewseters, the firm Dean had mentioned.

It turned out they were always looking for well-qualified affiliates.

Huh. How about that.

He looked at his watch. He had an hour before Faith said to meet them at the soccer fields. He reached for his phone. Dani answered on the first ring.

"So your bodyguard idea may have some merit," he started.

"I know." He could hear her smirk through the phone.

"But I can't use Ryan's girlfriend like that."

"I think it's called networking."

"It doesn't feel right."

"Fair enough. But I can mention it to her—"

"Nope."

"Zander!"

"But thank you for the push in the right direction."

"No kidding I pushed you. I'm surrounded by stubborn men who all need—"

He laughed. "I said thank you."

"Okay. You're welcome." Dani's radio crackled in the background. She must be out in the ambulance. "I gotta go."

"Save a life!"

"That's the plan, big brother."

Zander rocked back in the computer chair and looked at his phone. His thumb itched to text Faith and tell her the progress he'd made today—but he didn't have her number. He needed to fix that tonight.

In the distance, he heard the front door open and close. Pushing away from the desk, he headed into the kitchen, where his mother was unloading groceries on the counter.

Anne Minelli, as always, was put together. Her short hair was neatly set in a bob and she wore black dress pants and a blouse—her standard uniform from years of running a cafe and catering business.

"Let me do that for you," he said, moving past her.

"You don't know where anything goes," she fussed. "Sit down and have a cup of coffee. Tell me when you're going to marry and give me grand babies."

"Rafe and Dani are doing that."

She sniffed. Zander fought hard not to roll his eyes. He loved his mother dearly, but she was hard to please. "Olivia took what, seven years to agree to one baby? And Dani is too young still."

This time his eyes rolled themselves. Olivia and Rafe

had a rocky first marriage and there was a two-year break in their relationship where his brother buried his head in the sand. And Dani could very well be knocked up now, the way Jake looked at her.

Zander thought of how Faith had felt in his arms the day before. How much he was looking forward to watching Eric play soccer tonight.

He'd never thought about kids, other than thinking they were fine in theory and messy in practice. But Faith's kid? He was awesome. Funny and smart, a mighty little man in a small but perfect package.

Someone—a Mr. Right kind of someone—would take one look at Faith and hop right on the Anne Minelli life plan. Marriage, babies, even a minivan.

Faith having babies with someone else?

Jesus, the thought made his stomach flip over.

Of course, the thought of Faith having babies with him did the same thing.

One fucking afternoon of kissing and you're going to strange places in your head.

There was no way he was telling his mother about that.

Instead he grabbed the box of ziti and opened the cupboard where Anne had always kept pasta. He may have been away for a long time, but some things never changed. "You make the coffee, Ma. I've got the groceries."

"What aren't you telling me?" She narrowed her eyes and looked right at him.

He sighed. He couldn't lie to her. So he went with misdirection. "Dean Foster wants to go into business with me."

"I like him. But he's another one who needs to marry soon. As soon as you start getting grey hair, women won't think you can chase after toddlers."

"Dean runs triathlons." And Zander didn't think his friend had any grey hair yet, but he hadn't looked closely.

She frowned. "That's not a selling point, dear. Women want men to be present. Equal parents. Not a man with an expensive hobby running around in circles and buying expensive bicycles."

Or who load up their motorcycle and drive across the country. Go backcountry camping for twenty days.

"Minivans and college educations aren't cheap, either."

"Don't be argumentative, Zander. And providing for our family is the most rewarding thing your father and I have ever done." She handed him a steaming mug of rich, Italian coffee. Only the best food and drink in the Minelli house, that had always been the rule, even when his parents didn't have much.

He pressed his teeth into his lower lip to keep from challenging her on that point. *She'd* always put the kids first. His father...well, his father was a man, and Zander's first lesson in life had been that sometimes family shit was too much for men. It was entirely possible his mother had no clue that he remembered their brief separation.

Now wasn't the time to bring it up. He took a sip of coffee. "Well, I'm never going to want a van, but when I move back in the spring, I'm going to need a house."

She raised her eyebrows, clearly wanting more. Give Ma an inch...

His mouth went dry and he took another sip. Still dry. *Man up, Minelli.*

"With...bedrooms. Plural." It was all he could give her.

As if she knew her oldest wasn't nearly as mature as her youngest, Anne just nodded. "Bedrooms. Plural. That's a good start."

Zander rolled that conversation around in his head as

he made his excuses and headed over to the soccer field. He'd told his mother the truth—he was going to watch a friend play an evening pick-up game.

He didn't tell her the friend was four years old.

Or that his friend's mother had the sexiest mouth Zander had ever kissed, and he'd jerked off the night before imagining her kissing him...on her knees.

He shook his head at himself. Thinking about buying a family home scared him shitless, but he had no problem with a dirty fantasy about Faith. He really was an overgrown teenager.

At the park, he found them easily. Eric was on the edge of his team huddle, extra little compared to some of the bruisers he played with. Faith stood nearby, a plaid blanket hanging over her arm.

"Hey," he greeted her as he drew alongside.

She grinned back. He was glad to see she'd returned to her regular uniform of denim and cotton tees as well.

"No lawn chair?" All the other parents had coolers and chairs and veritable camps set up. Faith just had the blanket and two bottles of water.

"I always mean to bring one..." She shrugged. "And then I forget. When I get here, I tell myself to put one in the trunk when I get home. And then I forget."

He laughed and reached for the blanket. "May I?"

"Please."

He walked further down the field, away from the other parents, but still central to the action. He wouldn't interfere with her watching her son play...he just wanted some privacy while they did it.

He set down the small brown paper bag of treats his mother had sent along—chocolate chip cookies, because apparently she thought grown men had the appetites of children.

She wasn't wrong.

He sat down and stretched out, watching Faith hover near the players until the coach sent the first batch of kids —including Eric—onto the field.

Then she came and sat next to him, and started talking.

She didn't stop for twelve minutes. It was adorable.

She told him about the pick-up games, how they'd evolved from the more formal league that finished earlier in the summer. It was more than a little nice to stretch out in the late sun, wiggle his fingers in the grass, and just chat with Faith.

"How'd work go today?" she asked him, stealing his own line.

"Good. I actually thought about calling or texting you but..."

She bumped her shoulder against his, keeping her eyes on the field. "You asking for something?"

"I don't know. Do you give your friends your number?"

"Usually." She grinned. He loved the way it transformed her profile—she was beautiful when she concentrated on something, when she got flying on a subject she was passionate about, but when she smiled, her eyes crinkled up and her cheeks turned into two shiny pink apples. She was always gorgeous, but when she smiled? She was prettiest girl for miles.

Zander wanted to make her smile more often.

He turned just enough to make sure his words were for her ears only, but not so much that he wasn't still watching the field. "But not if they kiss you senseless behind a bakery?"

She tilted her head to the side, thinking. He breathed in the scent of her. No perfume today. Just shampoo and sweet woman. His mouth watered to taste her neck and find out just how soft she would be if he held her in his lap. If she was ticklish when he explored under her t-shirt and just what kind of bra she was wearing that made her breasts look that round and inviting.

Right on cue, the ref blew her whistle for half-time. Faith held up Eric's water bottle. He scanned the line of parents, looking for her, and when he saw them sitting together, his little face lit up.

"Zander!" he yelled, and Zander's chest constricted. Had anyone ever been that excited to see him before?

"Hey, bud!"

"Did you see me play?" Eric stopped in front of them and Faith slid the water bottle into his hand. He kept going. "I was a *forward*. And after half-time, I'm going in goal! Did you see?"

"I did. You're fast out there. You make a great forward." That was a bit of an exaggeration—but only because few of the kids maintained any position. But Eric had been fast, and kept control of the ball. Zander was legitimately impressed with the kid's speed.

"Thanks!" He turned to his mother, finally, who just laughed. "I'm hungry. Did you bring snacks?"

"We're going out for burgers after the game," Faith said, clearly a reminder of a previously explained plan.

"But I'm hungry now!"

Zander cleared his throat, but the second he did, he thought better of just offering the treats without checking first. He looked at Faith, hoping she spoke Pig Latin. "Oco-late-chay ip-chay ookies-cay?"

Eric giggled and Faith blinked. "What?"

"I-bay ought-bray ookies-cay." Zander stretched out the words more this time and she watched his mouth. She got it on the third word, her eyes lighting up.

"Oh! Yes. That would be fine." Another smile, and this time the pink blush traced down her neck and disappeared into the v-neck of her t-shirt.

Pig Latin.

It was going on the list with apple pie.

He reached for the brown paper bag and pulled out the smallest cookie and offered it to Eric, who also gave him a wide-eyed look.

Did nobody ever make these two people feel special?

He'd have to make more of an effort.

When? Out of nowhere, a black cloud appeared over his happiness. He was leaving in two days.

But he was coming back.

He just needed to make a case for why Faith should wait for him.

He'd start with hamburgers and asking her more about her books. It was all he had on short notice.

"Are you sharing those with anyone else?" she asked, breaking into his deep thoughts.

Oh, and cookies. He gave her a promising grin. "All my cookies are yours if you want them."

She just laughed.

For the second half, Eric started in goal, just as he'd said. It wasn't the easiest position for him, because he couldn't jump high enough to get the balls that sailed in near the top of the net, but he only let in two goals and he stopped twice as many more.

At the end, after the players all exchanged handshakes and Eric came sprinting back to them, his hair plastered to his face with sweat, it was Zander that he high-fived first.

Then he slid his hand into Faith's while Zander folded up the blanket and they all walked together to Faith's tiny car.

"Will you follow us to Mac's?" she asked, tilting her face up to his.

"Yep. See you there."

He beat them, in fact, because he'd parked closer to the entrance of the park, and could manoeuvre his bike around the slow moving parade of exiting vehicles.

Arriving at the diner first was a good thing, because Rafe and Olivia were there as well, waiting for takeout.

"A craving for meatloaf and mashed potatoes," Olivia admitted, patting her now prominent pregnant belly. Prominent but cute—pregnancy suited his sister-in-law.

Zander thumped his brother on the shoulder. "Cook your wife a good dinner."

Rafe scowled. "I tried. She prefers Frank's potatoes."

"Fair enough, so do I." He glanced out the window. "Listen, I'm here for dinner with friends and I don't want you to make a big deal about it."

Rafe's frown turned into a gleeful grin. "But because you're telling me about it, I know it *is* a big deal. Is this Faith?"

"Jesus. Don't you old ladies have anything else to talk about? When she and her son come in, pretend you don't know me."

"But I've known you my entire life. The day I was born you poked me in the eye. This is going to be hard to pull off." Rafe groaned as Olivia covered his mouth with her hand.

"We'll get our food and leave without making any eye contact," she said sweetly. Too sweetly, because she continued with a level threat. "Provided that tomorrow we get the skinny. Got it? You've been holding out on everyone except Dean, and that's not fair."

Zander knew the bastard wouldn't keep that secret.

He didn't say yes but he didn't say no. Honestly, he didn't have anything to share with his nosy but well-meaning family.

This was why he'd left Pine Harbour twenty years ago. Everyone else thought life was a joint exercise when Zander barely had a handle on doing a solo run at it.

Frank, the cook and owner of Mac's, dinged the bell and Deena the waitress bagged up Olivia's requested dinner. Zander stepped out of the way, breathing a sigh of relief that they were leaving before Faith and Eric arrived —and not a minute too soon, because the little hatchback pulled into a spot just as Rafe and Olivia headed outside.

He held his breath, watching as his brother not-so-subtly gave Faith the once-over. And Eric. There was that tightness in his chest again. He wanted to run outside and wrap them up in his arms.

But he didn't need to, because Eric was running inside, straight to him. The little guy reached way up high and pulled the door open, then flew into Zander's arms.

"I want a cheeseburger," the kid pronounced. "They make everything better."

Up until this moment, Zander would have agreed. Now he was pretty sure that it was hugs from a four-year-old that held that trump card.

CHAPTER NINE

THURSDAY DAWNED GREY AND RAINY, which matched Faith's mood. Zander was leaving the next day and she hated how much that upset her.

She distracted herself by having Vera kill a nasty group of vampires.

Faith hated vampires.

She took a break when Eric got up and they read some books after breakfast, but when she kept trailing off mid-story, he finally sighed and asked if he could play on his tablet for a bit. She ignored the guilty pang in her gut and agreed. She left her office door open so she could hear him playing in his room—first on the tablet, and then when his timer went off, with his Lego and blocks as he recreated the video he'd just watched.

Twice she pulled out her ponytail by accident. Three times she stabbed herself in the scalp as she shoved pencils into the elastic, then yanked them out again as she made notes to remember. Her monitor was growing quite the multi-coloured post-it fringe—it was alarming.

A quiet knock at the door dragged her back to reality.

"I'm heading to Owen Sound to do some grocery shopping," Miriam said. "I'll drop Eric at the library on my way."

"Thank you! And remember that we've got that picnic for dinner tonight, so you don't need to rush back." Faith tried hard not to turn red. She'd told her mother about it in the loosest of terms over breakfast, and Miriam had assumed it was with a friend of Eric's.

"I won't—I might go see a movie."

"Okay, have fun."

She listened to her family get ready as she turned her attention back to the post-it notes. God, she had a lot more to layer in. She rubbed her eyes. Maybe she should plot them all out into future scenes, get them off her monitor.

She preferred to write in a linear fashion, but some characters—Deacon—would get in her head, and as she wrote one thing, it felt like an echo of something that should happen later on.

She needed to get the man out of her head. He didn't need to be in this book.

Except that she felt very much, deep down, that he did.

Vera needed him.

She rubbed her eyes again, and scribbled *why Deacon?* on another post-it note. It was there, niggling at the back of her mind, but it wasn't enough to trust that the character had a reason for showing up in the book—she needed to understand why, in her kick-ass heroine's series, on book four a hot guy shows up and takes over and it's a good thing.

It didn't sound like a good thing.

It sounded dangerous and distracting and unhelpful.

It also messed with her plan for this to be the last book in the series, the grand finale. Because she was rounding the corner into the third act and while the monster of the week was being conquered, new plot lines were popping up.

A corrupt mayor.

A new, deadly drug in the underground club system.

And Deacon.

With a gasp, she sat straight up and tightened her ponytail. Three more books.

It was a seven book arc, not four, with a slow-burning love story over them all—and more books wasn't a problem, but...had she set it up well enough? And could she wrap up this book in a way that would satisfy her urban fantasy readers, giving them a satisfying conclusion before turning the series into a romance of sorts?

And did she even want to write a romance?

That had been her passion, back before she was published, before she had Eric.

Before Greg died.

When she worked at the Toronto Public Library, she'd dreamed of writing Regency romances. Dukes and seasons and clever, scientific-minded heroines.

And then life happened, and she couldn't imagine weaving a fantasy that could be believable.

She'd lost her faith in that romantic ideal.

Demon-slaying aligned better with her reality in more ways than one.

Spinning around in her chair, she grabbed the printed out copy of chapter one from the top of the book case and started reading.

Forty-five minutes later, she put down the third chapter and opened a web browser window. Her best writing friends had a private group online that any of them could use to vent or brainstorm or just hang out in when procrastination was the order of the day.

FAITH DAVIDSON: So... I think I'm going to expand the Darkness Rising series. Vera's found a love interest. Thoughts? I can see three more books, and while I thought it would be a bit of a mess, now that I've re-read the first three chapters that I wrote in this book, I think I've been setting it up all along. Is that possible?

INSTEAD OF REFRESHING the page waiting for a response, she got up and went downstairs to get herself a can of pop from the pantry.

She stood there for a minute, warring with herself before she dragged over a chair and hauled down the box of Halloween treats that she'd pretended were in fact for the holiday, still two months away.

Ha. She nabbed two of the snack-size bags before carefully closing the box up again.

As she returned the chair to its rightful place, she reasoned that after the salty, she'd need something sweet, and she grabbed a chocolate bar from the secret stash, too.

Reinventing her entire series—and her author brand—was scary stuff. The treats were totally justified.

When she got back to her computer, both Gillian Ford and Samantha Harcourt had weighed in. The fourth member of their self-named Quill Quartet, Cecilia Dark, was on a social media hiatus while she finished her book.

For the best—Cecilia would tell her not to do it. That she wasn't known as a romance author and going soft could be the kiss of death.

Faith knew that. And still her heart pounded harder as she read the responses.

SAMANTHA HARCOURT: Yes! Come to the dark side. Who is the hero? Is he a demon? Make him a demon. Ooooh.... Or a vampire.

GILLIAN FORD: She hates vampires.

SAMANTHA HARCOURT: So? Readers don't.

GILLIAN FORD: Also, Vera's a vamp slayer. Focus.

SAMANTHA HARCOURT: You don't even write romance!

FAITH SNICKERED. It was true. Gillian wrote cozy mysteries. The closest she got to romance was a double entendre over a whimsically splayed dead body.

GILLIAN FORD: Maybe I'll follow her lead and mix sexy firefighters into my next series.

SAMANTHA HARCOURT: I'm loving all of this. Go on....

GILLIAN FORD: Faith first. Honestly? I think your readers will want more Vera, and any guy she's going to fall for is going to be bad-ass, right? So it's all good. Do it. Trust your gut!

THAT WAS THE PROBLEM. Faith *didn't* trust her gut. Her gut had her kissing Zander even though he was completely wrong for her.

For a second, she thought about changing the subject. Her girls had held her up when Greg died, helped her figure out what she could write that would make enough money to support herself. Samantha had even flown up to be with her and Miriam when Faith's father died eleven months later and she'd fallen apart all over again.

She would tell them about Zander. Soon.

After the week was over and he'd left her, because he was just her Mr. Right Now. Mr. One Week.

Mr. Awesome With Eric.

She dropped her head to the desk, ignoring the quiet beeping of her computer as her writing friends continued to discuss the pros and cons of Faith finally getting back into writing romance.

Given how hopeless she was at managing her own love life, she hardly felt qualified. But maybe by the time she got to the next book, where Vera and Deacon would stop threatening each other with swords and start getting naked, she'd have a more recent reference point for what that was like.

Not that she'd ever stabbed anyone, and she managed to write that just fine, but watching dirty gifs on Tumblr was a poor substitute for Zander.

She sighed, breathing his name. Not that they'd have a chance to do anything tonight. Or ever.

Two days until he got on a plane.

If only she'd been brave enough to suggest he come over when Eric was at the library.

On her desk, her phone lit up. Her cheeks turned red as she glanced at the screen. Her filthy subconscious must have sent out a bad boy bat signal.

"Hi," she half-squeaked, half-breathed. Not a sexy combination.

"Did I interrupt your writing?" Of course he sounded sexy as sin. Not fair.

"Uhm…" She sat up straighter and pasted on a smile. Telephone speaking rule number one. "Nope! I was just brainstorming the next book in my series."

"I know we made plans to have a picnic dinner, but if I came up your direction sooner than that…?"

"Yes!" She leaned back in her chair. Too excited. "I mean, sure. Whenever."

Jeez. Overcompensating much, Faith?

But Zander didn't seem to notice. "Yeah? Really?"

"Uh-huh." She glanced in horror at her t-shirt and sweat pants. No, not whenever. She needed time to not look like a scary hot mess. "Well, give me fifteen minutes."

"I'm leaving right now. You've got twenty-five."

— —

ZANDER CLIMBED the steps to Faith's house. The flowers he carried were a big gesture that showed his hand. But he wanted Faith to know how interested he was. He wanted her to see that even if it pushed her out of her comfort zone, because he didn't have a lot of time this visit.

Be a gentleman, he told himself over and over again as he waited for her to answer the door.

His resolve lasted until he saw her.

She stood in her foyer in a bathrobe, her hair still damp from a shower.

He grabbed the doorframe to keep from lunging for her, but he couldn't keep himself from doing a head-to-freaking-adorable-bare toes once over. On the way back up, his grin got painfully big. "Did I drive too fast?"

"I'm terrible with time. Something you should probably know about me." She swallowed hard, and he watched her throat work before dragging his gaze up to her dusky pink lips, swollen from the warmth of the shower.

"I'm on vacation, what do I care about timings?" His biceps flexed on their own accord, hungry to wrap themselves around her. He tightened his grip on the open door frame, crushing the stems of the wild flower bouquet he'd all but forgotten about.

"Oh, that's a relief." She blinked almost shyly. "Aren't you going to come in?"

Hell, yes. But first... "Where's Eric?"

"Library program." She gave him a surprisingly flirty look that made him glad he'd called and asked if he could come around early.

"When I let go of this door, I'm going to kiss you."

She beamed. "So let go."

His first thought as he pulled her into his arms, kicking the door shut behind him, was that her eyes were extra blue right out of the shower. The next was that her mouth was extra soft, like velvet.

Then the flowers hit the floor and he stopped thinking.

Where their first kiss had been gentle, this one was an immediate clash of two people in need. Her hands went to his neck and up into his hair. His arms banded tight around her and his palms cupped the swell of her ass beneath the soft terry cotton.

He was painfully aware that only a soft belt separated him from the naked woman he'd been dreaming of all week.

That frustration poured right out of him as they kissed. He couldn't hold back, and thank Christ, she was just as desperate—she moved restlessly against his body, pulling herself tighter into his embrace as she breathed him in, her tongue inviting his right into an X-rated kiss that had him hard as a rock in seconds.

He wove one hand into her silky hair, the cool strands doing nothing to douse his ardour for her. With an insistent tug, he stilled her movements, slowing his caress of her mouth to an erotically glacial pace.

They weren't going to do more than kiss, so this was going to have to rock her world.

With his other hand, he lifted her hips into his, rocking her slowly against his body as he stroked his tongue against hers, thrusting and twisting until she was mewling in his arms.

And then, dying a little inside, he stopped, pressing his lips to her cheek, then her ear. "I wanted to do that yesterday."

She shook in his arms, her cheek rubbing against his as she whispered back, "Me too."

He kissed her again, softer this time, more exploratory. He was still learning the taste of her, what she liked and how she reacted. She sighed as he sucked gently on her lower lip, a sound of pure desire that worked its way right to his balls.

They needed to stop before he did something stupid like sliding his hand inside her robe and finding out just how sweet and heavy her breasts were. If she was wet for him and if she liked him sucking anywhere —everywhere—else.

With a Herculean effort, he licked his way to the corner of her mouth and pressed one last, chaste-ish kiss there before pulling back. "Go put clothes on."

Her eyes were glazed and heavy, and she blinked slowly twice before responding, her gaze pinned on his mouth.

Oh, fuck.

"Really?"

"No. Yes." He made a strangled animal sound in his throat and let her go completely, picking up the flowers and handing them over before crossing his arms for good measure. "Yes. Get dressed and give me a minute to think about math."

He watched as she ducked her head, sniffing the flowers with a smile that made his balls ache. Then she twisted away from him and moved up the stairs. Every third step she glanced back in his direction, and his dick told him how much being noble sucked.

Yep, pretty much.

It didn't take her long to put on jeans and a t-shirt, and as soon as she was back on the ground floor, he leaned in and gave her a regular, quick little kiss.

That felt surprisingly good, too.

"Hi," he whispered, keeping his face close to hers. "Sorry for interrupting your work day."

"I was already thinking about you and feeling distracted," she said, blushing.

"Good." He took a deep breath. "We should get out of the house. You want to go for a ride?"

She froze, then shook her head.

"It's safe." He cleared his throat, not wanting to lie to her. Not that he'd be able to—Faith was whip-smart, and wary enough to question everything. "Well, safe enough. We can just go around town. Slowly. I brought a second helmet. It's my brother's, but I'm not sure he's ever even worn it."

"How about we go sit in my backyard instead?" She worried her bottom lip between her front teeth, and in that moment, he'd have done anything for her.

"Sure." He let her lead him through her house—which was surprisingly large inside, and had an amazing kitchen that opened up onto a large, terraced backyard. She'd stopped long enough to put the flowers in water and grab them drinks. When they got outside, she pointed to a cushioned bench tucked up against the back wall of the house, under the shade of a soaring maple tree.

When they sat, their knees bumping and hands brushing, she didn't speak right away. Instead she looked at him. He could feel her gaze on his neck, his jaw, his brow. Her fingers followed, tracing the top edge of the cityscape tattoo that decorated his shoulder. Her hand curved down his arm and she tugged up his t-shirt sleeve.

"I could just take it off," he said roughly, and she leaned in to kiss his clothed biceps.

"That would be dangerous," she whispered. "What is it?" Her fingers followed the links of ink. Each brush of her flesh against his made his nuts ache a little more. "Oh! Toronto!"

"Yeah."

"Did you ever live there?"

"No. I just wanted an ice rink and a city behind it, and the artist had lived in Toronto. He did this sketch of city hall, and I knew that was it."

She turned her finger so the tip of her fingernail outlined the drawing of the kid playing hockey. "Is this you?"

He shrugged. "It's representative."

"Hmmm." He turned just in time to see her duck her head and press her mouth to his hot, bare skin.

His muscles jumped beneath her lips. "You make it hard to be a good guy."

She smiled against his skin. "Sorry?"

"Tell me why you don't want to go on my bike."

She sighed and turned her head, resting her cheek on his shoulder. Her body curved around his arm, soft moulding around hard—a perfect fit. "It's a long story."

"How much time do we have?"

"Enough."

He wiggled his fingers and she laced hers around them.

"My husband had a racing bike. Not like yours. It wouldn't be comfortable to ride across the country on."

And it would be built for speed. He could see the puzzle pieces, but he might be wrong.

"When he died, I sold it. We didn't have any life insurance, you see, other than a bit through his work. All of a sudden I needed to make every penny count. I didn't get very much for it. And I got so mad at him."

He squeezed her hand, trying to convey whatever one should say, without knowing exactly what that was.

She sighed. "It was a stupid thing to lose my shit over, but that's how grief is sometimes. That was the first time I'd gotten mad that he'd died. It wasn't even a bike accident—but it was similarly stupid, and I saw the bike as a symbol of his choices, I guess. He was waterskiing and did a flip. Landed badly on his neck and he was dead before they got him out of the water."

Zander burned, angry on her behalf. And also angry for her husband, because how many times had the guy probably done something similarly exciting and lived to crow about it?

Every damn time until the last.

Life was unfair. "I'm sorry," he said roughly.

She lifted her head and gave him a sad smile. "I'm usually fine. I've done the counselling thing and I've got a bereavement group that I lead. I've moved on with my life, ya know?"

"It's okay if you're not fine, though. Sometimes or regularly still. Especially if a bonehead like me suggests you do something reckless."

"I used to love that reckless, adventuring spirit. Love it in men, and in myself."

"Nothing wrong with that. There are ways to do things safely. A sedate, grandma-esque tool around town, for example." He winked, to be light, but he wasn't playing off her concerns.

He got it—better than she might think.

"I don't..." She winced. "I don't want half-measures, either. You know? I don't want to go to a gym with a rock wall. If I'm not climbing anymore, I'm not climbing. Full stop."

"You climbed?" He shifted closer, wanting to know more about that. He wanted to know everything about her. But it also seemed like a happier place to steer the conversation toward.

"Yeah." A tentative smile curled up her face. "I wasn't great or anything, but I really enjoyed it. Especially rappelling."

He laughed. "You'd make a good private recruit."

"I really wouldn't. The first time someone tried to get me out of bed at five in the morning I'd be court-martialled for what I'd say to them."

"Not a morning person. Noted."

She blushed, and he thought of all the possible thoughts spiralling through her head to make her cheeks turn pink like that. The two of them waking up together. Naked. He'd make mornings so good for her...

"Don't!" She pointed her finger at him. "Get that thought out of your head." She hesitated, and then went there. "Not if you're not going to do anything about it."

Time slowed to a crawl, and the hot summer afternoon suddenly felt like the surface of the sun. Zander could feel sweat rolling down his back as he weighed his options.

They were both hungry for each other.

This wasn't the time, though. "What? I just want to take you for a ride around town, Ms. Davidson. You have a filthy mind." He mock nipped at her fingertip and she laughed.

Then she sighed and her face slid back to that serious, thinking expression she wore so often. Her mom face. Her writer face. He got that those were two important hats for her to wear, but she needed a way to find the joy of adventure, too. Not in this moment, though.

She gave him a little shrug. "I need to get Eric from the library in an hour."

"I can do a lot in an hour." Now he was just having fun making her mind go to the various filthy places. Because even though she was blushing, her eyes were wide and bright and glued to his face. She wanted more and damn it, he wanted to give it to her.

In every imaginable way.

But the first time he made love to her, he didn't want it to be rushed. And on a selfish note, he didn't want her to be able to run away afterward—not until he'd made sure they were okay.

"I could do even more if we had a whole night." He took a deep breath. "You can slug me if this is too presumptuous, but is there any way you could get away tonight?"

Her face transformed in an instant. Distant, hungry longing shifted to a bright, sparkly conspiratorial look. "Maybe."

"It'll take me a bit of time to figure out where we should go—and later on I'll tell you about just how damn nosy my family is."

She laughed. "I bet they love you."

"Like Lenny and the mouse."

She threw her arms around his neck, her entire body shaking with glee. "A Steinbeck reference. If you can find us a quiet place later on, I'll reward you for that."

CHAPTER TEN

"DID you have any trouble getting away?"

Faith shook her head. Her mouth was too busy licking and kissing Zander's jaw to actually use words.

She'd ducked out of having to explain anything directly to her mother by dropping Eric off at Ryan Howard's place for dinner and a play date with Maya—an acceptable alternative to a picnic with Zander, although she felt a pang of guilt about the change of plans. Miriam had gone to the early show and would pick him up before bedtime on her way back up the peninsula. She hadn't even blinked at Faith's texted request.

Ryan, on the other hand, seemed to know exactly what she was doing. The knowing look he'd given her when she dropped off her son made her wish the ground would open up. But there'd been an understanding edge to it—unlike her mother or Zander's family, he wouldn't relish in her embarrassment, she knew that. And her secret was safe with him.

Now all of those thoughts faded away. Zander had

texted her a cryptic question—**do you have GPS?**—and then sent her coordinates for where to meet him when she responded that of course she did, and she even knew how to use it.

It turned out that Zander's snowmobile trail knowledge had other advantages. At the end of a dead-end road ten minutes north of Pine Harbour she found Zander's bike. Parking next to it, she got out and followed her phone's instructions down a small trail through the woods, and came out the other side to a secret paradise.

The beach was small, hemmed in on either side by pine trees and rising rock. Waves crashed on enough boulders in the private bay that she doubted it was safe to swim in, but the shore had a decent amount of sand, and closer to the woods, soft grass and pine needles made an equally nice base for a couple of tents.

Or tonight, just one.

Zander rose from his seat next to a small fire he'd made and approached, an easy smile relaxing his normally sharp features.

Camping looked good on him.

"This is nice," she murmured as he pulled her close for a soft kiss that quickly heated up.

He groaned as she slid her hands under his shirt. "Found it my last year of high school. I'm sure other people use it, but I've never seen anyone here."

She nodded, only half listening. Which was terrible. Zander was interesting and this place was beautiful.

But he was more beautiful, and since he was leaving the next day, and she'd finally admitted just how much she wanted him...now she really wanted him. Over and over again.

He spun them around, pointing her to the campfire. His tent was set back toward the woods, and between it and the fire lay a thick blanket. On it was a picnic basket and a small cooler.

"Hungry?" he asked as he tugged her down to the blanket.

Her only response was to roll on top of him and kiss him again.

That's when he asked her about getting away without difficulty.

The man asked way too many questions.

He laughed and rolled them both so they were on their sides, then he cupped her cheek and finally stopped talking.

After a time, when she was finally drunk on the taste of him, sated for the time being, he pulled her to sit between his legs, her back against his chest, and they ate cookies and drank coffee from a shared thermos as they watched the sun set over the lake.

"Thank you for tonight," he whispered, his lips caressing the curve of her ear.

She rolled her head back. "It's been a wonderful week. Better than I ever could have imagined, really. I'd given up on the idea of having a social life."

"I have to admit I wondered why you're still single."

"Fear, mostly."

"Mostly?"

"There's also the other side factor—grown men on the prowl are worse than teenage boys." She hesitated, but something about Zander made her want to tell him everything. "I did try dating, about a year and a half after Greg died. When Eric was sleeping through the night and my mom had moved in with me. I wasn't looking for anything romantic, just..."

He tensed around her, and she worried she'd made a mistake. Of course he wouldn't want to picture her with other guys, not that anything had happened. But she'd wanted it to. Getting laid had been her goal for a bit, and when she hadn't been able to find a healthy, safe way to do that with someone who sparked the right kind of feelings, she'd buried those feelings deep.

"You deserve the world." His words were slow. Careful. Rough with an edge of something she couldn't name—but it felt sharp. Possessive, like her pleasure might be a responsibility he wanted.

Zander sparked all the right kind of feelings.

He lightened his tone a bit. "But I can't deny that some of my feelings for you are of the teenage-boy variety."

He was always doing that—hedging his bets, dialling back his intensity because he didn't want to alarm her, maybe. Or maybe even now she was sending mixed signals. Time for that to end.

"I'm a big girl, Zander. I know that I said some things...I was scared. Am still scared, since we're being honest." She twisted in his arms, sitting sideways so she could see his face. "But I want this—I want *you*—more than I want to be alone. So you don't need to make a joke. Unless you're making me smile, because I like that."

"Yeah?" His face lit up.

"Yeah. Tell me what you want. I promise I won't run scared. Not tonight."

"I want to hold you naked in my arms and make you moan." He rolled his shoulders and pulled her closer—enough that she had to tilt her head back to still see his serious expression. "In a perfect world, I'd want more."

"But you're leaving tomorrow." The words were hard to say.

But not impossible.

She was stronger than she gave herself credit for.

"I am."

He'd been brave and said what he wanted. Now it was her turn. She ran her finger along his jaw, down his throat. Watched his Adam's Apple bob and savoured the heat of his taut skin. Then she buried closer still, hoping that she could get deep enough that *yes* wouldn't be a possible answer to her next question. "Are we saying goodbye?"

"That's up to you." He exhaled roughly. "I don't want to."

"But you're leaving."

"I'm coming back. Do you want this to be goodbye?"

She shook her head.

"Then it won't be."

What would it be, then? The start of a relationship on hold?

"It doesn't have to be," he said stiffly, and she realized with a pang that she'd asked that selfish question out loud.

"I didn't mean—"

"Shhh," he murmured, relaxing his body around her. "We're getting off track from my charming camping seduction."

She laughed despite her mortification. "Really, Zander, that's just my inner neurotic girl talking. I don't have any expectations other than I want to keep building our...friendship."

He didn't say anything for a bit. He just held her and touched her, whispered his lips against her ear and down her neck. Finally, when she was well and thoroughly undone, he rolled her onto her back. It had gotten dark while they talked.

"I am your friend, no matter what." He gave her a stern look, one she could imagine him pointing at children who got too noisy. The fondest kind of stern. It looked good on him. "But I want more. I want to hear your secrets and soothe your frustrations. Cheer your successes and be someone you can lean on."

"How many friends do you have like that?"

"None."

She believed him. There was a raw look in his eye that promised while he may have said more than he'd intended —or maybe she was reading clearly between the lines for the first time in days—he was making her promises that he'd hold up. "I'm going to miss you something fierce."

"Then we'll just have to make a memory tonight that will keep you warm while I'm gone."

It was keeping her more than warm right then. He kept talking, in between kisses and caresses, and slowly her shirt got worked up her torso. It felt like the most amazing kind of agony, that slow creep of his palm up her side. An inch at a time, then he'd stop. Squeeze, stroke her with his thumb. Return his attention to her mouth and her neck.

He was making her squirm in the best way possible, and by the time his fingertips grazed her bra, she was aching for more. Her nipples rubbed against the inside of the lace cups, making her already hot and heavy flesh even more so as he cupped her breasts.

Holding her breath, she watched as he ducked his head, his face disappearing in the shadows. His breath drifted over the valley in the middle, then up one swollen slope. Through the lace, he outlined her nipple, tracing the tight nub until she cried out for more.

Then he sucked, right through her bra, making the delicate fabric wet and clingy. When he moved to the other side, the warm summer night's breeze was a second tongue, lapping at her exposed body.

He settled between her legs, not grinding—just there. Hard and ready. More teasing.

She was going to explode from the delayed gratification. Lifting her hips, she took on the task of remedying that herself.

At the first roll of her hips, Zander paused his worship of her breasts. At the second, he redoubled his efforts, helping her get right to the brink—then he reared up and reached for the waistband of her jeans.

Oh no.

She wanted to be naked with Zander more than anything else in the world.

But even under the cover of darkness, she realized she wasn't quite ready for Zander to *see* her naked.

She grabbed at his wrists and tried to pull him back down on top of her. Maybe they could just dry hump. That had been hotter than it sounded. It had been hotter than her fantasies, and she was a writer with a pretty expansive vocabulary and a deep understanding of the dirty side of the Internet.

He wouldn't be deterred. His fingers slid beneath her waistband, making her soft tummy quiver, and not in a good way. Okay, mostly a good way with just an edge of fear. But she still pushed at his hands.

He gave her an amused look. "Stop batting my hands away. I want to feel it when you come."

She sighed, suddenly nervous, and he gave her another look, this time one of dawning awareness. She tipped her head back. The stars were so bright tonight. "I've got battle scars," she whispered. "Stretch marks and a c-section incision that didn't heal properly. You've only seen the good bits."

Zander settled back on the blanket beside her and nuzzled into her neck. "Seriously? You don't think I've got scars? Let's go toe to toe."

"Yours are different." He was beautiful. All sculpted muscle and delicious shadows. "New plan. I'm going to touch you."

"Be my guest." His voice was low and rough, like a tumble of falling rocks. *Danger*, her heart thumped. He rolled away from her and pulled off his t-shirt, baring the tattoos that had caused her so much anxiety just a few days earlier. The flickering light from the fire caught the edge of a raised scar on his rib cage, and she sucked in a breath as she reached out and traced the knotted tissue that looked suspiciously like a slash in his skin.

"What happened?" she asked in a quick rush, then shook her head. "No. I don't think I want to know."

"You don't. But it's okay, I'm alive and here. That's all that matters."

"Hardly," she murmured as she let her fingers rove over his torso. Under her touch, his skin pebbled and his muscles flexed. His gaze was riveted on her face, like he couldn't believe they were doing this. That didn't make any sense. She was the lucky one, getting free reign to explore his perfect body. She circled her index finger around three faint white lines on his shoulder. "This looks older."

"Bike accident when I was a kid. Flew over the handle bars and landed in some gravel, shoulder first." Lifting his right arm over his head, he distracted her with his flexing biceps, and she didn't notice his other arm scooping her by the hips and hauling her on top of his body. "Come here."

Laughing, she kissed his chin. "I'm right here, no need to manhandle me."

"Oh, there's need."

Right. She could feel his need squarely pressed against her pelvis now. It matched the heat flaring inside her, making her wet and achy.

"But first..." he wiggled his raised arm. "Keep going. We're looking at all my horrible flaws."

She couldn't really see his arm anymore. He was holding her too close, and his gaze was too piercing. Too hot and demanding of kisses. "You don't have any flaws," she breathed, brushing her lips against his. "You're perfect."

"You only see the good parts, babe." He sucked her lower lip between his, licking the captured flesh in a teasing motion before pulling her closer for a deeper kiss. By the time they broke apart, she was panting for more. "Look at my stretch marks."

She stared at him dumbly for a second. "What?"

He laughed, his entire body shaking beneath her. "On my arm."

Tipping her head sideways, she looked closely at the underside of his upper arm. Barely visible thin white ribbons ran from the top of his curved biceps muscle into the dark, silky hair in his armpit. "Oh, but those are barely—"

He rolled her quickly onto her back, muffling her shriek with a hungry, demanding kiss. "Barely noticeable? Not what you notice when you look at me? Trust me, babe, I only see the good parts on you, too."

— —

SHE SIGHED and dug her nails lightly into his back, her eyelashes softly fluttering as she breathed his name.

A surge of emotion overtook Zander and his throat felt thick as he kept talking.

"Let me in, babe. Let me make you feel good." She'd had her turn. Now he wanted to explore every last perfect inch of her body, as long as she wanted him to. "Tell me to stop and I will. Any time, no questions asked. But I want you, Faith. I want to make you feel so good you forget everything else for tonight."

He lifted his head just enough to bring her eyes into focus. He liked being so close that everything was blurry and they shared the same air, but for this, he needed to know he wasn't crossing a line.

"Yes." She smiled tremulously as she reached for the button on her jeans. The glint of steel balls grabbed his attention. Her other two piercings were both in her navel, and that was hot as hell.

"Hang on," he whispered, covering her hands with his. He ghosted his lips around the twin silver barbells, one through the skin above her belly button, the other right below. "How did I miss these?"

He glanced up at her, but it was a rhetorical question. She gave him a shaky smile.

"Any more?"

She laughed and shook her head. He pressed his mouth more firmly into the soft skin below the piercings, right above her waistband. It felt like heaven against his lips. There wasn't an inch of her body that didn't turn him on.

"Let me in, Faith," he finally rumbled, releasing her hands. He could worship every inch of her again once they were both naked.

The rasp of her fly was the sexiest sound he could imagine, and he slid his hands around her hips, beneath the denim, helping her strip down to her lace panties.

His girl wore lace beneath her distressed-by-real-life jeans. The bra had been gorgeous, but somehow he hadn't registered it as an actual lingerie set until he saw the bottoms.

Moving lower, he brushed his mouth over the lace that hid the heart of her, then slid his palms under her gorgeous ass and lifted her bottom. He traced her sex through the panties, loving the way she bucked her hips as he reached her clit. She was so responsive. So sexy.

And all his, at least for tonight.

He kissed her harder there, then lower, breathing in her musky sweetness, letting it fill his head and take him to a more primal place. His lips moved along the edge of the fabric, then onto the inside of her thigh. She shivered when he grazed the softness there with his teeth, a barely whispered plea the only sound in the night air.

"More…"

Oh, he'd give her more. He nipped her again, then sucked on the skin, loving it with his tongue. It would probably leave a mark she'd see for a few days.

Nothing compared to the mark she was leaving on his heart.

Fuck, he needed more of her. His pulse hammering hard, he jerked her underwear to the side and dove back in, licking her up and down until she was groaning his name over and over again.

He reached down and unbuttoned his jeans, shoving them down his hips and kicking them off into the sand in the darkness beyond their little world of blanket and bonfire. A woodland creature could wander off with them for all he cared right now. His cock throbbed to be inside her, but when that happened, it wouldn't take long until he exploded, and she needed to do that first. On his tongue.

He squeezed the back of her thighs, spreading her wider still as he stroked his hands to her knees then back up again. All the way to her core. He couldn't get enough of touching and tasting her, because she was a goddess. Soft curves. Wet heat. Responsive as fuck. He looked up at her through hooded eyes. One hand was braced against the blanket as she arched her back.

The other was inside her bra, playing with one of her nipples.

He just about died.

"You're so beautiful," he rasped, and when she looked at him, her lips parted and swollen, he knew that moment would be burned into his memory so he could replay it again and again.

"You can tell me that whenever you want, soldier," she whispered.

He responded by sliding a finger inside her. "Beautiful," he repeated as she gasped, holding his gaze. "So tight. God, that's beautiful, Faith. So greedy for my fingers."

He didn't care if he was repeating himself. It deserved to be repeated. He'd send her text messages every day reminding her of this gift she'd given him. This connection.

"It's been a while," she panted, half-laughing. But she was mostly dazed, spun-out on desire, and Zander was so fucking proud he did that to her. Could give that to her.

"How long?" He growled the question, not really wanting to know the answer, because he wanted to be the only person who could do this to her.

She blinked at him, and he knew the answer before she said it—and he was glad he'd asked. "Since Greg."

"Oh, fuck." His heart cracked and he surged up her body, not stopping his ministrations to her most sensitive parts as he kissed her. "I'm sorry. I'm rushing you. I thought...I mean, you said you'd dated."

A lazy, amused smile crept across her face as she nuzzled him. "All aborted efforts. I wasn't ready then. I am now. I'm ready for you."

She felt more than ready. Slick and swollen. He still hadn't made her come, but now he needed to be inside her more than he needed to be a sex god. He added another finger, stretching her with two digits. He teased her entrance with a third, but she whimpered, so he eased off.

"Can I be on top?" she asked, kissing his chest.

He rolled onto his back, reaching for the picnic basket as he stretched out. "There's a box of condoms in there, hang on..."

She laughed as she wiggled out of her underwear, then straddled his thighs and loosely circled his cock with her fingers. His hips moved with a life of their own, rocking up into her touch as he tried and failed to grab the edge of the basket.

"Uhm..." She shifted higher up his thighs, rubbing her

pussy against the underside of his cock. "I have an IUD," she whispered.

His dick strained hard against her hand and Zander tried to think clearly. That guy was not in charge of this conversation, as much as he might want to be. God, she was wet. He bucked against her. "I've had two physicals since the last time I had sex," he admitted. "Are you..."

"I haven't been with anyone since before Eric was born." She licked her lips as she looked down at him. "I trust you. And I want you inside me. Just you. Nothing between us."

He rolled up, wrapping his arms around her as she ground against him. Taking her mouth in a hot, desperate kiss, he told himself this was a bad idea. He'd never had sex without a condom. Not once in his thirty-seven years. Tonight was not the night to break that record.

But Faith wasn't like any other woman. He trusted her, too.

And more than that, he was pretty sure he was falling in love with her.

Fuck, fuck, fuck.

How could he be sure that wasn't his inner caveman roaring? Or even just his cock making more of the hottest sex of his life than it should?

"I'm sorry," she whispered. "I shouldn't have..."

"No." He shook his head. "It's okay. I've never gone without condoms before. I'm just...fuck, Faith." He laughed as she pressed up on her knees, wiggling her hips around until she'd notched them together. "Tell me this isn't reckless."

She did an agonizingly slow swivel of her hips. "Can't do that." She grinned at him. "Wanna do it anyway?"

He nodded, settling his hands on her hips. "Yes."

With a breathy exhale, she lowered herself onto him. Inch by glorious inch, she surrounded him with her heat, then paused. It was nearly impossible not to pulse up into her, pushing further, but he held himself still. Waiting.

This was her show. He'd wound them up, now she was riding him and she got to set the pace.

Her pace ended up being deliciously, tantalizingly slow.

It was perfect.

She kissed him softly as she rose up, then sank again, taking more of him. Up, down. Deeper. With each lift, her muscles flexed beneath his hand, and inside, different ones —softer ones—squeezed him tight. And then she'd lower herself, blooming for him as he surged into her, and she'd make these noises.

Breathy moans and groaning sighs. Earthy, wonderful sounds that told him she was building toward a climax. Anxious, desperate noises when she got closer still, when she lost her rhythm and he needed to take over.

He took them back to the slow grind, using his mouth and his hands to make love to every part of her body. Her neck. His mouth on her breasts. God, he loved the taste of her skin and the rub of her nipples against his tongue. How wide her hips were as she straddled him and how responsive her clit was when he found it with the pad of his thumb, squeezing his hand between their bodies.

When her orgasm hit, rippling through her body, he almost tumbled over that cliff with her. Instead he breathed in the beauty of her as she became completely undone, and told himself to be patient.

They had all night.

And if he played his cards right, they'd have forever.

She wasn't ready for that, of course. She'd said as much.

But as he rolled her onto her back, kissing her softly until she was ready for him again, he made promises.

Silent ones. To himself and to Faith.

And when he finally found his release inside her, when she clung to him once they were both spent, he whispered the barest essence of those promises to her.

"I've got you, beautiful. I've got you."

CHAPTER ELEVEN

"HE'LL BE BACK for the wedding," Dani said with more than a little amusement as their mother fussed over Zander. He was unpacking his saddlebags and figuring out what he could leave in Pine Harbour and what he needed to take back to the base.

"I know, but we've hardly seen him this week. He was gone all last night, for goodness sake. Didn't roll in until seven this morning smelling of bonfire."

It was so inappropriate to pop a boner in front of your mother, so Zander kept his head down and tried not to think of making love to Faith. Twice next to the fire, and when that burned out, again in the tent, slowly, because she'd been sore and tired, but he couldn't get enough of her. And then she'd woken him up at five this morning, kissing her way down his body, proving that she also had a hunger for the magic they made together. At least he wasn't the only depraved one.

Fuck. Math. He needed to think of math. Not bonfires and blow jobs and dark-haired writers with sparkling blue eyes.

Even his mother's voice wasn't the cold shower he really needed. "And the wedding weekend is going to fly by so fast," she continued. "When will you get in, Alessandro?"

He stifled a laugh. She only called him that—his father's name, his namesake—when he was getting ready to leave her.

It never stopped him from going, because he was a terrible son.

He was his father's offspring in more ways than one.

Tamping down that bitter, never-spoken thought, he glanced up at his hovering mother. He hadn't booked his flight yet, but he needed to figure out a way to do it and steal some time with Faith without her knowing. "About that...I think I'll get a rental car for the wedding weekend."

Both women protested. It wasn't the Minelli way. Even though the airport was three and a half hours away, someone always came to pick him up. Tom would be driving him there later today.

"Leave it alone. I can't take someone away from wedding preparations for an entire day, not when they stock perfectly acceptable cars for just such a purpose right at the airport."

"We can argue about that later. Just remember when you book your flights that the rehearsal dinner is on Thursday night, not Friday."

"Ma," Dani interjected. "Zander doesn't need to take that many days off."

"I'll do my best."

"I know you will, my darling. You and Tom will be the most eligible bachelors. Don't pass up this opportunity to find someone, hmm?"

Oh, shit. "Do not try to fix me up with anyone."

"Why not?" This time it was Dani who asked, and from the stricken look that crossed her face as soon as the two words were out of her mouth, she'd said them without thinking. "I mean, of course not. It's not a good time."

He cleared his throat. He hadn't asked Faith to come to the wedding yet, but now he needed to—and more importantly, he wanted to. "It's actually a just fine time, but I may have a date for the wedding."

"You may?" Anne pitched her voice into that *tell your mother everything* zone that gave him chills.

"I have someone that I'm going to be asking. And if she's busy, I don't want to be fixed up with anyone else." He stood and nodded down at his small backpack. Everything he needed for his flight. But first he had a phone call to make. "Excuse me."

He strode outside and dialled his brother's number. "Tom? I need a favour."

— —

THE DOORBELL RANG and Faith pushed away from the kitchen table where she was working on a puzzle with Eric and her mother. "That'll be dinner," she said, but neither of them were paying any attention. Not even Eric, who normally needed to be the one who answered the door.

It was a really good puzzle, and it had been a long day. She'd already explained to Eric that they weren't going to see Zander again for a while, and that was okay, because he had to go and work with the army and protect the country.

She lied like a pro.

It *was* okay. Of course it was. He had an important job, and he was coming to the end of that responsibility, anyway.

Then he'd move to Pine Harbour and they could... date. The thought made her warm all over like a school girl who'd just been invited to the prom. Only in this case, the prom wouldn't happen for six months, and when it did, would be more likely to be a jeans-and-t-shirt-type dance at the legion.

In other words, perfect.

But waiting for that...and telling her son to wait...that was agonizing.

Faith had been focused so hard on being *smart* and *safe*, she hadn't given any weight to the possibility that they weren't the same thing.

Because saying goodbye to Zander hadn't felt safe at all.

So she'd ordered fish and chips and planned a movie night. She'd curl up with Eric and try desperately to stop thinking of the calendar in terms of days and weeks. Months would be so much easier to count down. And if she held her breath for thirty days at a time to get it done, so be it.

She'd been frozen before.

And Zander had taught her that the thaw could be lovely. She just needed to be patient.

She grabbed her purse from the closet and muttered something rude under her breath when the delivery guy knocked again. Mighty demanding knock from someone who wanted a tip.

But on the other side of the door stood a man who could be as demanding as he wanted.

"Zander," she breathed, not caring at all that she was blushing or sounded like an infatuated teenager. "I thought you'd gone!"

He grinned, every inch the charming rake she'd been smitten by. "I may have changed my flight to tomorrow."

Her heart beat faster, each flutter more reckless than the last. "Yeah?"

"Except for my brother Tom, my family all thinks that I've left already. So...I was wondering if you and Eric wanted to have dinner with me."

"Absolutely." She couldn't breathe properly. "If you... where are staying tonight?"

"Tom's."

Her mind was racing. "You could stay here. Not in my room, because of Eric, but...we have a guest room."

"I don't want to impose." He raked his gaze over her and she wondered for a moment if maybe she had really just gone up in flames. Nope, no scorch marks. But whew...the heat that rolled off him when he looked at her was insane. Had it been like that all week and she just hadn't noticed?

And he didn't want to impose. Silly man. She stepped back and opened the door wider. "Come in. My mom is in the kitchen so I'm going to have some awkward explaining to do when Eric starts jumping all over you, but she's generally pretty cool. And we can discuss the rest later."

He stepped into the foyer and looked past her, but she could hear Miriam and Eric still loudly arguing over the puzzle. She hopped up unto her tiptoes and kissed his cheek, and he cupped her jaw, holding her in place so he could kiss her lips.

"Gotta do it right," he whispered against her skin.

Her chest ached as her heart doubled in size.

"You do everything right," she murmured, reluctantly stepping back.

"Except for the part where I fly across the country tomorrow." He gave her a pained look.

"You can't help that." She rolled her lower lip between her teeth. "And now we've got a bonus night. We're just waiting for delivery—fish and chips again, but there will be plenty to share."

He beamed. "And I've got more chocolate chip cookies."

"That's a very fair trade."

"I'll go get them." He stepped toward the door and their hands came up, linked, between their bodies.

When had she slipped her fingers into his?

And why was it so hard to let him go and get cookies?

She lingered in the doorway, watching him bound to his bike. Behind him, a car pulled into the drive, and he stopped and waited for the delivery guy. Before she could say anything he'd pulled out his wallet and handed over three twenties, accepting the bag of food with a wave and a thanks.

He's leaving in the morning. Apparently her heart hadn't just exploded, because now it was very solidly, very painfully thumping in her chest.

She didn't want him to go.

She wanted this—him in her driveway, him walking up the steps with a bag of food, him leaning in to kiss her forehead—

"Faith?"

But her fantasy didn't include her mother catching a stranger kissing her on the forehead.

Zander froze, then stepped to the side and gave her mother his most charming smile. "Delivery?"

Bubbling, unstoppable laughter shook Faith's body and she doubled over. When she stood up again, tears were streaming out the corner of her eyes. She shooed Zander in, muttering something about finding Eric.

Which left her standing on the front step receiving a what-the-hell look from her mother.

"Who is that?"

"That's Zander."

"He's...tall."

Another laugh ripped out of Faith's mouth and she wiped her eyes again. "Yes, he is."

"Why are the fish and chips being delivered by a tall drink of water on a motorcycle, all the way to our kitchen table, with a pause for a kiss for you?"

"That's not exactly what's happening."

"So the fish and chips guy didn't just kiss you? I mean, they are pirates. I wouldn't put it past them."

Faith sighed. "He's not a pirate."

"Are you going to tell me anything else?"

"Are you going to stop asking me questions long enough to give me a chance?"

Miriam's eyebrows hit the roof. And she pressed her lips together.

"We met last week, at Greta's. He's in the military and he's been a wealth of knowledge for my latest book. He's from Pine Harbour and was visiting for the week, and tonight..." She didn't need to justify it to her mother. She was a grown-up.

But maybe she needed to justify it to herself.

"He's flying back out west tomorrow. So tonight he's staying here."

Miriam's expression didn't move.

That could be good. It could be bad.

Faith was too rattled to tell the difference.

"Not in my room," she hastened to add. "He'll sleep in the guest room."

Still nothing.

"What?"

"Well, if it were me, I wouldn't have him stay in the guest room, but I suppose that makes sense with Eric," her mother finally muttered.

"Mom!"

"What? He's very tall."

Faith was starting to understand where she'd inherited her taste in men.

"Okay, don't say anything like that to him." She yanked the door open and pointed inside. "Let's go."

— —

FAITH'S FAMILY was totally different than the Minelli clan. They argued silently, for one thing. Over dinner, when Eric didn't want to eat the frozen peas Miriam added so there would be something green on their plates—"Because coleslaw isn't a vegetable", a statement of Miriam's opinion that Faith vehemently denied as fact—all Faith had to do was give him a raised eyebrow and he shoved a spoonful in his mouth.

And when he said, "yummy," with a grimace that said the exact opposite on his face, nobody reamed him out.

There were still rules, and rebellion, but both were muted.

Zander thought it was delightful.

For a guy who'd spent his whole life surrounded by ever increasing noise—quarrels, arguments, lectures, drill sergeants, explosives, war zones, motorcycle engines and helicopter rotors—this quiet family dinner was an unexpected balm.

After dinner they cleared the table, but dishes were just scrapped and stacked next to the sink, to be done after Eric went to bed, so they could squeeze in a promised family movie night before it got too late.

Chores taking a back seat to fun? Zander could get behind that, too.

In the cozy, book and photograph lined family room that overlooked the garden, an armoire opened up to reveal a decent sized flat screen TV. Eric hopped on the shabby chic sectional and demanded that Zander sit right in the corner—"So Mommy can sit on one side and I can sit on the other!"—and that sounded damn perfect.

Faith hid her blush by scurrying off to the kitchen to make popcorn. When she came back, Miriam had taken the arm chair. She stood in the doorway for a minute and Zander could feel her watching him reading the back of The Lego Movie DVD case with Eric.

"This looks like it might be scary," Zander mock whispered, stealing a look up at Faith. She handed a bowl of popcorn to her mother, then disappeared again.

Eric nodded solemnly. "It's okay to hide under the blanket."

"Duly noted."

When Faith returned, she didn't bring more individual bowls of popcorn, but rather one big bowl. And she put it on Zander's lap.

Eric curled up on one side of him, and while Faith left a bit more room on the other side, her arm did brush his on a regular basis as they watched the movie. And when Eric squealed and grabbed the throw, hiding behind both it and Zander's arm, Faith teasingly did the same on the other side.

And she stayed there for the rest of the movie, her cheek pressed against his biceps.

So did Eric.

Zander couldn't imagine a better last night on the peninsula.

Once the credits rolled, it took Faith half an hour to put Eric to bed. Twice he got up, once to give Zander another hug goodnight and again for a glass of water.

If Zander had been the adult in charge, Eric probably never would have gone to sleep. One adorable tilt of his tousled blond head and that gleeful dimpled smile, and Zander would have put on another movie and made more popcorn.

He was a sucker, and he wasn't ashamed to admit it.

He also didn't mind either of those interruptions to the otherwise one-on-one time he was having on the main floor with Faith's mother.

Miriam was lovely, of course. And she didn't have anything on the shark-attack approach that his own mother preferred. But there was no mistaking the fact that she too was a mama bear.

He liked her.

But he also feared the way she looked at him, because in Zander's experience, mothers *knew* things. So he wondered…did Miriam know how much Faith was afraid of making a mistake? Of diving recklessly into a doomed adventure?

Could she see that Zander desperately wanted to be more than an adventure? More than a delayed rebound guy? More than a "right now" fling?

She didn't say anything. She just washed the plates and handed them over, and he did what any sane man would do—he dried them and pretended he had better answers to the obvious questions—because the truth was pretty damning.

Yes, I had sex with your daughter last night. Yes. I'm covered in tattoos and drive a motorcycle. Yes, I'm leaving tomorrow.

But like her daughter, Miriam didn't need to say anything. She just looked at him from time to time, eyebrow raised ever so slightly. He stood straighter and squared his shoulders. Yes, he knew how special her daughter was. He saw how strong she was, even when she didn't feel it in herself. He saw her wanderlust spirit and her need to protect her son and he loved both equally. Fiercely. Yes, he was leaving, but he'd come back.

He was already thinking about how he could re-jig his monthly leave days, usually used for shopping trips into the city or personal appointments, and fly back once a month until his contract was up in March.

He wouldn't leave Faith and Eric hanging.

"Can you put this bowl on the top shelf?" Miriam asked, interrupting his thoughts. She was holding the glazed pottery dish she'd served the peas in, which she'd just dried herself, and pointed to the fourth shelf in the extra tall cupboard. He'd noticed her use a footstool to get it down earlier. That stool was now folded up and tucked in a nook beside the fridge.

"Yes, ma'am."

"Faith says you work out west."

"I do. That's coming to an end."

"And then what?" She gave him that appraising *mother knows* look that said she saw him, too.

A week earlier, he'd ridden off the ferry wondering that exact same question. Now he felt a lot more comfortable in his answer. "Then I'm moving back to the peninsula. I'm from Pine Harbour. Got a lot of roots here."

"Big family?" For someone who didn't talk a lot, Miriam suddenly had a lot to say. Or ask.

Her right, of course. Zander nodded. "Two brothers and a sister. They're all in the area."

"And you joined the army and travelled far and wide." She smiled, but there was a tremor of tension in her brow even as she did it.

"Got it out of my system," he said evenly. *For the most part*. But the thought of not being able to pick up and go— of maybe having some responsibility beyond a job— suddenly didn't terrify him.

"Good to know."

And that was that. She pointed to the cupboard again, he put the dish away, and returned to drying plates.

When Faith came downstairs, she'd changed out of her jeans and t-shirt, and put on a simple black jersey dress. Bare legs. Bare feet. No jewelry and just a bit of lip gloss, maybe.

She took his breath away.

"I'm going to bed," Miriam announced.

"Night, Mom," Faith murmured, but her gaze didn't leave Zander's face.

He slowly dried the plate in his hand, then reached up and put it on the shelf without breaking that connection.

"You can leave the rest to dry in the rack," Faith said, coming closer.

"It's no problem," he said gruffly.

Miriam smiled at him from behind Faith.

He tried and failed not to turn red.

CHAPTER TWELVE

THE HOUSE WAS SUDDENLY VERY, very quiet.

Faith stood in the doorway, watching Zander dry the last two plates and listening to her mother climb the stairs at the same time. At the top of the landing there was a door to the granny flat above the garage, where Miriam had made her own space. Faith tipped her gaze up, staring at the ceiling as she heard the door open, then some rustling around. Miriam went into the main bathroom between Eric's room and the spare room and got the baby monitor Faith had left on the counter.

Her mother knew her so well, for better or worse. Miriam knew that Faith needed someone else to keep an ear out for Eric...and that she wanted to be alone with Zander.

From the way he was blushing, he knew all of that too.

And the house was too damn quiet to share that knowledge in any other way than with equally embarrassed looks.

She crossed through the kitchen to the living room and turned on the stereo, which they kept tuned to public radio, and on a Friday night, that meant a weekly lecture series. Someone was talking about the meaning of "self" and individuality.

An excellent question for the end of a week where Zander had made her reconsider every notion she had about herself. He'd stormed into her life and given her ideas and fears and hopes and desires, and now they had one more night, a bonus chance to say goodbye properly.

He was done with the dishes, and he met her in the middle of the room. She looped her fingers through his. She couldn't imagine a more unexpectedly natural feeling in the world than holding his hand, ready to lead him away from this domestic scene to something more private.

She'd been a mother for so long, and *only* a mother, that she'd thought this selfishness would be harder.

From the second he'd been born, her son had owned her heart, and raising him—getting to see him grow and learn—it was a gift. It didn't feel hard fought at all, and she knew she was lucky for that. But the few times she'd tried to take something like this for herself, it had felt *wrong*.

This ease with Zander shook her to her core because this wasn't supposed to happen.

Not with him. Not to her.

She wasn't this lucky.

She led him down the hallway to the small craft room tucked in behind the living room—the furthest point in the house from her mother's room, safely tucked around the corner from the living room. It had a long, comfortable couch...and the door locked.

She whispered for him to pull it closed behind him while she moved further into the room to find the lamp.

The click of the latch was like a starter's pistol—both in

imagined volume and in a metaphorical start to this most private part of what had been an unexpectedly lovely evening already. He'd closed the door before she got the light turned on, and then he was behind her, his arms around her waist and his mouth on the back of her neck. Her fingers slipped off the plastic knob and she fumbled for it again, then gave up, turning in his arms.

The moonlight streaming in the window was enough for now.

They tumbled together onto the couch, touching in a quiet, reverential moment of reconnection.

He captured her face between his hands and kissed her softly at first, then more insistently. She started to climb into his lap and he dropped his hands to her hips, stilling her movement. "Your mom? Eric?"

"Mom took the monitor for Eric's room into her apartment, which is on the other side of the house. We probably shouldn't get naked, but we won't be interrupted unless the house is on fire."

"I'm resourceful. There's a lot we can do without getting naked."

The first thing he did was ruck her skirt up to her waist. Under her dress she was wearing black boy short panties, and he slid his hands under the stretchy cotton, cupping her bottom.

Then he surprised the hell out of her by continuing to make conversation. "Hey, so...I'm back next month for my sister's wedding."

"Yeah?" She beamed at him and kissed the corner of his mouth. A bonus visit, maybe?

"And I want to ask you to be my date."

Wow. "Okay. You should do that."

"Ask you?"

"Yes."

"I will."

She laughed. "When?"

"When I get up the nerve." He squeezed her butt cheeks, and she wondered how he could doubt she'd be all over that.

She rolled her hips, finding him hard and ready. Big Zander might be nervous, but Little Zander had no doubt of her interest, and the feeling was obviously mutual. "Zander, I'm going to say yes."

"People will see us together," he said, completely seriously.

She cackled and nipped at his jaw. "Babe, I think that ship has sailed."

"My mother will be there."

"So? You met my mother tonight."

"There's no comparison."

"I can handle it."

"Then will you be my date next month? Wear something pretty and dance with me under the stars?"

She hummed against the warm, tasty skin of his neck. Poor guy had walked right into this and she was feeling playful. "Gosh, I don't know…"

He flipped her onto her back and covered her with his body, his mouth hot and demanding as he pushed his tongue into her mouth. Oh, was he going to punish her for being lippy? Because she was pretty sure she'd enjoy that.

"You're a minx," he growled, reaching for her hands and pinning them above her head on the couch seat. "I love this couch, by the way. It's nice and long. Perfect to stretch out on and take my time in working you up."

"And then getting me off, I hope?"

"Greedy much?" He shifted his weight, holding her

wrists with one of his hands while he used the other to push her dress even higher. He groaned when he found she'd ditched the bra when she got changed. "Oh, fuck, Faith."

She breathed a heady, aroused sigh as he circled his palm ever so lightly over her right nipple, pulling it into a tight, aching point as if by magic.

"Wait." He pinched that peak and jerked his hand out from under her dress. "Wedding date? Yes?"

"Yes!" She hissed it to keep from yelling at him. "Please don't stop."

His teeth flashed white in the darkness. "I love how sensitive your breasts are, because I think they're fucking gorgeous and could happily feast on them for hours."

Yes, yes, yes. "Less talking, more touching." She closed her eyes. "Please?"

He chuckled, resuming his attention. Right. Left. Right. Between her legs, she was growing so wet she could feel it. She tugged her arms out of his loose grasp and reached for his belt. Even before she got his jeans unzipped, she was palming his erection, tracing the length and glorious width of him with her other hand. And then she had his hot flesh circled with all her fingers, and he was clumsily reaching around her to tug her underwear off.

They didn't need to talk about it.

He slid inside her, both of them still fully dressed, his belt rubbing against the back of her thigh as she hitched her leg around his hip, pulling him closer.

Her breath caught as he stretched her wide, filling her up and shoving all her thoughts right out of her head.

That ache. It was beautiful and perfect and not enough, never enough, because she wanted more. He pulled out, all but the tip, and that delicious rub of his cock at her entrance again made her gasp. Now she was stretched and more open for him than before, and when he thrust deep, it went all the way to her cervix.

Again he was bare inside her.

She clenched around him, wanting to hold on tight to this moment of being one.

And all of a sudden it was too much.

"Wait," she gasped, rolling her hips, releasing him from her body.

He lifted up, and she was glad for the darkness. She didn't want to see the look of confusion on his face. She turned, kissing his arm as she settled on all fours. Zander hesitated for a second, then slid her dress up her hips, baring her from behind.

She felt his fingers first. He found her still wet, still ready, because she wanted this...she just needed it to be sexy fun times with a friend.

She squeezed her eyes shut. What a joke. She was falling so hard, so fast, when she hit the ground she was going to shatter into a million pieces.

But she didn't want it to be tonight. Or next month.

"What's going on?" He tugged her dress down a bit and kissed her shoulder, his breath warm and steady there. His fingers still worked between her legs, keeping her warm there, too. Not steady, though. She wasn't steady in the least.

So she didn't answer, because what would she say? He was perfect and she wasn't...

She bit her lip so hard she was pretty sure she'd just made herself bleed.

Thankful again for the darkness, she arched her back, sliding her wet slit messily against his hand. "Fuck me, Zander."

"That's what you want?"

"Yes." Her heart slammed against her ribs. She wanted lots of things.

He probably didn't have any clue how he looked at Eric. Looked at her. How loving and gentle and *ready* he was.

She didn't deserve him. But she still wanted every amazing part, anyway. She was totally greedy for him, and not just the sex.

But right now, yes, she wanted sex. Just sex. No more feelings. She wanted him to obliterate all these thoughts and fears, and fill her with all the pleasure she knew they could make together.

She opened her mouth to tell him again what she wanted, and that's when he practically lifted her off the couch by the hips and slammed home, his cock filling her to the point of ache, exactly as she'd demanded.

He was fucking her. Hard.

He set a blistering pace, all the nerve endings inside firing as he pistoned his hips. She stretched like a cat, rubbing her heavy, swollen breasts against the couch at the same time as she shamelessly presented more of her sex to him.

Filthy words flooded her mind. Things she wanted him to do to her. Things she wanted to do to him. Together. Apart, while the other watched. She swallowed a moan as his grip on her hips tightened, as he held himself deep inside her for a second, his thrusts getting more erratic.

He was fighting for control, too.

Good, she didn't want to be alone in her insanity. She snaked a hand between her legs, meaning to touch herself and get herself closer to release, but then her fingers touched his balls and he gasped.

Oh, yes. Cupping her hand around his sac, she squeezed, contorting herself into a pretzel so she could drive him crazy and grind against her own arm at the same time, and generally be a filthy, dirty, sex-happy slut for him, and herself.

"Yes..." Zander breathed roughly, like he was fighting for control. Now that she had a hold of him, he couldn't move very far, but he snapped his hips, rocking the head of his cock over some magical button deep inside her.

She bit her lip to keep from crying out as the swirling sensations came closer. Tighter. They wrapped right around her, so intense the edges of her vision started to dim.

"Come for me, babe. Come around my cock. Do it. Doit doit doit...Aaargh..." He lost control as she started spasming around him, and he fell over her, pushing her to the couch.

His mouth found her neck, then her ear, and he whispered things that made her blush as he held himself deep inside her.

She was going to have to get this couch steam cleaned, and until that could happen—at the earliest possible moment—she'd have to lock this room.

Totally, completely worth it.

But oh jeez, he was dirty.

And so was *she*, apparently.

She pushed her face into the couch cushion and grinned secretly to herself.

— —

SHIT. Zander had just... no, he didn't want to name what he'd just done to Faith. He'd practically reamed her in a back room of her house while her mother and son slept upstairs. And even worse, she'd gotten scared of the intimacy, and he'd ignored that because having her on all fours had made him so hard he couldn't think straight.

He was an asshole.

He couldn't risk going in search of a washcloth, so he pulled off his t-shirt.

"What are you doing?" Faith asked dozily, rolling onto her side as he tried to shift her legs.

"Cleaning you up."

She laughed. "Can you grab the light? I've got baby wipes stashed in like every room of the house, but especially in here, because of paint and glitter glue."

Nothing quite took the heat out of a post-coital moment like talk of glitter glue. He stood and found the lamp. Squinting against the sudden brightness, he kept his back to Faith for a moment, needing to compose himself. But before he could figure out what he was thinking, what he wanted to say, she sighed and stood up, following him across the small room. The crinkle of plastic accompanied her slide against his back, and she wrapped her arms around him, an open baby wipes container in her left hand.

"Here you go," she whispered, pressing her lips against his spine.

"Do you—"

"I got one."

He nodded.

"I'm glad you're here tonight," she said softly. "So, so glad. It's kind of crazy, though, right?"

Did she mean falling in love after a week? It hardly felt

like the most dangerous thing he'd done in his life. Driving around a poorly mapped mine field took that prize, and he'd fucking survived that. "I've done crazier things."

"Come back to the couch." Her arms slipped away, and he cursed himself for not holding on to her.

He tucked himself away and zipped up his jeans.

When he turned around, Faith had curled up on the couch. She was looking at him with a surprisingly open, happy look on her face.

Maybe he hadn't gone too far.

"You okay?" she asked, holding out a hand. He took it and sat beside her, tugging her into his side. Her back fit right there, perfectly, like his chest had been carved just to hold her against him. Of course, he was supposed to be comforting her, not the other way round.

"Of course." He buried his face in her hair, breathing her scent deep into his lungs before slowly exhaling. He wrapped his arm around her waist, like just holding her might ebb some of the tension away. It didn't work. So he went for honest confession instead. "I don't want to hurt you."

"What are you talking about?" She tried to turn, but he banded his arm tighter around her waist. Emotional dumps weren't his strong suit. He didn't need to get lost in her eyes at the same time.

"That was rough."

"That was *hot*," she said softly, and damn if that didn't make his balls throb. It had been hot as hell—when he wasn't thinking too much about it. "If or when you hurt me, I promise it's not going to be because you held me down and made me come so hard I almost blacked out."

"If or *when?* What does that mean?"

A long pause flooded between them, ratcheting up his pulse before she answered. He could feel her nibbling on her lower lip. "Well…you know…"

"I don't. And since I'm heading back to work tomorrow, don't you think we should clear this up now?"

"No?" She twisted again, and this time he let her because he wasn't going to hold her against her will. She didn't go far, though, just spun around and planted her hands gently on his chest, pushing him back against the arm of the couch. Then she wiggled into the space between his body and the back of the couch. Instantly, his panic eased.

She worked her fingers slowly down his chest in a lazy walking-man pattern. "Maybe let's back up to talking about how hot it was. I might be out of practice, but I think when I turned around and said—"

"Minx," he whispered, and she laughed.

"You don't want me to say it again?"

"Didn't we learn last night that I'm an insatiable ogre when it comes to you? Yes, I want you to say it again, and then I'll flip you over and do it. Hard." He tried like hell to ignore her shiver. He couldn't.

"Then what's the problem?"

"I wanted tonight to be—" Fuck, he was going to lose his bad-ass infantry soldier status if he admitted this. "Special."

The giggle-snort in response was not reassuring.

"I can bench my body weight."

"Wow," she gasped, wiping at her eyes as laughter still wracked her body. "That's a terrible attempt to change the subject."

"I'm saying I'm strong."

"And kind, and brave, and responsible. And…a giant

girl when it comes to negotiating a friends-with-benefits thing."

"That's not what this is, and you know it."

"Okay, that was the wrong phrase, but it's not like this is…"

"What?" He sat up, pulling her with him. "This isn't real? Because it's pretty fucking real for me, Faith."

Her mouth dropped open and she frowned at him. "You're the one who called yourself my Mr. Right Now."

"That was before. Hell, I want to bring you to my sister's wedding. And you said yes. I want to introduce you as my girlfriend."

Her eyes were big, wide, and suspiciously bright. "You said you're not that kind of guy."

"Maybe I didn't know that I was."

Her cheeks turned pink and she shook her head. "Don't say that kind of thing. Not if you preface it with maybe. I can't go there, you know? It's too much, too soon."

Shit, he did know that. He needed to shut himself up and the best way to do that was to pull her tight and kiss her senseless.

"Ignore the maybe," he said, his voice strained as he pressed his forehead against hers once she was breathless and he'd laid the physical claim he couldn't say out loud. Her lips were red and swollen, and he stroked his thumb across her mouth, around the bottom curve of her lower lip, then ghosted it over the cupid's bow of her upper lip.

"I'm going to miss you so much." Her voice cracked.

He wrapped his arms around her, holding her tight. "I'm coming back, Faith. No maybe about that."

CHAPTER THIRTEEN

SEPTEMBER BROUGHT the start of school, edits on Faith's finished book, and daily video calls with Zander, usually after dinner in Tobermory, which was about the time he got home from work in Wainwright. Most days he was still in his camo fatigues, which Eric loved—and it didn't take Faith long to figure out that's why Zander didn't change first before he Skyped them.

Right now, Eric was holding the iPad at the table, sitting with his back to Faith so she could see the screen over his shoulder as she tidied up the kitchen. She watched with amusement as her son tested his new best friend with spelling words.

"Brontosaurus."

"B-R-O..."

She went to the front hall to get Eric's backpack as Zander kept spelling. When she pulled out his lunch bag, it felt suspiciously heavy. *Damn it.* She should have checked right when they got home from school, but her mom had been raking leaves and they'd gotten distracted by jumping into the pile and taking some impromptu family pictures.

"Eric, honey, say goodbye to Zander," she said when she returned to the kitchen.

He groaned, but when she wiggled her fingers, he handed over the iPad.

"Go find a book about dinosaurs for us to read together, please." She waited until he was upstairs until she collapsed on the couch and gave Zander a sad face. "He didn't eat his lunch again today."

"Ahhh, shit. I'm sorry, babe. Did you talk to his teacher about that anxiety you were worried about?"

Yeah, and it had been a bust of a conversation. "She thinks he's just too busy talking with his friends."

"What does your gut tell you?"

"I don't know. I'm worried I'm being paranoid."

He gave her a gentle but firm look. "That's not an answer to the question."

"I think he's struggling."

"Then keep on it. Trust your gut." The screen blurred as he moved through his small apartment, then he propped his phone against something in his bedroom and she watched as he first stripped off his uniform shirt, then the skin-tight, olive-green t-shirt underneath. He came closer to the screen—maybe his phone was on top of his dresser?—and then stepped back and pulled on a basic black t-shirt.

"Shame to cover that up," she whispered, and he winked at her.

"Got a book, Mommy."

She jumped up as Eric leapt onto the couch beside her, the iPad tumbling out of her hands. When she picked it up again, Zander was biting his knuckle to keep from laughing. She could feel her cheeks were on fire. She covered her face, then waved at the screen. "Okay, we're going to go read that book."

"I'm going to finish getting changed and hit the gym."

It was the most mundane, ordinary conversation, but as they said their goodbyes, Faith felt refreshed.

Three weeks had gone by, and there was no sign of Zander losing interest. She'd been afraid that when he wasn't near her, he would change his mind. Go back to being the guy who lived just for the present, and since his present reality was thousands of miles away...

But while he was there, he was also still here in her kitchen, in her living room, and some nights, after Eric was asleep, they'd call each other again, and he'd be in her bedroom, too.

It was easy and wonderful, and almost too good to be true.

She tried not to think about that last point too hard. He'd be back in another week for Dani's wedding, and she'd have a chance to hold him in her arms. Feel his strength and refill the hope bank a little more.

— —

ZANDER SAT through the rehearsal dinner at his mother's cafe trying hard to contain his impatience. His sister was getting married. That was important. Jake was a great guy —even better. But they were going to do this again in another two days, and there was only so much polite, multi-generational friendly conversation he could make when he hadn't seen Faith in a month and he was probably missing Eric's bedtime and why hadn't he invited them to this?

Right. He was trying not to rush her.

That was rolling around in his head as he finally made his goodbyes, taking his dessert to go. It had required admitting to his mother that he was going to "his friend's" house for the night, but she'd put two pieces of chocolate tart in his takeout box, so that was something. And his sister just gave him a thumbs up as he kissed her cheek and apologized for ducking out.

No ribbing.

No demands for information.

The distraction of a wedding was proving to be a good time to show a slice of his personal life to his usually meddlesome kin.

Arriving at the little house overlooking the harbour in Tobermory was like coming home, although he was smart enough not to say that to Faith. She needed a long, slow courtship, he'd realized once he'd arrived back in Alberta. With some distance, he could see how the week of constant, escalating tension between them—good tension, holy shit—had been too overwhelming.

How he'd overwhelmed her.

So now he was playing a long game. He was all in, but she didn't need to know that yet. He could show her, because deeds felt good. Right. And where words could be doubted, his actions would build a solid, dependable foundation for Faith to believe they could build something real on top of.

He pulled out his phone and texted her. **I'm sitting in your driveway like a creeper. Wasn't sure if I should knock, don't want to wake up Eric if he's asleep.**

Ten seconds later the front porch light turned on, and ten seconds after that she was in his arms on the front walk.

She was salty-sweet softness and unexpected steel. Her mouth crashed into his and her hands dug into his shoulders as he lifted her in the air, not caring if anyone saw how much he'd missed her.

"He's asleep and my mom is gone for the night," she whispered, nuzzling against his neck as he lowered her slowly to the ground.

He picked up his duffle bag from where he'd dropped it and followed her straight to bed.

— —

THE SECOND FAITH'S front door opened on Saturday afternoon, a wave of calm settled over Zander. He'd only been gone for five hours, but it was enough to once again remind him that this was where he belonged.

He hadn't let himself in—there was something formal about coming to collect her as his date for his sister's wedding, so he knocked and waited for Miriam to open the door.

"Faith is upstairs changing her dress for the fifth time," she stage-whispered.

From upstairs, Faith groaned and called out that she could hear them.

"You look lovely," Zander used his sergeant's voice to make that clear, even though he hadn't seen her yet. He had no doubt she'd take his breath away, she always did.

She appeared at the top of the stairs, and lovely didn't cover it. She was wearing a strappy, sky-blue chiffon dress that floated down her body and skimmed the top of her bare knees. A dark blue wrap was fisted in one hand and her other was thrust toward him, holding a pair of flat silver sandals with straps that would probably wind around her ankles and drive him mad. "Can I wear these? Should I wear heels? That seems impractical for a dock wedding, but I don't want to—"

He held out his hand and crooked his index finger. "Come here."

"Nope, can't do. I still have to do my makeup. Yes or no on the shoes?"

"Yes."

She grinned at him. "Ten more minutes."

"Sounds good. Where's Eric? I'll go hang with him until you're ready."

"He's out in the backyard," Miriam said, shooing him in that direction as she moved to follow her daughter upstairs.

"Thanks." He found Faith's gaze again, holding it for longer than was probably decent. He didn't care. "You really look extra beautiful today."

She twirled away, her skirt lifting high enough on her legs to give him a glimpse at her thighs. Gorgeous.

Outside, he found Eric stretched out on a blanket with a bucket of Lego and a hardcover kids' reference book about construction vehicles. He was building something similar to what was on the page.

Zander dropped down beside him. "Hey."

Eric flashed him a grin and kept building. They'd hung out for hours the night before, from the time Zander picked him up from school with Faith to the extra-late bedtime since it was a special occasion. Eric had been like a spider monkey, all over Zander and full of silly giggles, but now Zander was already part of the background again. The resiliency of kids always shocked the hell out of him. He hadn't been this strong when he was four.

He rolled onto his back and watched the clouds, asking Eric a question or two about what he was building. Apparently the spies at his spy base needed custom-built dump trucks and bulldozers for an undercover something.

After a few minutes, Eric pushed aside his project and rolled over as well, using Zander's arm as a pillow.

"Look at that cloud," Eric said, pointing at a low-lying puffy dragon riding a motorcycle.

"And there's a horse," Zander added, but as a wispier altostratus cloud floated behind, Eric pointed out it had transformed into a unicorn. "Good point."

"There are a lot of clouds today. Is it going to rain on your party?"

"Nah. It rained last night, and some of those clouds are left over from that. Did you know that? Those streaky clouds, they come *after* a storm, not before."

"That's weird."

"Yep. Science is often weird. And cool."

"What kind of cloud is that one? It looks full to *bursting*," Eric asked, pointing at a cumulus cloud.

"That's a marshmallow cloud."

"No it's not."

Zander laughed. "No. It's called a cumulus cloud, and it is full of water vapour, but it's a hungry cloud that wants to get bigger, so it eats all the water droplets and doesn't let them go until it gets big enough. So it floats on by, getting bigger and stronger and eventually will rain somewhere else."

"When it gets to China?"

"Maybe, sure." Zander hesitated, then turned his head and looked at Eric. "Are you a hungry cloud? Are you eating all your food and getting big and strong?"

Eric gave him a confused look.

Shit. He should mind his own business. "Never mind."

"I eat my lunch sometimes," Eric said, his voice extra small. Smart kid, figuring out where Zander was going—where he had no right to go, though.

"That's good."

"Do you always eat your lunch?"

"Every day."

"Do you ever run out of time?"

Awww, poor kid. "Sometimes. Especially if I'm thinking hard about something."

"Like what?"

"Football. You. Work, sometimes."

"My mom?"

Hell fucking yes. "Sure thing. I think about your mom a lot."

"Me too."

"Your mom wouldn't want either of us to worry about her so much that we don't eat our lunch, though, right?"

"I guess."

"What are you thinking about at lunch time?"

"My spy base."

Zander laughed gently. "Yeah?"

"I wish I could go to spy school instead of regular school."

"I'm pretty sure you need to finish regular school first. Spy school is like college." Zander squeezed Eric close in a little kid version of a one-arm bro-hug. "We should go inside. Your mom is probably ready by now."

"Are you taking her to a fancy ball?"

"My sister's wedding. Which is going to be like a ball, but outside."

"My mom got married in a church."

"Lots of people do."

"Where did you get married?"

He laughed. "I've never been married."

"Why not?"

"That's a big question."

Eric gave him a look that said, clearly not, it's only two words. Did four-year-olds understand the idea of a loaded question?

"How about, it's a small question with a big answer?"

"Okay."

One of Zander's favourite things about talking to Eric was how he just bounced along. Were all kids this agreeable? Or smart? Or funny?

Eric rolled over on his tummy, more interested in talking than getting up and going inside. "I don't want to get married."

"Why not?"

Now it was the kid's turn to laugh. "I don't know!"

"I'll tell you this much. My sister? Today is the best day of her life. She's over the moon happy about this wedding. And if you grow up and fall in love with someone, and they get that happy about having a party to celebrate your love, you might just change your mind."

"Nope." Eric poked at Zander's suit jacket. "I don't like clothes like this. I only like jogging pants."

Zander knew the feeling. "It makes girls happy, though."

"I like to make my mom happy," Eric said quietly.

"Me too, bud."

"Is that why you're wearing the suit?"

"Nah. This is for my sister. But I asked your mom to come with me because I knew she'd have fun getting dressed up."

"My mom?" Eric shook his head. "She hates getting dressed up."

She might stress about it, but the twirling skirt and bright eyes he'd left inside said otherwise. "You think?"

"That's what she says."

"Life lesson number one, Eric. Girls don't always say what they mean."

"That's weird."

"Yep."

"Hey, do you want to come to the park with me tomorrow?"

Zander's chest squeezed tight. "I...I'm getting on an airplane tomorrow. I'm flying back to my army base."

"Oh."

"Next time I visit, okay?"

"When will that be?"

Shit. Not until Christmas. "Maybe in the winter. Can you still go to the park in the winter?"

"I think you can. But my mom says it's not safe."

Zander couldn't quite figure that one out, but he'd already learned not to disagree with Faith's mama bear instincts. "Does it get slippery?"

"I guess."

"I'll be back for a week at Christmas. We'll do lots of fun stuff. Safe, fun stuff," he hastened to add, because he wasn't going to promise anything he couldn't deliver.

"Like what?"

"I don't know yet. I'll talk to your mom and find out what we're allowed to do."

Eric giggled and buried his face in the blanket.

Zander cleared his throat. "You know, even at work I need to get permission to do things. We have to fill out a threat assessment and get five different people to sign it."

Eric lifted his head and gave him an appropriately scared look.

"Right? It could be way worse. How much paperwork does your mom require for a park visit?" Zander hopped to his feet and held out his hand. "Come on. Let's go tell your mom she's not as bossy as a Canadian Forces base commander. She'll get a kick out of that."

— —

FROM THE UPSTAIRS WINDOW, Faith watched Zander help Eric fold up the blanket they'd been lying on together, then she turned to her mother who was fussing about what earrings she should wear.

Nothing dangly, Faith thought, remembering the brush of Zander's lips against her neck.

"Mom..." God, this was harder than she thought. "If I didn't come home tonight...?"

Miriam nodded. "I'll make pancakes in the morning and distract Eric."

"Am I being foolish?"

"I can't answer that for you. Do you love him?"

Faith jerked her head back, alarm zinging through her body. "What? No." *Not yet. It's too soon.*

"He's flown across the country to see you."

"He flew back for his sister's wedding."

"Honey, most of the time, for a family wedding, there's a lot of milling around and pictures being taken before the ceremony. Most brothers of brides don't leave town to go pick up a date, and lie down on the grass and have a deep and meaningful chat with a four-year-old."

"Do you think we're distracting him from something more important?"

Miriam laughed. "I think to that man, *you* are more important."

Well, that did nothing to calm the nerves zinging around in her belly. "He's not moving here until the spring."

"Good." Her mother handed over a pair of simple diamond studs. "That's probably how long it will take you to figure out whether or not you can love him."

"What are you now, a relationship expert?" But Faith said it softly, because between the two of them, her mother was the expert. She'd had a better marriage than Faith had, longer too, and now she'd shifted into happily dating a new man with zero drama.

Faith had no clue how to do zero drama. It sounded nice, though. Like something she might want to try if she could lock down her overactive imagination long enough to be a normal person.

CHAPTER FOURTEEN

ERIC DETOURED to the couch and Faith's iPad as soon as they were back in the house. He waved as Zander bid him goodbye, but his attention was already elsewhere.

As a door opened again upstairs, Zander's focus shifted as well. He straightened his tie and squared his shoulders, proud and yet nervous about introducing Faith to his family.

Faith ran down the stairs, stopping on the second to last step. She'd put her hair up in a fancy twist, but already the shorter pieces around her face were coming out. Her makeup was subtle, but...damn.

"You look incredible." When she beamed at him, he swivelled his index finger in the air. She wanted compliments? He'd give 'em to her all night. "Turn around, let me see this dress."

She hopped down the last step and spun in a slow circle. If her mother hadn't been watching, he'd have dropped to his knees and worshiped her as she deserved. Since they had a chaperone he settled for taking her hand and brushing his lips against her delicate knuckles. Her fingers were paler than they'd been in the summer—he'd noticed the last two nights that she was losing her bare whisper of a tan already.

He got halfway hard thinking about her porcelain limbs wrapped around his darker body as he made love to her.

Not a great start to an entire day spent with other people, including his mother.

He cleared his throat. "Ready to go?"

The wedding took place at Dani and Jake's house, a gorgeous custom-build at the end of a road that butted up against the provincial park just outside of Pine Harbour. Zander parked his rental car on the side of the road, behind a long line of other vehicles. It looked like the entire adult population of the peninsula had turned out for the wedding, and still more were arriving behind him.

The ceremony was at a brand-new dock Jake had built for Dani, way at the far end of their property, where a forest spilled out to a rocky descent down to the lake—but Zander's brand-new brother-in-law had put in stairs, too.

"This is stunning," Faith said as they made their way down the stairs to the water's edge. Most of the guests were milling around an open bar serving champagne and beer out the side of the boat house.

"None of this existed at the start of the summer. Jake's been busy."

"Does he like boating?"

Probably nobody else would have noticed the hitch in her voice, and Zander knew Faith wouldn't want to make a big deal about her own past on a day like today, but he still took her hand and lead her through the growing crowd, over the pine-needle covered path to the back door of the boat house, where he opened the door and ushered her inside—to show her Jake and Dani's matching kayaks.

"Only the sedate paddling kind," he murmured.

She let out a shaky breath. "Was that silly?"

He shook his head. "And I really just brought you in here to steal a moment of privacy. You okay?"

"Yep." She reached for him, touching his waist briefly, then fiddling with his jacket lapels and finally pressing her palm against his cheek. "Thank you. I'm not anti-boating, I just... I've met Dani and Jake, and I was surprised to see this kind of elaborate building down here. I didn't think..."

"That Jake was a pretentious ass?" Zander laughed. "He's not. But he and Dani have been a long time coming, and he wanted to do this right. Make it right, a little bit, because he's secretly loved her since...well, since a time when he was way the fuck too old for her."

"Really?" Faith's eyebrows shot up and she grinned. "That sounds dirty."

"Hey. That's my baby sister you're talking about."

"Oh. Sorry." She winked and pressed up on her toes, brushing her lips against his. "Let's replace that mental image with one of me in one of your t-shirts and no panties, yes?"

He growled and hauled her against him.

Yes.

— —

"MRS. MINELLI, it's so nice to meet you," Faith murmured,

hoping the faint residue of colour in her cheeks from Zander's scorching kiss in the boat house could pass as artfully applied blush. The freshly almost fucked look, so in this year.

Anne Minelli gave her a practiced smile that gave nothing away. "The pleasure is ours, of course. Zander's kept you a well-guarded secret. But I understand you are a successful author."

"Ma…"

Anne fluffed her hand in the air. "Oh, Zander. I'm just making conversation."

Faith laughed. "I don't know who has been talking me up, but yes, I write books. And some people like them."

"There was a feature display of them at the library, my dear."

Now she was blushing for a whole other, more accept-able reason. "One of my fans is Chloe Dawson at the Pine Harbour Library, yes."

"She's the one with the…" Anne trailed off and glanced away from Faith's own nose piercing. Becca had a hoop through her eyebrow, but Faith wasn't about to finish that sentence. Or snarkily add *"the masters degree in Information and Library Sciences?"* because while that was totally on the tip of her tongue, there were some instincts you stifled the first time you met your boyfriend's mother.

Zander's father, on the other hand, seemed totally lovely, and chose that moment to change the subject to dinner. Then it was time to take their seats, and Faith could let loose the breath it felt like she'd been holding in her chest the whole exchange.

As soon as they were seated, Zander took her hand and casually started rubbing his thumb across the inside of her wrist. Back and forth. Back and forth.

The man was going to make her combust and the ceremony hadn't even started yet.

They were sitting with the other guests on lovely, padded white folding chairs. Some on the wider part of the dock that was built into the hill, some on the boardwalk that surrounded the boat house, and others on the two landings on the wide staircase that wound up the hill into the forest. She was sitting with Zander and his family on the left hand side of the dock, and Faith was glad for the friendly face of Olivia Minelli, who served as a buffer between them and Zander's parents.

Dani and Jake had gone without a wedding party, Olivia explained as they sat waiting for the bride to appear at the top of the hill, because of the size of the dock. Olivia would be Dani's witness on the marriage certificate, and Dean would be Jake's, but they were sitting with everyone else until that point in the service. The other brothers would all have speeches and toasts during dinner.

Jake stood alone with the minister on the dock, pride of responsibility—for marrying this woman, hosting this celebration—projecting loud and clear. He didn't need a best man to hold him up.

A string quartet had been playing quietly for the last half hour, and when the minister raised his hands, they paused playing for a moment while everyone stood, then started again, shifting from the standard classical fare to… it took Faith a minute to place the cover of Led Zeppelin's "All of My Love."

This was going to be a fun wedding. Zander needed to keep his hands to himself so she could focus.

Dani stopped at the top of the stairs. She walked herself down the aisle, as it were, going slowly like she was taking her time to soak it all in—and the whole time, she only had eyes for her husband-to-be. The chemistry zinged across the gathered witnesses and was almost embarrassing to watch, but something about the construct of a wedding that made the personal moment worthy of public celebration.

And this was a wedding unlike most—even unlike Faith's own, which until this moment she'd thought had been pretty special. When she and Greg got married, though, they were focused on throwing a perfect party, not on having the perfect ceremony. They'd been best friends, lovers, and co-conspirators in knowing that a wedding wasn't necessary except for social reasons.

Nothing about this moment felt driven by social propriety. Faith hardly knew these people and yet she *knew* this was a moment years in the making. Years, Zander had told her, spent apart, filled with longing.

She dug furiously in her clutch for a tissue. There was no point pretending she was going to get through this with dry eyes.

After dabbing away her first tears, Faith took a deep breath and tried to take in all the details.

Dani wore a simple dress and carried a large, hand-tied bouquet that had sprigs of berries and greenery zinging off in all directions. It was simple and eclectic, and perfect for a lakeside celebration of love. As she got closer, Faith realized the dress wasn't actually that simple in the details. The raw-silk, strapless sheath had a subtle layer of lace peeking out from the top of the fitted bodice—it looked like she'd been wrapped tightly in the lace, then bound again in the luxurious silk.

Faith approved. She also loved how the dress barely skimmed the ground, revealing glimpses of Dani's ballet slippers—a seriously genius idea. She remembered her own three-inch heels and the boned corset that had left painful red marks on her mid-section by the end of the night.

Zander shifted behind her, brushing closer.

But Jake and Dani made a breathtaking couple, him in his dark blue suit and polished brown leather shoes, her with a barely-there veil that fell down her back, somehow affixed by magic in her loose dark waves. And when it lifted on the wind, Faith realized there were a million tiny buttons running down the back of Dani's dress.

That dress was perfect. Simple from afar, but up close...whoever made it was a design goddess. And it wasn't Faith's fault if such perfection whipped her girly insides into a bit of a "what if" fervour.

As the couple turned to face each other, the minister indicated for the crowd to take their seats again. Zander stretched his arm across the back of Faith's chair and tugged her hand back into his lap as she leaned into him.

She shot him a quick, sideways glance.

He was staring straight ahead.

So it was just his body that was making a possessive, public claim on her.

Not that she minded. With the way her heart was bouncing around like a cheerleader high on life, he could make all the claims he wanted today. Today, she was a sucker for romance and one particular man in a perfectly tailored charcoal suit.

The ceremony was short and sweet, with Dani and Jake each reading their own vows.

Jake went first, his rich voice carrying easily across the wind and water, up into the trees that surrounded them. "Eight years ago, I was sitting on a dock just like this one, and I blinked. That was all it took, and in that moment you went from being little Dani to being *my Dani*. You stole my heart on a dock, Daniella Minelli, and I couldn't tell you. Not then. But I can tell you now, and yet that doesn't seem quite enough. So I built you another dock, just so I could stand here and say...keep it. It's yours now, forever and ever. Today I stand in front of our family and friends and promise you my love will never waver, my devotion will be sure, and my support is constant and unconditional. You are the light of my life and I am honoured to be your husband."

Water-fucking-works.

Dani needed a tissue, too, but after she dabbed her eyes, she squared her shoulders—a move that Faith recognized as a standard Minelli "here we go" gesture—and pressed one hand to her chest as she squeezed her other hand around his. "I've only got room in here for one heart, so if I'm keeping yours, you need to hold mine for safekeeping, and I know you will. You are the best partner, the best husband, the best lover and friend a woman could ever want. I love your honour and your integrity. I can't wait to build a family with you, and sit on this dock in our old age, when we look back on eight years as just a prequel to our entire lives spent loving each other." She took a deep breath, and Faith realized that those weren't written vows. They'd just said what was in their hearts. It blew her away. Their formal vows did, too, and when Dani repeated what Jake had added to his own vows, the tears started all over again. "Jake Foster, today I stand in front of our family and friends and promise you my love will never waver, my devotion will be sure, and my support is constant and unconditional. You are the light of my life and I am honoured to be your wife."

There was an exchange of rings and an epic, bride-tipping kiss followed by a fist-pumping jump in the air by the groom, but Faith was lost in the vows. They'd waited so long to tell each other how they felt. God, the angst of that... she sighed and rubbed her chest.

"So you like weddings, eh?" Zander asked quietly against her ear as they stood and followed the couple up the winding wooden stairs. The rest of the wedding would take place in the field behind the newlyweds' home. They'd passed the white marquee tent on the way down to the lake.

"Doesn't everyone?" Faith said lightly, but the real answer was no, she normally didn't. Not like this.

Today was something entirely unexpected and wonderful and, the more she thought about it, just a little scary.

As they climbed the stairs, Zander's hand rested lightly on the curve of her hip, his arm wrapping around her back, and when they got to the top of the stairs, he took her hand, weaving his fingers around hers.

Definitely possessive. She wasn't the only one who liked weddings.

Alarm bells clanged in her heart and she took metaphorical wire cutters to the leads. Not today. Today she'd pretend all of this made sense.

There were some family photographs that needed to be taken—casual, fun, quick pictures, and somehow Zander pulled Faith into one with just the married couple and them. Dani and Zander in the middle, big brother and little sister, with Jake and Faith on either side. Then he was whirling her into the tent and finding her a glass of champagne, introducing her to family friends and second cousins.

By the time people were getting seated, her head was

spinning. Dani and Jake appearing in front of them again, this time making their rounds of the guests in the tent before dinner, was a welcome moment of familiarity.

Jake and Zander shook hands—a funny formality, but weddings were full of them—and Dani gave Faith a tight hug, bending a little because all Minellis were tall and Faith was…not.

She decided to take the conversation to a really important place. "I need to know…your dress, where did you get it? It's just amazing."

Dani smiled and leaned in. "Shhhh. We're not talking about the dress in front of the men."

Jake laughed and wrapped his arm around his wife's waist. "Is that because I'll have a heart attack if I know how much it cost?"

"Says the man who built me a boat house and a dock just so we could have our wedding ceremony down at the water."

"That's a yes?"

"That's a 'don't worry about it, we're never doing this again.'" She gave him the sweetest, most hopeful look, and the tough-as-nails contractor melted right in front of them.

"So they're happy." Faith whispered the understatement as the couple moved on down the row of rectangular tables set up, family style.

"Disgustingly so, yeah." Zander winked at her. "Not a shabby way to spend the rest of their lives, don't you think?"

CHAPTER FIFTEEN

DINNER HAD BEEN LOVELY, and the speeches were great. Even the DJ was awesome, but after spinning Faith around the dance floor a few times, Zander was aching to escape and take the dance to a more elemental level.

"What's with the long face?" Dani asked as she breathlessly grabbed his hand and pulled him onto the dance floor from where he'd been standing at the side, waiting for Faith to finish talking to his father, who apparently had a secret love of Buffy the Vampire Slayer and Supernatural, and was keen to discover that Zander's new girlfriend wrote about demons and angels and everything in between.

"No long face. Kind of stunned at the ridiculous expense you two went to for this party, but—"

She whacked him on the shoulder. "Shut up. You look like you'll be the next one down the aisle, and I doubt you'll do it in jeans and a Harley Davidson t-shirt."

"Whoa, what?"

She gave him a knowing look. "I recognize the way you look at Faith. I see it on Jake's face every day."

Zander looked at Faith like she was a filthy goddess. "I really didn't need that comparison."

"Don't make me punish you with details of how I want to get knocked up on our honeymoon."

"Jesus. Okay, uncle. Yeah, I like Faith."

"Like?"

He sighed. "It's complicated. She's not ready for more. And I'm not moving home until the spring, so we've got time. But yeah...she's special. It's just hard when we don't have the time or space to date, be alone, all the usual stuff." That was all his sister was getting out of him. It was more than he should have said to anyone, but a bride on her wedding day shouldn't be refused.

"Awww!" She squealed. "But no alone time sucks."

"I'm a big boy, I can be patient."

"Where are you guys staying tonight?"

He blushed like a damn little girl, then gruffly admitted that Tom had agreed to stay at Matt Foster's for the night.

"Private cabin? I've just one question for you, big brother." Dani arched an eyebrow. "Why are you still here?"

— —

FAITH HAD LEFT Zander's father and gone in search of her date, but he wasn't on the dance floor. Before she could turn around and look for him in the darkness, she felt him slide up behind her. The stroke of his fingers on her neck had her primed even before he wrapped his arms around her waist and said, for her ears only, "I think we've celebrated long enough, don't you?"

"Depends on what you had in mind next," she whispered back at him, keeping her eyes on the dance floor. "I got all dressed up. It would be a shame to go home so early."

"And what if I suggested maybe you don't go home tonight at all?"

She'd already told her mother that she might stay in Pine Harbour. Her cheeks had been on fire the entire time they'd had *that* awkward conversation, but that had nothing on the heat that engulfed her now. "Then I'd say... lead the way."

He groaned into her hair before straightening up and pulling her backwards into the night. "I already collected your purse and wrap and they're in the car."

She giggled and ran with him around the side of the house, only slowing as they stepped onto the road. "I'm guessing your mother will have a cow when she realizes you ditched?"

"Pretty much. But since I'm leaving early in the morning to fly across three provinces, I don't really care. I cleared it with the bride, and that's all that matters."

"You asked Dani if we could duck out?"

He laughed. "Actually, it was her idea, although it wasn't hard for her to pick up on the fact that I was projecting a very strong desire to be alone with you."

"Strong desire?" she asked as they reached the rental car. Her breath hitched as he spun her around and bracketed his hands on the car on either side of her shoulders. At some point in the night, his jacket had come undone, and she slid her hands inside, smoothing her palms over his tight waist. The muscles flexed through the thin cotton dress shirt. "That sounds...vague. Be specific."

"I want to take you somewhere and make you scream. Fill you up, get so far deep inside you it's hard to know where I end and you begin." His breath was ragged and rough as he pressed against her, hip to hip. "I want to strip you bare and make love to you. Fuck you. Have another round of the best sex of my life, because you are my addiction and my favourite treat."

"I'm your favourite treat?" That was the silliest thing to pick up on, but she liked it so much.

"Chocolate ice cream and warm raspberry sauce has *nothing* on you, babe. You're perfection."

Oh, she was done for. "You're sure it's okay for us to leave?"

"We saw the speeches. Now it's just people getting drunk and making fools of themselves."

Fair enough. "Where are we going?"

"My brother's place. Tom's," he added, since he had two brothers. "He has a cottage with a dock. It's private. And he's crashing at Matt Foster's tonight...so it's all ours."

Her pulse picked up. "Oh."

"Is that okay?" He gave her a concerned look that made her heart melt.

She nodded like a bobble head. It was more than okay. "Perfect," she breathed.

Tom's place, it turned out, was six minutes away, north of the park.

Getting there felt like it took a lifetime—exquisite torture as they drove in silence, the warm late summer wind swirling through the open windows. Zander's hand twisted around hers, holding her fingers against the hard, straining muscles in his thigh.

He parked next to the small, wood-sided house that was indeed quite private. The lake here was more sheltered, the house sitting on a small cove. She left her purse in the car but slung her wrap over her shoulders as she followed him onto the property.

High overhead, the moon was bright, and the waves lapped gently against the shore. The house had a decent sized wraparound porch, and that's where Zander stopped. He obliterated almost all of the scenery when he moved closer and slid his fingertips along her jaw, reaching into her hair to loosen her French twist. "Do you want to go swimming?"

She smiled and shook her head, letting her hair down. God only knew where those bobby pins went. "I didn't bring a swimsuit. I thought we were going to a wedding, not stealing away for some alone time." Okay, so she had a toothbrush and a spare pair of underwear in her clutch. She'd hoped they'd be alone. But swimming?

"Should we head back?" he asked with a wink.

"Not in the least." She swallowed hard. "I missed you, Zander. Like this. Alone. I'm sorry that we can't get more time like this."

God, that was hard to admit, because it opened her up and revealed her to be needy for him.

Zander, bless his heart, just kissed her lightly and tugged her toward the dock. "Let's go skinny-dipping."

"The water will be freezing!"

"I'll keep you warm."

"This is crazy."

He grinned wickedly and worked his tie loose. Faith's ovaries clenched as she watched Zander slowly strip out of his suit. Tie first. Jacket next. Then his shirt, one button at a time, until his chest was bare to the moonlight and his clothes were in a pile on the porch steps. He toed off his shoes next, setting them more neatly beside the jacket and shirt.

She stopped him when he reached for his belt. "Let me."

He hissed as her knuckles made contact with his abs —the muscles pulled tight as she teased him, carefully avoiding the erection eagerly straining to be touched. Her mouth went dry as she unzipped him and his cock practically leapt into her hand, tenting his boxer briefs like they could hardly be a barrier to his need to be in her hand.

There was no doubting how much he wanted her. He showed her that at every opportunity, and right now was no exception.

She was a lucky, lucky woman.

He got rid of his pants, then turned her around. His turn to do the unzipping. And the touching. As soon as her dress was open in the back, he was shoving it away and pulling her bare back against his chest. He cupped her breasts and kissed her neck, and prowled after her when she grabbed her dress and climbed the porch, looking for a better place to hang the delicate fabric.

He took it from her and carefully hung it on a finial beneath the porch light, then with a quick brush of his lips against her cheek, he shucked his briefs and grabbed two blankets from a chair in the shadows, and took off running for the lake. She pulled off her bra and panties and made chase.

He was already coming up from beneath the water, taking a big breath of air, as she hit the dock and ran past the blankets he'd dumped there. Without hesitating, she dove in.

It was fucking cold.

"You jerk!" she shrieked as she came up for air right in front of a laughing Zander. "We're going to get hypothermia!"

"Come here," he said mock-gruffly, his eyes dancing in the moonlight. "You just need to keep moving."

He kissed her and wrapped her in his arms, and sure enough, as her legs slid around his and her hands found his shoulders, then his chest, she started to warm up. But that didn't change the fact that it was still damn cold.

"Maybe this was hotter in theory than in practice," she said, her teeth chattering.

"Not a chance," he whispered against the wet droplets of water running down her neck. "But I did bring blankets for a reason."

This was where Faith had an advantage. She nipped at his lower lip, then shoved him away before turning and slowly rising out of the water. Tom's cottage had a decent walkout beach, so she didn't have to haul herself up on to the dock.

She could feel Zander's eyes on her swaying ass as she took her sweet time exiting the water.

By the time she was back on the dock and leaning over for the blankets, he was right behind her.

Still watching.

He was right—there was no chance this could be hotter in theory.

Breathless, she wrapped herself in one blanket and turned to hand him the other.

He was right there.

She decided to torture him. "What were you and Eric talking about this afternoon?"

He swallowed his tongue. Yeah, she'd just brought up her kid instead of climbing him like a tree. She winked and gave him her best innocent expression.

"Guy stuff. Looking at the clouds."

"Fascinating."

He narrowed his eyes and his lips quirked. Damn. Her upper hand hadn't last long. "Lots to see in the sky at night, too."

He whipped off his blanket and spread it on the dock, then pulled her down with him. He lay on his back and pulled her close, covering their wet bodies with her blanket. At some point they'd need towels, but this worked for now.

She sighed, ridiculously happy. "Another night lying on a blanket with you...you're starting to broadcast your moves, Mr. Minelli."

"Good."

He kissed her, slowly and sweetly, then faster, hungrily, before pulling back to show her the Big Dipper. Then they kissed again, and he told her about satellites and commercial flight patterns. He had an answer for any question she could think of, inspired by the lights and movement in the sky, and she soaked up every last bit of Zander-wisdom.

Under the blanket, he kept touching her. Stroking her hip, kneading the skin at the base of her spine. Drifting lower to cup her bottom and pull her closer and closer, until she was shamelessly plastered against his thigh.

His body had just the right amount of hair. Generous across the chest, then just a narrow line bisecting his abs, past his belly button, and widening again, thicker and darker at the groin. His hip was surprisingly smooth under her hand, but then the hair, which was silky on his torso, grew wiry on his legs, and the rub of that against her thighs was pleasantly but persistently distracting.

She rolled her hips, rubbing against him more deliberately than before, and he stiffened between them. She loved that pulse of his flesh, the first bead of moisture against her belly or her hand. Her tongue, too, and she wanted that now. Wiggling her way under the blanket, she kissed her way down his stomach, tracing the firm ridges of his clenched muscles with her tongue.

Six glorious licks later, she was exactly where she wanted to be—on her knees, making her boyfriend rapidly come undone. His hands tightened in her hair as she licked him from root to tip, then circled his glistening crown with the flat of her tongue. He tasted like clean skin, but with each swipe she got a fresh burst of salty, musky desire. It filled her senses and scrambled her brain.

She tried to tell herself that how she reacted to him—so hungry for his taste, desperate to please him and with an ever-present ache to have him literally inside her—was because it had been so long since she'd last experienced this kind of passion.

She was kidding herself. This connection was unlike anything she'd ever had.

"Suck harder," he instructed, sliding his hands to cup her face. That was certainly different, too—Zander wasn't shy about taking what he wanted, or praising her. "God, your mouth. So wet, babe. So fucking wet."

She flicked her gaze up to meet his. His face was mostly in shadow, but she could feel the cocky pride. He knew what that word did to her, how it made her wet between her legs, too.

He mouthed it again, nearly silent this time. "So. Fucking. Wet."

A helpless whimper escaped her stretched-wide mouth and he jerked his hips, shoving himself hard against her tongue. Oh, yes. She swallowed hard, taking him into her throat. With a groan, he held her head still and pulsed his hips, rocking the head of his cock against the back of her throat until she almost gagged. Then he pulled her off and rolled her onto her back, his thumb replacing his erection in her mouth.

Spun completely out of her mind with need for him, for his skin and taste and his very being, she sucked greedily and moaned when he pulled out.

"Need my hands. Gotta worship every inch of you." He circled her breasts, wide, lazy loops that barely grazed her skin but still raised almost painful goosebumps. He licked those away and repeated the pattern, with tighter and tighter circles, until his breath brought her nipple to a hungry peak.

"Suck harder," she said, echoing his earlier instruction, and he did, laughing quietly against her skin.

Her back arched off the blanket, slamming their bodies together, and then all seduction efforts were lost, and it was a mad, lusty scramble to get him inside her and get their hands on each other's bodies. One of his hands pulled her leg up high and stayed there as he slid through her folds, holding her wide open as he fit them together.

God, he felt bigger than before. Wider, thicker. She bucked, wanting to shove herself up and onto him. She wanted to feel every last inch of him, wanted him to possess her as thoroughly as he'd promised earlier. But then she gasped at the first cleaving stroke, and he shook above her.

"I'm fine," she breathed. Claimed. Marked. Branded, maybe forever. Whatever, no biggie. She clung to him and he seared her mouth with a lip-bruising kiss before returning his attention to her breasts as they rocked, fitting themselves together as tightly as humanly possible.

"I'm not sure I am." But he was. He was *so* fine. Even as he lost a bit of control, his breath getting ragged and his movements growing more desperate, he still made her pleasure his pleasure. Heat bloomed deep in her belly as he found all the right buttons and pushed them in the magic sequence that unlocked her orgasm in record time. And then he stretched it out as he drove himself harder into her body, carrying her climax until his own joined the party.

The look on his face matched the day's theme—possession—but there was more there, too. Disbelief. Wonder, maybe, although it was hard to understand how Zander Minelli could be surprised by good sex. Great sex, even. The man had moves that had moves.

And some of his best were post-coital, as he stroked her back to Earth and kissed her in a way that promised more, much more.

"Wow," she breathed.

He kissed her shoulder. "You getting cold?"

Hardly. "We should go inside, I guess."

"We don't need to." He tugged her against his chest and stroked his fingers through her hair. "We've got all night."

Right. And then back to real life. Long distance phone calls and planning for a Christmas visit. *Which is what you wanted, right? Slow and steady?* They'd talked about it in the restrained way that distance demanded. They were on the same page. She didn't even hesitate before thinking about him as her boyfriend.

But doubt still lingered that they'd last. Faith closed her eyes and burrowed tighter into Zander's chest. Maybe she'd find some answers in the solid warmth there. Somewhere between the tattoos and the scars, writ in invisible ink, was the secret to dating a bad boy and not losing one's heart, and Faith desperately needed that insider information, because Zander was doing the world's slickest impression of actually being a keeper.

"Your brain is whirring pretty loud there," he said, and she caught her breath. He sounded chill. Calm. But there was an edge to his voice, and if she hadn't been with him, up close and personal in all the most intimate ways, she might have missed it.

"Big day today," she answered carefully. "Stirs up a lot of stuff in a writer's imagination." *A woman's imagination, too.* "Don't worry about it."

"I do, you know. Worry."

She nodded. She did know. Neither of them had seen an intense relationship coming.

"Faith—"

"Any chance we might find hot chocolate inside?" She rolled up to her feet, stealing the blanket and wrapping it around herself.

Zander stared up at her, every inch a naked god stretched out on the dock. Raw, masculine, powerful. His jaw worked silently for a moment before he jumped up to join her. "Yep. Marshmallows, too."

"Good." She stepped backwards, slowly, watching him advance on her.

He stopped her when they got to the porch. "Today was amazing," he murmured, making a fist in the front of her blanket and tugging her close. "You are amazing. There's nothing imaginary about how I feel about you, you got that?"

Did she get that? She heard him. She even felt it to be true in moments like this. It was when he left her and life was still the same as it had been before—when The Zander Effect was diminished due to lack of proximity, if not lack of effort—that was when she started to worry.

And the higher the peak, the harder the fall. She took a deep breath. "One thing at a time, mister. Let's start with hot chocolate."

He shook his head. "One of these days, we're gonna have to talk about this."

She nodded. "But not tonight, okay? Today was perfect." She stuck her tongue out at him. "You are perfect."

"Brat."

She kept going. "There's nothing imaginary about how perfect I think you are."

"Now you're just talking about my ass."

"Mmm-hmm. Indeed I am."

"Hot chocolate?"

She bit her lip and nodded.

So he made her hot chocolate and ran them a bubble bath for two, because he really was perfect.

CHAPTER SIXTEEN

IT WASN'T that she expected dating someone who lived on the other side of the country to be easy. But then it *was*, for weeks on either side of his trip home for the wedding, so when their first fight happened, over something kind of stupid, it took her by surprise.

Eric's birthday was almost a month after the wedding, and in the weeks between, a steady stream of boxes had been delivered to their house, that Faith had ordered because she lived in the middle of nowhere and hated shopping in malls, anyway. Mostly presents and birthday party supplies. The vast majority of the time the couriers showed up during school hours, so Eric had no clue, but the few times he had been home and gotten curious about the increase in brown cardboard boxes—"Is that for me? Is it the robot dinosaur I saw a commercial for?"—she'd distracted him with Anne Minelli's chocolate chip cookies.

She had a regular supply of them now, because Zander had tasked his friends with bringing them to her and Eric. Twice a week, one of the Minelli brothers, or a Foster substitute, would drop off a Tupperware container and a note from Zander. Always something funny and cute and very much PG-13, because it was a guarantee that the "delivery men" would read them.

Everyone had a price for doing a favour, clearly.

So the cookies worked to keep Eric from peeking at the boxes before she could hide them. And Faith kept a checklist in her office of everything she'd ordered, and when the last box arrived, she breathed a sigh of relief. Hiding things from Eric was getting harder and harder.

A few days later, on a glorious, unexpectedly warm day, when she walked to get Eric because it was just that lovely outside, they returned home to find two more boxes stacked against the front door.

"Can I help you open them?" Eric asked hopefully.

She wracked her brain.

"Uhmmm..." She looked at the two packages, then picked them up and inspected the return addresses. The first was definitely for her—lingerie, so he didn't need to open *that* one. The second was from a bigger online store, and she was pretty sure it was books she'd ordered a while back. They weren't presents, he could open that one. "Take the big brown box, sweetie. This one is mine."

She jogged upstairs and stashed the itty bitty silk scrap of nothing in her bedroom closet.

As she headed back to the kitchen, she heard Eric grunting in determination. His little fingers scrabbling at the tape, then cardboard ripping.

Then a gasp, and a laugh of disbelief. "Skates? No way!"

What?

He repeated the words, this time shrieking them loudly. Yep, he definitely said skates. As in, okay on a cute pair of pyjamas she'd bought him for his birthday, but not so much actually on his feet, what with being blades and causing head injuries and so forth.

Faith skidded to a stop next to the table, where Eric was jamming a shiny black winter-sports helmet on his head. He shook his whole arm, index finger extended, at a pair of black and white hockey skates on the table.

Skates.

"You got me hockey stuff?" His mouth hung open in disbelief.

That made two of them that couldn't quite believe what was happening.

"This...wasn't me." Her mouth dry, she reached past him and grabbed the packing invoice. At the top in big block letters it read *GIFT RECEIPT* and below that was a message.

Eric bumped into her arm and his little, happy voice read it out loud over her shoulder as she took it in.

HAPPY BIRTHDAY, **bud. I'm sorry I'm not there. We'll use these at Christmas.**

Zander

OH, no. No, no, no.

"Can we call him, Mom? This is freaking awesome."

Awesome? When did her kid start talking like a teenager? Maybe around the same time he somehow wiggled a secret desire to play hockey into a conversation with her boyfriend.

Yeah, she'd be calling Zander all right. "I think he's probably still at work, baby." She glanced at the clock. Four o'clock in Ontario meant it was two in the afternoon out in Alberta. "I'll send him a thank you note on my phone, and maybe we can video chat later."

She sagged back against the kitchen counter, letting him play with the world's greatest gifts because there was no point closing the barn doors now that the horses had fled and joined the Calgary Flames.

Or something.

Fingers shaking, she typed out a text to Zander. **Skates?**

His reply was immediate. **They arrived?**

She growled and stalked to the craft room for some privacy. She tapped his name, then the phone icon. If he could respond to a text, he could talk on the phone. Hopefully.

He answered on the first ring. "Uh oh."

"What?"

"You're calling me instead of texting. Were the skates a bad idea?"

"Yes!" She took a deep breath and lowered her voice. "Zander, why didn't you ask me first?"

Stunned silence was the only response. She tried to picture his face. Was he annoyed she'd called him during the day and yelled right off the bat? That would be fair. She was overreacting. She couldn't help it, though.

"Well..." He sighed. "Okay, in hindsight I can see how I may have overstepped. But they're skates, Faith. Every boy needs a pair of skates."

"Not my boy." God, she hated the defensive, brittle tone in her voice. She'd worked so hard to be chill, and it had all been an act. She wasn't chill in the least when it came to recreational activities. She was uptight and over-protective, and she knew that it was about Greg's death and entirely irrational. She also didn't try very hard to curb herself. "Hockey isn't safe."

"I'm not going to argue with you, babe."

"But you don't agree." Something creaked over the phone lines, and he sighed again. She echoed the sound. "I'm sorry. I interrupted you at work."

"I'm just sitting in my office, it's fine." Another creak.

"What are you doing right now?" The tension ebbed from her voice and she closed her eyes. "Tell me what your day is like."

"I thought you wanted to have a fight."

"Never."

"It would be our first one. Might be a fun milestone."

She laughed quietly. "Tell me about your day."

"We're planning a week-long Arctic exercise for the end of the month, so I'm filling out forms for that. All computer stuff."

"I have a hard time picturing you behind a desk."

"Well, it's an Army-green metal desk, and my feet are propped up on an ammo can that has my name stencilled on it, if that helps."

"Are you in uniform?"

His chuckle rumbled through the phone. "Yes. Always."

"That was a stupid question."

"No such thing. I'm sorry I didn't ask about the skates. It was just a spontaneous thing. I was online late the other night, and there was a countdown sale to midnight. It would have been like two in the morning for you, not that I even thought about calling. I just clicked on them because…"

"Every boy needs a pair of skates?" She repeated back

his earlier, not incorrect, defense. "Is it a lost cause, me trying to keep him safe?"

"Babe, you can keep him safe while he learns to play hockey. Whether or not he plays on a team, that's a different question. If he's ever allowed to play contact, that kind of thing. But just learning to skate? That's a rite of passage. And can be totally…"

"Boring?" She perked up at the thought of boring skating that might drum an interest in hockey out of her son forever.

"Safe. And still interesting."

"Not too interesting."

This time his laugh wasn't restrained, or quiet. He guffawed hardcore, but it warmed her in a weird way. Like he was laughing at her in a way that meant he'd always be laughing with her.

"Lost cause?"

"Nothing boring about hockey, babe."

"Shit. I was worried you'd say that."

In the background, another man's voice spoke. Zander muffled the phone for a second, then with a rustle he was back. "I gotta run. Can we continue our first fight later on?"

"Sure." She grinned. "Eric wants to say thank you."

"Video call?"

"Definitely."

— —

ZANDER KNEW he'd messed up, not checking first, but it

had been a genuine mistake and Faith was a reasonable woman.

It would be easier when he was back on the peninsula. He looked at the brown paper envelope on his desk. He had a career planning meeting in two weeks time, and he'd put off signing the discharge forms inside the envelope. He grabbed the envelope and slid out the sheaf of papers. A quick click on the pen he always carried in the breast pocket of his uniform, and he hovered his hand over the signature line.

"Are those your discharge papers, Warrant Officer?"

He looked up and nodded at Captain Diwali, his commanding officer, who'd silently appeared in the doorway of Zander's office. "They are."

"You still planning on signing them?"

"Yessir." Nothing would stand in his way of getting out now. If he was formally asked not to, he'd give that due respect, because there was a way things were done in the forces, and when an officer asked you to wait, you waited. Officially. But this NCO had two important reasons back home to be done with the army. He'd given the crown two decades of service. That was enough.

"I'll miss working with you. Anyway, that's not why I stopped by. We've been contacted by 32 Brigade. They want to attach to our Arctic training."

"Another week?"

Diwali nodded. "The week before."

"As in, three weeks from now?" Zander cursed under his breath. "Who's organizing troop lift?"

His captain just looked at him blandly.

Zander threw his hands in the air. "Come on."

"They can do it."

"But I need to tell them that. Got it." He scowled at his

boss, who retreated to a safe distance. Zander called after him, "You know, this is why I'm signing those papers!"

Diwali hollered something back, but Zander missed the exact words. He was already firing off emails to get an ORBAT, adjust accommodation and weapons requests, and have the safety plan approved. The whole time he was thinking about how he would describe what he was doing to Eric. Teach him that the ORBAT was the order of battle, a fancy word for the list of everyone involved in an operation.

It would have to wait until another day. Some days when he called, Eric was full of questions about the army. Tonight would be all hockey, all the time, and that was just fine by Zander.

Sure enough, as soon as he got home and called them, Eric grabbed the iPad from his mom and propped it up on the table so he could give Zander a very detailed tour of the skates and helmet. Then the skates again.

"They're pretty nice, bud."

Eric screwed up his face. "I don't know how to skate, though."

"I'll teach you."

"But you live a plane ride away."

Zander nodded. "I know, but we'll have time to learn at Christmas." He held up his own skates which he'd pulled out of his storage locker. "See? These are mine, and I'll bring them home."

"You'll definitely be home for Christmas?"

Zander hesitated. It was a knee-jerk reaction. Twenty years in the army, and he'd learned not to promise anything like that. In the background behind Eric, Faith looked up from what she'd been doing with Miriam in the kitchen.

Zander looked back and forth between her and Eric. "That's the plan, yep. And you know where I'm going in a few weeks?"

"Where?"

"Pretty close to the North Pole."

Instead of being impressed by Zander's impending proximity to Santa Claus, Eric just blinked at the screen, his brow furrowed.

"What's wrong?"

"How long are you going there?"

"Two weeks."

"How are you getting there?"

"On a military plane."

"Why can't you drive?" With each question, Eric's voice got smaller and smaller.

Faith pulled her eyebrows together and came closer. She leaned over Eric's shoulder and looked right at Zander. "What's going on?"

"Nothing." Shit, no, not nothing. Zander took a deep breath. "I'm going on an exercise up north. I mentioned it earlier. There aren't any roads that far north, bud."

"Are there polar bears?"

Faith squeezed Eric's shoulder. "I'm sure he's not..." She'd trailed off when Zander tried to give her a look. "Okay, that's enough questions about top-secret army stuff, right?"

She tried to make light of it. Eric was having none of that. He glared at Zander. "But you're coming here after that, right? You're coming back?"

Zander kept his voice calm, even though he had an impending sense of doom telling him it didn't matter. "Yep, I'm coming back real soon."

"My dad didn't come back." He said it matter-of-factly,

but Zander could see Faith's reaction over Eric's shoulder. It cut her to the quick.

Zander didn't have an easy, comforting comeback. There wasn't one. He tried not to see Faith right there, tried not to feel the pain radiating off her so sharply he could actually feel it on the other side of the country, and he couldn't just let the silence stretch. "He would have if he could, bud."

He took a deep breath. Maybe Faith needed to hear that, too. He didn't know anything about her ex, not really, but he knew something about the human spirit, and he'd lost people over the years due to combat and mental health-related problems. Whether it was an act of war or a tragic accident, every dying man's last thought was for his family. His wife. His child.

"We'll go skating, I promise. I love you, and I don't want you thinking about me not being there, okay?"

Eric gave him a long, solemn look, then turned and glanced back at his mother. "Can I go play now?"

"Yeah, honey. You can for a few minutes. Then it's story and bedtime, got it?" Faith took the iPad, the video on the screen swinging wildly as she told her mother she was going upstairs for a few minutes. Zander's heart hammered in his chest. Had he said too much? Over-stepped? Fuck, he hadn't seen that coming.

"I'm sorry," he said as soon as she was looking at him again.

She didn't say anything.

"Something else we should have talked about first?"

She closed her eyes and shrugged her shoulders slightly. "Yeah. Maybe."

Maybe? "I didn't know what to say."

Fatigue tightened her brow and tugged at the corners

of her mouth. "What you said was fine. Just…Don't make him promises you can't keep."

"I can keep them."

"You told my son you love him," she whispered, propping her forehead in her hand. She'd curled up on her bed. He wanted desperately to be there with her, to hold her and let her get it all out. "Do you have any idea what it will do to him if you flake?"

Yeah, he'd said that he loved the kid because he *did*. But someone wanted to take things slow and it sure as hell wasn't him.

At least, it wasn't him now. Shit. He couldn't remember a time before Faith made him want things that weren't on offer.

He couldn't get mad at her. It wasn't fair. But the burn in his gut didn't feel fair, either. "You don't think I know how serious it is to tell someone they're loved? To tell a child that I'll never leave them?"

"Do you?" She shrugged, a little gesture that said way too much. "You're a great guy—"

"Stop saying that." His voice was cold as ice now. He needed to hang up. They needed to try this again another day when their feelings weren't so unexpectedly raw. He knew that, and yet he couldn't stop. "My earliest memory is of my father calling my mother a bitch and walking out. I must have been three. And it happened more than once, until one day he didn't come back for a while."

She stared at him in obvious disbelief. "But your parents…"

He laughed, not caring if it sounded hard and unfeeling. "Yeah. My mother dragged him back, and I guess he realized it was easier with her than without. My entire life, I've known that my parents love each other, but there's a part of them that hate each other, too. And we never talk about it, so welcome to my dirty little secret."

"No," she whispered. "That's not true. They're so happy together."

He clenched his jaw. "You've met them once, Faith. Don't tell me anything about their marriage."

She pressed her lips together. Even across the wobbly Internet connection, he could tell her eyes were welling up with tears. "But you get to tell me about my son?"

"No, babe. I was trying to tell you about *me*. Not Eric. *Me*. That I'm going to be there for him, no matter what. But you don't believe that, do you?"

"I said I don't know."

"That's not what you said. You questioned my word."

"Okay, I don't know what I meant. I'm…" Tears were flooding her cheeks now and in the background he heard her bedroom door open. Eric asked if she was okay, and she waved him over.

Shit, shit, shit.

He felt impotent to fix his blundering.

"Zander, I gotta go," she whispered. Her fingers reached for the screen, and he reached out too, wanting to touch her if only through glass and fiberoptic connection, but instead of touching his video image, she disconnected the call.

It took all his willpower to not throw his phone across the room.

CHAPTER SEVENTEEN

ZANDER'S first text message pinged her phone before she went to bed that night.

I'M SORRY. **Call me back?**

HE HAD nothing to be sorry for. She'd lost her shit over old ground. So much for being ready to date. So much for the past being settled. It was her apology to make, and she couldn't. Not yet. She sobbed herself to sleep, smothering her cries in her pillow, wishing everything was different. Easier, less fraught with history that was not of Zander's making. She came with so much baggage, a lot of it unexpected and messy.

The next morning, he tried to call and she let it go to voice mail. She listened to the empty message over and over again. The silence followed by the nearly imperceptible sigh, then a click. *To listen to this message again, press three. Beep.*

She zombied her way through breakfast and let her mom take Eric to school. When she climbed back into bed, her pillow was still damp. She lay down on it anyway.

The next text message ping made her cry before she even read it, and her heart cracked once she did.

WHAT DID **you pack in Eric's lunch today? I hope he eats it. I'm sure it's delicious.**

A HAM and cheese sandwich with cucumber slices and goldfish crackers on the side was hardly gourmet, but it was Eric's favourite. And she desperately hoped he'd eat, too. She worried about him so much.

Maybe Zander did, too.

It's pretty fucking real for me. He'd said that their first week together. Did he still feel the same way? Would they even make it to the spring? Long-distance dating was hard enough. Long-distance fighting was a recipe for disaster.

BABE?

THAT ONE-WORD MESSAGE DESTROYED HER. She knew she just needed to talk to him, but she didn't trust herself to say the right things that would protect their new relationship. So she turned her phone off, and left it off for three days.

She buried herself in edits and marketing plans, and rewarded herself for any reasonable amount of productivity with a curl-up on her bed where she let herself wallow in sadness. She hugged a pillow tight and tried to figure out how to be a better girlfriend.

Turning on her phone would be an excellent start.

But for some reason, she couldn't bring herself to do that.

At the very least, she should tell him that she knew he was a good man. That she saw his patience and his kindness, and she'd quickly learned to appreciate it—really—but now that she knew the root of it, she was even more touched. She was so angry at his parents, at his father, for not knowing the impact their fighting had on his child.

Every time she thought about him hearing that at the age of three, she started crying. No wonder he was a life-long bachelor.

At least he'd learned to live his own life differently. On his own terms, sure, but with kindness. He was the most considerate boyfriend she'd ever had. If he ever decided he wanted a marriage, he'd make a wonderful husband.

A wonderful father.

The kind who knew how scary it would be to be abandoned, either by fate or by choice.

Her phone was a heavy weight in her pocket as she watched Eric swing across the monkey bars. They'd stopped at the park on their way home, but that had been a mistake, because she looked at the curb and the bench and the swing set and heard Zander in each of those places. Felt his gaze and smelled his unique scent that had imprinted so successfully on her.

So much for just being her Mr. Right Now. She'd gone and fallen in love with someone who wasn't available on her terms. Their first fight had been over *nothing* and it had still slayed her soul. What would it be like when their fight was over him wanting to ride his bike to Central America or climb a mountain?

She wanted those fights, though. They scared the pants off her, that was definitely true. But better to have them, to have *him*, than not.

She pulled out her phone and turned it on, and after it connected to the network, a dozen messages flooded in. The most recent was a re-iteration of some of the previous points, all pulled together in a plea that finally snapped through her frozen attitude.

I KNOW I OVERSTEPPED... **Fuck, Faith, I'm no good at this, I get that. But I didn't mean to hurt you. Please let me call you. Give me a chance to say I'm sorry straight to you.**

BLINKING BACK TEARS, she typed in a quick response. **I'm sorry.** *I miss you.* But she couldn't add that, her fingers wouldn't tap the keys. She couldn't do this at the park. **I'll call you tonight.**

"Faith!"

She turned, looking for the female voice calling her name. From across the grass between the playground and the fire station and ambulance bay, Dani Foster waved at her, then broke out into a jog. She was in her paramedic's uniform.

Faith took a deep, fortifying breath. If he'd sent his sister to play peacemaker, that wasn't going to go well. Faith didn't want anyone else to know just how neurotic she was. So when the other woman stopped in front of her, she went on the offence—small talk, wedding-style. "How was your honeymoon?"

Dani grinned, looking just like a prettier version of her brother. "Not nearly long enough. If our entire family wasn't on the peninsula, I'd be tempted to move to the Caribbean, because oh my God, that water is blue. And Jake could wear board shorts year round."

"I went to Turks and Caicos on my honeymoon, I know what you mean. It's just gorgeous." Faith laughed. "As is your husband, of course."

"I'm biased, but I know, right? Speaking of handsome men, I have two pictures for you." Dani reached into the large pocket on her pant leg and pulled out a cream envelope. "Our photographer gave us all the digital files, too, so if you'd rather, I can email them to you? But I really love how these prints turned out. Way better than when I get them run off at the grocery store. I figured giving them to you made more sense than Zander, since he'll just be packing stuff up and bringing it back here soon enough."

So he hadn't told anyone about the fight. She gave a sigh of relief and flipped the flap up, then tugged out the glossy images. The first one was of the four of them, and they were all laughing. "This is a great shot," she murmured, and then her voice caught in her throat as she flipped it over and caught sight of the image beneath it.

Her and Zander, maybe just a few seconds later? The photographer had zoomed in as Zander turned to her and brushed a lock of her hair behind her ear. Her face was tipped up toward his and the look on his face… "Oh."

"You guys are perfect for each other," Dani said. "I know Zander said you want to take things slowly, but the way he looks at you…"

Faith blinked back tears. *It's just a picture.* They'd both been swept up in the emotion of the day, that was all. "Thank you." Her voice was thick and she coughed to cover it up.

"What's that, Mommy?" Eric appeared at her side, tugging on her arm. The kid was getting too good at his stealth-mode sneak up.

"Careful of your fingers," she whispered, dropping down to his level. She showed him the two pictures, and he reached out his index finger to touch Zander's face on both pictures. Heart. Splat.

"I miss Zander," he said.

"Me, too."

"Me, three?" Dani added and Eric laughed.

Faith sighed. She needed to stop being so damn sad, so damn scared, and get over herself. She stood up. "Dani, this is Eric, my son. Eric, this is Zander's sister."

"I know."

"You do?" asked Dani with an amused look.

He nodded. "Zander told me all about you."

Oh dear lord. Faith pressed her lips together and tried to keep a straight face. Dani looked like she could handle crazy kids. "What on Earth did Zander tell you about Dani?"

Eric rolled his eyes. "I can't tell you. They're boy secrets."

Dani laughed. "That means Zander called me a crazy bride." She shrugged. "He wouldn't be completely wrong."

Eric frowned. "No...he said you were on the moon happy, and it was a man's job to keep you there." He nodded, proud of himself for remembering that. "And that's cool, because I want to go to the moon."

Faith stared at Eric, then looked at Dani, and as soon as their eyes met, they lost it.

"On the moon?" Faith repeated after she got her giggles under control, her voice still cracking with amusement.

"Keep me there?" Dani wiped at her eyes as she took a deep breath. "Oh kid, you're a keeper. You're going to make someone very happy someday."

"I know." He sighed. "Then I'll have to stop wearing sweatpants. But Zander promises there's cake."

— —

ZANDER'S PHONE lit up and skittered on his bedrooms' fake wood flooring. He had it on vibrate out of force of habit, but ever since Faith had sent her short response earlier that day, he'd been on hyper alert waiting for her call. He shoved the kit he'd been packing out of the way and lunged for the phone.

It was just a regular call, no video. His chest seized up and he told himself to settle the fuck down. "Hello?"

"Hi." Her voice was so small, it broke his heart.

"Babe." He swallowed. "God, I've missed you."

She sniffled.

"No tears," he whispered.

"I'm so sorry, Zander. I've been awful."

"No, no, no. You've been scared. I get it. It's okay."

A long, slow, reedy exhale filled his ear. He wanted to feel that breath on his neck as he held her close. "I've missed you, too."

He pressed the phone so close to his ear that it pinched his skin. "Then that's all that matters, right?"

"Your sister found me and Eric at the park today."

"Yeah?"

"She had a picture of us from the wedding that she thought we'd like."

"And did you like it?"

Another sound that suspiciously hinted at tears. "Yeah."

He laughed gently. "Good."

"I'm scared, Zander."

He wanted to tell her that he was, too, but that would be a lie. The truth was, they weren't in the same place. Maybe they needed to talk about that. "What do you want?"

"I don't know." But it sounded like maybe she did, so he took a leap.

"I think you know what I want. I've hinted at it already, but you've said that you wanted to take things slow."

"We've only known each other a short time. I think that's fair."

Maybe it was. But how he felt about her wasn't reasonable, or fair, or rational. It didn't feel like he'd known her for a short time. He knew she was a free spirit and a proud mother. A loyal daughter. A writer who could weave magic out of twenty-six ordinary letters, turning them into words that entertained and bewitched.

He knew her.

And he knew himself.

"I lied to you, Faith. I don't want to be your Mr. Right Now, and you already know that. I want to be your Mr. Right, period. But it's more than that. I want you to trust me with your deepest fears and I want to take care of you."

"I think I want that, too."

Think? Fuck, this was hard. He could practically hear his mother, his brother, his sister all telling him to wake up and get with the program. Love was hard. Falling in love was the easy part. Keeping one's shit together while the person you love freaks the fuck out—that was the real challenge.

But inside the doubtful wrapping was exactly what he'd been hoping to hear all this time. Despite her fear, Faith wanted him. He'd spent a fair bit of time thinking about how to take their relationship to the next level. Over the phone on the tail end of a fight wasn't one the scenarios he'd considered, but he didn't want to wait any longer. "Well, I know I want that. And I know it enough for both of us. But you can't shut me out like that."

"I'm really sorry."

"Do it again and I'm showing up on your doorstep," he said gruffly. "And then I'll be court-martialed for going AWOL, so that would be bad."

"Zander, don't you dare risk something like that, not for me."

Not for her? Crazy woman.

"Of course I'd do that for you. *I love you.*"

It would have felt a hell of a lot better if at the exact same moment she hadn't said, "I don't think we should do this on the phone."

CHAPTER EIGHTEEN

"WHAT?" Faith couldn't have heard that correctly. Not after her silent treatment and hysterical meltdown.

Zander cleared his throat. "Maybe you're right."

"No, say it again," she whispered, her pulse was flying.

"You sure? Because even a guy like me can be sensitive about—"

"I just meant you shouldn't joke about going AWOL." She couldn't breath. "Say it again, Zander."

"I love you," he repeated, more roughly this time. "And I wanted to wait until we were on the same page and in the same province to spring that on you, but it needed to be said. I don't want you to run scared because if you do, I'll just chase you, and like I say, there are consequences to that. So...don't be scared. I'll wait forever for you to be on the same page. But I'm done waiting without action, you know? I'm going to tell you how I feel, because you deserve to hear it."

"You love me." She felt faint. And warm, suddenly, after days of being cold to her bones.

"Very much. What did you think I was going to say?"

Her first instinct was that no way was she telling him the truth. But that flew in the face of everything he just said. She closed her eyes and winced. "There might be a small part of me that worried you might think this is all just a bit much. Want to take a break or something."

He laughed.

Laughed!

And not gently, either.

"It's not funny."

"It's a little funny, because..." He sighed and laughed again. "You know what? I think we've had enough for one night. Tell me about the plans for Eric's birthday party."

"Wait." She swallowed. "I love you, too."

"You don't need to say it just because I did."

"But I do. And you deserve to hear it, way more than me. You're lovely, Zander. And I've missed you." As soon as she said it out loud, the truth of that statement released so much tension from her body. "I miss you, actively. And this is hard, *because* I love you."

"You don't know how good that sounds." His voice poured more of that delicious warmth straight into her veins.

"Feels good to say, too."

"I miss you too, babe. Both you and Eric."

A pang of guilt sliced through her for keeping them apart the last few days. She'd lied to Eric—another pang, not the first she'd felt about it—and told him Zander had to work away from his phone.

"He's been sleeping with the helmet every night."

"Seriously? That's awesome. I'd love to talk to him in the morning, before he goes to school, if there's time?"

"It'll be early for you."

"I'll be up. It's fine."

"Then we'll do that."

He yawned. "I was up at dark o'clock to do my annual fit test. So I want you to crawl into bed and tell me about the birthday plans and anything else that I've missed in the last few days."

"Just like that?"

"Just like that. Can we switch to video?"

Her heart skipped a beat. "Sure."

She ended the call and switched to Skype. He wasn't wearing a shirt, which she found really distracting. And she wasn't wearing makeup and her hair was a mess, but on her preview screen it didn't look that bad. And it didn't really look like Zander was perusing her outfit, either. His gaze was locked on hers. "Hi."

She wiggled her fingers and gave him a small smile.

"Birthday party?" he prompted, and she nodded. She told him about the ten kids that would descend on her place in another week, a few days after Eric's actual birthday. They talked until they were both yawning.

"I don't want to say goodbye," Faith whispered, her head on the pillow.

Zander gave her an almost smile, but his eyes were impossibly warm and full of love. "Then just say goodnight."

"Night," she murmured. "I love you."

"Love you too, babe. Always."

— —

ZANDER'S PHONE rang at half past five the next morning. He jackknifed out of bed and hit answer. "Minelli."

Eric's little giggle made the heart attack totally worth it. "Hi Zander."

"Hey, bud. Getting ready for school?"

"Yep. You back from army work?"

Zander shook the cotton out of his head and tried to figure that one out. "Pardon?"

"Mommy said you went to army work."

Ah. "Yeah, I'm back at my base."

"I went to my base yesterday, too."

"Did you?"

Eric explained how they'd gone to the park and met Dani, and on the way back, he'd stopped in at his spy base and done some training.

Zander lay back down on his bed and listened to the story. It was fantastical and innocent. *Never grow up, Eric.* He was perfect just the way he was.

"What kind of tank do you drive?" Eric asked.

Zander held off on the lecture about how infantrymen didn't drive tanks, that was the artillery. "If we go in an armoured vehicle, it's called a LAV. Not a tank, and I don't drive it, but close enough."

"We have spy LAVs. I think we do, anyway."

"That's great. Do you by any chance have spy rations? Because if I get cabbage rolls again, I'm going to scream. So if you have a better food distributor, maybe we could tell the Canadian Forces."

Eric giggled. "Okay."

"Okay." Zander grinned. "Time for school now?"

"Yeah."

"Miss you."

"Miss you, too."

He heard that little voice over and over again all day, and it kept him calm until he got home and got to hear it again.

He was just marking time now. Worst kind of soldiering, but he had trouble caring.

His heart was in Tobermory, as simple as that.

If duty actually required his attention, he'd shift it, of course. But as long as he could get through his tasks on auto-pilot, he'd leave his focus where it belonged.

When Faith called back that night, after Eric was racked out, the last thing he wanted to talk about was work.

"Tell me about your writing instead," he said as he settled on his bed. Talking to Faith had become his anchor. He'd talked more in the last two months than in the twenty years before that, and it felt surprisingly good.

Sharing for the win.

But tonight he just wanted her to share.

"I don't know, how much do you want to know?"

"All of it. What are you writing?"

"Well, that book that I was writing while you were here, that's done, and I've gotten edits back on it. I added…" She stopped and blushed.

"Added?"

She scraped her teeth over her bottom lip. "Um…"

"Is it dirty? I approve."

She laughed. "Not really. A little. I added a new guy to the story, and instead of him being a secondary character, I think I'm shifting the series into the urban fantasy romance category."

"So Vera actually gets to keep a guy now?"

She stared at the screen. "Have you been reading my books?"

He grinned. "You're a good writer."

She squeaked and buried her face in the blanket.

"Faith?"

"Go away!"

He laughed and she peeked one eye up at the screen. "How many books have you read?"

"All of them. Can I have an advance copy of the new one? Who is this guy, anyway?"

— —

FAITH COULDN'T LOOK Zander in the eye. "He's...well, I started writing him that night we met in Greta's."

"The notes you were taking while we talked?" He sounded...proud.

She glanced up. "Yes?"

"What's his name?"

"Deacon."

He made a noncommittal noise and rubbed his thumb along his jaw. "Does he have the power to make Vera do things like...give him a blow job?"

So he'd read the second book, with the wizard who cast an uninhibited spell on Vera, great.

He winked at her. "I'm definitely hoping that the next dirty blow job Vera gives someone will be Deacon. I have to admit I don't much like the idea of her with anyone else."

Oh God, she was going to die from embarrassment. "She's only just met Deacon. Anything she did before he stormed into her life can't be held against her."

"I said *I* didn't like it. Deacon's a cool guy. He might even like to hear about some of those stories."

"It's not that kind of book. I mean, their relationship will grow, and Vera likes sex, but my readership doesn't like long sex scenes." Now she was just babbling. Nerves were shoving useless bits of information out of her mouth and she couldn't stop it.

Zander gave her a pointed look. He'd rolled onto his back and propped a second pillow behind his head. "Faith. Focus. I'm trying to suggest… you know. That *I* might like to hear some of *your* stories."

Oh. She blushed and dropped her face into the blanket again.

She'd never get enough of the sound of his laugh, even when she was burning up inside because he saw inside her filthy head.

"So that's a no to the video sexting?"

"It's not a no," she mumbled. Her breasts were already heavy and aching, responding to his voice and missing his touch. "It's a…give me a minute."

"Should I go first?"

She rolled onto her side and propped her tablet against the headboard. "Depends on what kind of stories you want to share."

"Fictional ones, of course. Bedtime stories about a beautiful writer and the handsome soldier who inspired one of her characters."

"Sounds like a cliché."

He laughed. "Take your pants off."

She did as she was told. "What kind of stories do you want me to tell you?"

"Did you do any experimenting in college?"

She laughed so hard she snorted. "I kissed a girl at a

house party once. Maybe twice? Truth or dare was a popular game."

"Where did you go to university?"

"Toronto. My dad was a professor, so I got free tuition."

"And little did he know you were kissing girls..." Zander winked, then rubbed his lower lip with his thumb. "I can't see all of you. Scoot back a bit."

She moved so she was laying sideways on the bed, her bare legs curled up in front of her. "How about you, any experimenting in the army?"

"No, but I can probably make up a shower story if you want to hear one."

She shook her head. "You know what I want to know about? Your first time. Provided it was when you were a teenager and the person you lost your virginity to is now happily married and driving a minivan."

He howled, then gave her a hooded, heavy look. "I think she is, actually. You really want to know about that?"

"How old were you?"

An adorable wince told her that yes, she wanted to know this. She wanted to know everything about him. "Fifteen."

"Zander Minelli! How scandalous."

"I went through puberty early. I already had chest hair. How old were you?"

"Seventeen. High school boyfriend. No clue where he is now."

"He was the same age as you?"

She nodded. "Wait, your first time was with someone older?"

Another wince. "It was the summer between grade ten and grade eleven, and Dean and I snuck out to a bush party, mostly seniors heading off to college in the fall, some people back for the summer. All college-aged, anyway. And we were so sure we'd be caught and kicked out for being kids, but we'd both sprouted up that summer, and they thought we were older than we were..."

"Where did it...happen?"

"Front seat of a pickup truck. It didn't last long."

"Awwww. Poor teenage Zander."

"The first time. I was ready to go again pretty soon, and she had a bunch of condoms—"

"Too much information!" But it wasn't, really. That happened more than twenty years earlier, and Faith could picture that teenage kid, so eager to be a man. It was an important piece of the Zander puzzle. "And then you left for the army two years later?"

"Yeah. Crazy to think about how much I grew up in those few short years."

"When did you first go overseas?"

He shook his head. "This is the wrong direction for this conversation to go."

"But I want to know!"

"And I want to watch you get yourself off, then tuck you into bed so you can sleep well and wake up early and get more writing done."

"I'm editing now. I don't do that before dawn. Not a morning person, remember? I only get up that early for words because I need total quiet."

"I'll remember that." He winked at her. "Okay, then I'll just have to make up a bedtime story..."

CHAPTER NINETEEN

"I'M NOT TIRED."

"Tough. It's a school night."

"But Mom! I'm five now!"

Nineteen hours into his next year of life and Eric had decided to sprout an attitude. It was a good thing she thought he was cute. "You will be an absolute bear in the morning if your head isn't on your pillow in ten minutes. And when you are a bear, I will point out that you had a choice to get enough rest and chose not to take it. Understand?"

"No."

"Of course not. Come on, upstairs."

She'd just pushed herself up off the couch, where she'd been playing Plants vs. Zombies and pretending she wasn't antsy about not having heard from Zander since the night before. And the last two nights, when they'd talked, he'd been...brief. Cryptic, even. And no video chat.

She was doing her best not to imagine why.

The ability to ask why and get a dozen evil, doomsday

answers was a writer's secret weapon—and a new girl-friend's certain undoing.

As Eric whined again about putting away his Minecraft reference book, the one that he couldn't even read yet, they heard a knock at the door.

Knock. Knock-knock.

Her heart leapt into her throat. She knew that sound. Knew the fist that made that kind of forceful alert of presence. That fist—and the beautiful man to whom it belonged—was supposed to be in Alberta.

She flew to the front door, but so did Eric, and the little bugger was faster than her. She laughed as he slid in front of her and put his hand on the door knob first. "I've got it."

Stepping back, she let him open the door for Zander.

God, he looked good. In person was so much different than on video chat. A billion times better, and yet already her heart ached because she knew he couldn't be here for very long, so she greedily soaked up every detail. The stretched-out, faded black t-shirt that used to have lettering but now just looked *good*. The jeans. The boots. The leather jacket slung over his shoulder.

So focused she was on gobbling him up with her eyes that she almost forgot she was wearing rolled up sweat pants and a sports bra underneath an oversized tank top that said "Hakuna Masquata: It Means Nice Booty".

Almost.

With a squeak, she stepped behind Eric, who wasn't big enough to hide anything.

And it didn't matter, because Zander gave them both a massive grin and swept them into his arms.

"Happy birthday, bud," he said roughly.

"Can I stay up late because it's my birthday?" Eric asked, earning himself a growl from her.

Zander laughed. "Seriously, dude? Don't get me in trouble."

"That's a no?"

"Is it a school night?"

Eric wriggled out of Zander's arms and jumped onto the staircase. "Maybe."

"Go brush your teeth," Faith said, then twisted to look at Zander's profile. He was right there. So close she could kiss his cheek if Eric wasn't paying attention. She turned her head back to her son. "Zander will read you a bedtime story."

Like a shot, her kid disappeared, and Zander squeezed her close to his side. "Surprise."

"No kidding. What are you doing here?"

"It's Eric's birthday." Just like that. Like, of course he'd be here.

Of course he'd be here. Her heart grew another size with the reminder.

Upstairs, the door between her mother's apartment and the landing opened. "Faith, did I hear—Oh, hello, Zander."

Faith hadn't told her mother that they'd had a fight. She hadn't told her that they'd made up, either. She'd been falling down on the sharing side of things, but she could scarcely believe she *had* Zander, let alone understand the details of *how*.

"Miriam," he said with a hint of laughter in his voice. He still hadn't let Faith go. This was well beyond a welcome back hug. He was just holding her now, and it felt wonderful.

"Is this another whirlwind visit?" her mom asked. God, the small talk. Faith couldn't handle it, not when she wanted to hit a pause time button and climb him like a tree. Although she did want to know the answer to that question.

She patted Zander's hand. He didn't take the hint and let her go. "I should go and check on Eric," she muttered.

"I'm fine!" her son yelled from upstairs.

"PJs!" she yelled back.

Zander kept talking to her mother like the yelling hadn't happened. "Yes, I've got a three day leave pass before I head up to the Arctic for two weeks. I wish I'd been able to get here before bedtime."

That was out the window, and Faith wasn't complaining.

"It's okay," she whispered, nuzzling closer. Upstairs, her mother followed Eric into his room and starting helping him with his pyjamas. Faith took advantage of the moment of privacy and flung her arms around his neck. "You're really here."

"I am." He grinned.

She returned the smile, suddenly giddy. "I love you, Zander. And I love that you're here."

When Eric came to get them, they were still embracing, and he slid between their bodies, getting in on the hug. Zander kissed Faith's brow, then she stepped away, watching as he flipped Eric upside down and carried him back to bed by his ankles.

Her son beamed the entire way.

Zander ended up reading both bedtime stories, and he didn't come to her room until Eric had passed out cold.

"Sorry I kept him up late, I meant to get here earlier, but my flight was delayed..."

She waved him off. "You're just in charge of getting him up in the morning. I recommend pancakes."

"Deal." He settled on her bed, watching her get ready for bed. She'd traded her ratty sweats for the silky scraps of nothing she'd bought just for him, and her skin started to warm under his appreciative stare. She picked up her hair brush and pulled out her ponytail. "Can I do that for you?"

She joined him on the bed, feet dangling over the edge, and he carefully brushed her hair. Each long stroke tugged gently on her scalp, and on the third pass, she groaned in pleasure. Behind her, he shifted, and when her hair hung loose and shiny around her shoulders, he gathered it together and twisted it to the side.

His hands pressed against her skin. Warm, a little rough, and ever so caring. He rubbed his thumbs down her back, between her shoulder blades, then squeezed her shoulders and rubbed up her neck. Again and again he repeated the massage until she was boneless. Then he tugged her back against him and just held her.

It was blissfully domestic.

"Seventy-two hours, eh?" she whispered.

"This time."

"Every time, it seems." She didn't mean it to sound like that, with that edge of snark that was really fuelled by fear.

But it did, and Zander didn't miss it. "So?"

"Nothing."

"No, you said it. Let's talk about it."

She sighed. This wasn't how she wanted to spend even a second of his limited time. "I'm just being silly."

"Then be silly out loud."

"Um...." She took a deep breath. "Are you sure you're this guy?"

"What guy?"

"Domesticated and tethered to one place."

"Ahhh." He shrugged. "I'm not sure where you got the idea that I'm filled with burning wanderlust. That's not all that I am."

"For now? Anymore? Because when I met you—no, stop giving me that look." Her back was to him, but she could picture the look he must be giving her. He chuckled, telling her she was right. "I'm not picking a fight, I'm just...it's hard to wrap my head around the idea that this —" She gestured around her bedroom, but meaning her entire house and town "—could ever be enough for you."

"You need to stop telling me what kind of guy I am." He said it gently enough, but it still scratched like a burr.

"You need to stop pretending that you aren't exactly that kind of guy! You already feel the itch, right? You've been back three times in four months. Don't tell me you wouldn't rather be exploring some far-flung corner of the world instead of being obligated to come here."

"Obligated? Babe, I promise you that's not the word I'd use to describe how I feel right now." He wrapped himself more tightly around her, his jaw twitching as he brought their cheeks together. He waited a beat, then whispered, "How about you stop pretending you wouldn't rather come with me?"

She had good reasons. "Eric has school. I have to work."

"And wanderlust is what vacations are for. I've worked hard for twenty years and I'm looking at starting a new company. I get not being able to drop everything. You think I don't respect that about you? I'll never try to tell you to work less. You work as much as you *want*. But there are other things you want, too."

Heat radiated off his body, seeping into her, carrying with it the confidence he felt. Was he right? She wanted so much more, it was true. But she'd lived that way once before. Greg had, too. She'd learned the hardest way possible that being an adult meant giving up the right to indulge all the wants of the human spirit.

Especially the wants that tugged one away from safety and security.

"Zander, I can't—"

"I know." He turned her enough to cup her cheek and he circled his thumb at the corner of her mouth while his dark eyes searched her face. "You're not there yet. Hear me say this: I don't need to take off on an adventure until you are by my side."

"But—"

"And yeah, it might not ever be your bag again." He lifted one eyebrow and gave her a bossy look that made her quiver all over. "You and Eric are more than enough adventure for me, right here in this little house. I will take all of my leave passes and mark them as destination Tobermory and Pine Harbour in advance if that would prove it to you."

"What if you just marked them as Tobermory?" Her heart was fluttering a mile a minute, but *yes*, this felt like the right step. "Would it be crazy to ask you to move in here when you come back?"

"Maybe. But crazy...now that sounds exactly like what kind of man I am."

Hardly. But she let him whisk her to bed, and when she

woke up in the middle of the night to find him rolling off the mattress, she tugged him back down beside her. There would be no more nights in the spare room.

Life was too short and precious for pretending he wasn't exactly what she wanted, every minute of every day.

— —

ZANDER'S ALARM went off at six. He hit snooze and rolled onto his back. Faith murmured something in her sleep and rolled too, resettling with her head on his shoulder and her hand on his stomach, warm and soft as her fingers unconsciously tangled in the hair there.

This is what happiness feels like. The house was quiet still, and he let himself sleep in a bit, drifting in that pleasant near-awake state until his second alarm went off. As much as he wanted to stay there all morning, they hadn't talked about Eric knowing they were sharing a room. With a groan, he shoved himself out of bed and carefully tucked Faith back in.

In the kitchen, he found pancake mix and whipped up the batter, then he turned on the TV and watched the news as he did his morning push-ups. He had a set of six different push-ups that he did most of the time—plyometric, walking push-ups, pike push-ups, etcetera. They worked his entire body and didn't require any equipment. As he finished his third set of the lot, he heard little footsteps enter the living room. He looked over his shoulder. "Morning, bud."

Eric yawned. "Morning."

"Pancakes?"

He nodded, then stared as Zander stood up. "You're not wearing a shirt."

"No, I—" *didn't sleep with one on* was probably too much information. "I didn't think anyone was up."

"Are you exercising?"

"Yep."

"I do exercises. Sometimes Mommy does yoga and I sit on her back."

"That's fun." Zander filed away the fact that Faith secretly did yoga. He wanted to watch. "Want to do some push-ups with me?"

Eric nodded solemnly and shuffled closer, still sleepy. He carefully pulled off his shirt and put it on the arm of the sofa and then planked next to Zander. That was how Miriam found them, Zander in his shorts, Eric in his PJ pants, neither of them wearing a shirt and both of them laughing like idiots as Eric pretended to correct Zander's form over and over again.

"Grandma, can you do push-ups?" Eric asked as he climbed onto one of the kitchen chairs.

"I can make coffee, sweet pea. That's my superpower. Now put on your shirt." She pointed at Zander, an amused smile dancing across her face. "You too."

Zander tossed it over to him, then headed for the stairs. Faith's mother was the only person on the planet who could make him blush. He jumped into the shower, then dressed himself properly for mixed company in a long-sleeved black Henley and faded blue jeans.

Faith woke up as he was threading his belt through his jeans. "Is Eric up?"

"Yep. And we worked out together."

"What? He wasn't grumpy?" She laughed as she pushed herself up in bed. She was wearing a silky camisole, but with the sheet held up in front of her chest, it was easy to imagine her naked. *Breakfast. Focus.*

He cleared his throat. "Nope, not grumpy. Although your mother chastised me for not wearing a shirt."

Faith giggled and shook her head. "You don't know my mother. I highly doubt she was chastising you. What did she say?"

"She told me to put on a shirt."

"Was she smiling while she said it?"

Zander groaned. "No, don't tell me."

"You were lucky she didn't pat your chest and compliment your form."

"Oh, Jesus."

"What? You're a beautiful, beautiful man, Zander Minelli. And we appreciate—" She shrieked as he dove onto the bed, silencing her with a soft, lingering, *thorough* good morning kiss. When he let her up for air, she sighed and snuggled closer. "I appreciate you the most, though."

"Lucky me." He pushed himself off the bed and held out his hand. "Pancake duty calls. Your mom is making coffee."

Faith grinned. "I'm the most spoiled girl in all of Tobermory today."

"Good." He dragged himself away before he molested her in a way that wouldn't be appropriate for a school morning.

Over breakfast they were all quiet, except for Miriam and Faith exchanging cryptic half-sentences about their day's plans.

"Mom, did you call—"

"Yes, I'll pick it up. And maybe for dinner...?"

"The fish? I think so. Zander?"

He gave Faith an amused look. "Do I like fish? Is that the question?"

"Yes." Her brows pulled together in a delicate frown. "Wasn't that clear?"

"Not even a little, babe. Yes, sure. I'm easy, I'll eat anything."

Eric shook his head. "I won't. I don't like steak. It's hard to chew. And I *really* hate mushrooms."

"Oh, you're missing out. Steak with mushrooms on the side...maybe some herbed butter, and mashed potatoes..." Zander's mouth was watering. "That's heaven, right there."

Faith groaned. "Well now *I* don't want fish for dinner."

He grinned. "Fish is good. Lemon, herbs, butter again, because that's the secret to good cooking. And rice instead of potatoes. Delicious. Asparagus or green beans on the side, and voila." The entire table stared at him. "What?"

"Zander..." Miriam cleared her throat. "Can you cook?"

"Sure."

She smiled enigmatically. "Good."

Faith's phone beeped. "Time for school."

"I don't want to go to school! I want to stay here with Zander!"

"I'll be there to pick you up as soon as you're done. And I've got work to do today, anyway. Not fun for a five year old."

"I like work. I do work at my spy base all the time."

"School, end of story," Faith said, firmly propelling Eric toward the front door.

Zander followed behind. "I'll come along for drop-off."

"Will you tell me about your Arctic training in the car?"

"Definitely."

Eric sped ahead and pulled open the back seat door of Faith's car. She turned and winked at Zander. "And then will you take me to Greta's for pie?"

CHAPTER TWENTY

"HOW MANY MORE DAYS NOW, MOMMY?"

"Three more days." Faith pointed to the calendar on the side of the fridge. They'd been counting down the days until Zander finished his arctic exercise. There was no cell reception where he was, they only had satellite phones. He'd had his turn to make a call home at the end of the first week, and that had re-doubled Eric's interest in knowing everything about what Zander was doing.

"How much snow is there?" he'd asked five times, at least.

Each time she said a variation on the same answer. "More ice than snow. But it looks like snow. It's white in all directions. Rocks and dirt, too, here and there. We can look it up on my computer."

Each night they looked at YouTube videos of life in the far north.

It was early November, and snow had yet to come to the peninsula, but it would soon. Every day was a little bit colder. The bright burst of autumnal colour that had greeted Zander's last visit was now gone. The leaves were still crunchy on the ground, but brown now, and the cloud-heavy sky looked greyer each day.

Or maybe that was just her mood.

If you fall in love with a soldier, this is the life. She told herself that over and over again. And two weeks wasn't so bad. She was selfishly grateful that she hadn't had to love him through his tours in Afghanistan and Bosnia. Her heart ached for the women that made that quiet sacrifice right along with their spouses.

"And when is it going to snow here," Eric asked next.

"That's harder to say," she answered, trying to be patient. His endless questions were really a mask for wanting to know when they'd return to their new normal. Zander calling each night, planning for the holidays. In less than six weeks, they'd have fifteen days all together. And they just needed to hold their breath and be brave until then.

It sounded melodramatic when she said it out loud—to Olivia and Dani when she met them at the diner in Pine Harbour for coffee, to her mother one late night when Faith couldn't sleep. But every time Eric asked another question, something twisted inside her. A dial of worry.

Three more days. Maybe the worry would ease when they got to see Zander's face on the iPad again.

— —

FAITH YAWNED and blinked at the white stuff falling from

the early morning sky. Eric would be happy, at least. She needed another cup of coffee.

She had a phone meeting with her editor as soon as she dropped Eric at school, and then, if her courier guy showed up early enough in the afternoon, fifty hot-off-the-presses novels to sign for giveaways. And Zander was coming home for a surprise visit.

He'd been back at his base for a few days, and he had another three day weekend which he finagled into four somehow. She wasn't going to question their good fortune. Two months apart would have been too long.

Her mother had left the day before for a week-long vacation with her "friend", Bill, who Faith had only met twice, and briefly at that. Miriam seemed content to keep that relationship separate from their lives.

As opposed to Faith, who had gone from flirting to dating to moving in with her boyfriend in what felt like the blink of an eye.

A very happy blink, but still.

And yet every time she thought of Zander, a happy calm settled over her. He was ridiculously good for her, and she wasn't going to sabotage those feelings in any way.

She poured herself another cup, then finished making Eric's lunch. He still wasn't up yet, so she grabbed her mug and went to wake him. When she knocked on his door, half-open, she was surprised to see him already dressed. He had his backpack on his bed. She set her coffee on his dresser and zipped it up for him. "What's in this thing, rocks?"

"Show and share today," he said as he crawled under his bed. He came back out with a plastic toy from a fast food restaurant, which he tucked into the outside pocket. "All set."

She'd made oatmeal, which he tucked into with more enthusiasm than he'd had for any meal all week. And before her alarm could go off, he cleared his bowl to the sink and was rifling through the front closet for his snow pants.

"I'm not sure you need them," Faith started to say, but that was silly. Better warm than cold, even for the short recess breaks.

He kept taking gleeful peeks out the window at the fluffy flakes now sticking to the window. The temperature was hovering right around freezing. A degree or two warmer and all of that would melt into slushy, muddy yuck.

At the very least, the snow pants would keep the rest of him clean and dry.

As they headed out the door, her phone vibrated with a text message from Zander. **Heading to the airport soon. See you tonight. XO**

Drop off was extra quick, just a kiss on the cheek and a rushed encouragement to have a good day, and then she scurried home again for her phone meeting, which ended up being more than an hour long. By the time she hung up her head was spinning from the mile-long to-do list for the new series arc. She tried to open her project file on the computer, but she couldn't focus, so finally she pushed away from the computer and put on laundry. Zander would be arriving in Calgary soon. He couldn't get a direct flight, so he had a two hour stop-over. At least he had a direct flight home.

She stopped mid-transfer of laundry from the washer

to the dryer and closed her eyes. She needed to cut herself some slack if she didn't get any work done today. It was okay to just be excited and distracted sometimes.

Like Eric and the snow.

Her phone vibrated on the kitchen counter at the same time as someone knocked at the front door. She ran for the door first—it was the courier, and she signed for the box of books. It was heavy enough to just leave on the foyer floor, and she wandered back to the kitchen to see who had texted her.

It hadn't been a message, though. She'd missed a call from the school.

Before she could dial back, it rang again.

The school calling back. Worried, she answered the phone. "Hello?"

"Mrs. Davidson?" an unfamiliar male voice asked.

"Yes?" Was Eric sick? Why wasn't the secretary calling?

"This is Will Kincaid, the principal of Tobermory Public School. Did you by any chance pick Eric up for an early lunch?"

White hot fear thundered through her body. "What? No...Where is Eric?"

A single, painful beat of hesitation was all she needed for that panic to explode. "We can't locate him, Mrs. Davidson. I'm sorry to tell you this over the phone. We're calling 911 right now," he said over muffled conversation in the background. "You should perhaps stay home until the police arrive, in case Eric is heading there..."

She didn't hear the rest of what he said, because she was already out the door, her phone still in her hand.

No.

No, no, no.

She starting screaming the word over and over again as she backed her car out of the drive, rocking wildly onto the curb. Her wheels spun on the snow-slick road as she gave it too much gas, and she jerked her foot back. *Get it together, Faith.* Heart pounding so hard it hurt her chest, she drove the two minutes to the school, eyes peeled for any sight of her son.

As she pulled into the lot, so did two O.P.P. cruisers. The police officers followed her inside. The principal was standing right inside the entrance. All the doors were closed, and two teachers were moving quickly down the hall away from where their boss stood. He held up his hand. "We're searching the school right now. All classrooms are locked down, and our staff members are going room by room—"

"When was he last seen?" Faith interrupted. "When did you lose my son?"

"He had gym class—that's right now, just ending. So we last saw him forty minutes ago. Lunch is next, so our hope was that..."

"Are you the mother?" one of the police officers asked.

She nodded. He introduced himself but Faith didn't catch his name. He asked for a description, which she gave with some prompting, then he started talking into his radio as the other officer ushered them into the school office.

She watched him through the glass pane in the office door as the principal started talking again. "My understanding is he asked to go to the washroom, and approximately fifteen minutes passed before it was noticed that he didn't return."

She spun around. "Aren't they supposed to go with a buddy?"

He shifted uncomfortably. "Yes."

"So that didn't happen?"

"Mrs. Davidson, I am so sorry—"

"I don't give a fuck if you are *sorry*. That didn't happen?"

His voice shook and at any other time, she'd have cared about his obvious pain. "It was an oversight."

The first police officer returned to the office. "We'll need some recent pictures…"

The next twenty minutes passed in a blur. A fire truck arrived, then more police. She was holding it together okay until Dean Foster strode in. He was in uniform, and everyone else looked his way, but he didn't stop and talk to anyone. Instead he bee lined to her, concern written all over his face, and at the sight of someone familiar, something inside her chest cracked open.

"I've got you," he said roughly as she clung to him. "We're going to find him."

"He packed some extra stuff in his backpack," she choked out. "I didn't realize it this morning, but it was heavy."

"Okay. Okay." He squeezed her shoulder and lifted her chin with the tip of his finger. "Zander's brother is the best Search and Rescue organizer I've ever met. They've already set up a command centre and they're gathering teams together. Can you think of anywhere Eric might want to go?"

She shook her head, trying to shake away the panic. She couldn't think. "He likes hiking." Her mind flashed with a memory from the morning. She'd gone to put a granola bar in Eric's lunch box and there weren't any left. "He took some snacks from the kitchen, I think. They were missing this morning and I didn't think anything of it…."

"No, you wouldn't. But it's good that you're remembering that now. There are snowmobile trails that run behind the school and out of town. We'll start there. And I'm going to be right here, right by your side, and any time you remember anything, you just tell me. Doesn't matter how random it is, got it?"

She nodded numbly.

"I tried to reach Zander," he continued. "His phone keeps going to voice mail."

Another bubble of pain rolled through her chest and lodged in her throat. "He's in the air. He's flying home for the weekend."

"Did Eric know that?"

She shook her head.

"Could he have overheard something?"

No. They'd only texted about it. "It was a last minute plan."

Dean pulled out his phone and fired off a message to someone. "We'll get a hold of him. When and where does he land?"

"Umm…" She closed her eyes. "He's got a connection in Calgary. He's probably going to land soon."

Someone came up behind Dean and handed him a coffee, which he pressed into her hands. "Drink this."

"I don't—"

"I'm also going to make you eat things from time to time." He guided her to a pair of stiff plastic chairs and sat them both down. He gave her a serious look that part-terrified, part-reassured her. "If Eric's taken off on a little adventure, it might take us all day to find him. You're going to need your strength. It's my job to make sure that you keep it."

She took a sip of coffee.

"And I want you to go home. I'm going with you, but right now there's a constable standing guard there, and if Eric makes his way home, it's better that he finds you than a policeman."

"I want to join the search party." She was losing her voice, and it came out in a rough whisper. Maybe he hadn't heard her. "Dean?"

He shook his head. "Not yet. Let's let the S&R teams do their thing."

He held out his hand and guided her outside. He wanted to take her back to her place in the cruiser, but that was ridiculous. It was a few blocks, and she'd driven her car here.

Reluctantly he agreed to follow her, and she had a few moments of stunned, surreal silence as she drove home. There was a cruiser in her driveway so she parked on the road and stumbled out.

It was cold, she suddenly realized.

She'd left the house without a coat or her purse.

Dean met her in the middle of her lawn and pushed her up the stairs and past the uniform standing guard at her front door. She hadn't locked up—was pretty sure she hadn't even closed the door, although the police officer must have done that when he showed up.

"Thank you," she whispered as she passed. She wasn't feeling very grateful for anything, but the ingrained reaction took care of itself.

She didn't realize her phone was ringing until Dean stopped her and reached for her hand. He held it up in front of her.

Zander.

"He's just landing in Calgary," she whispered.

Dean looked at the screen. "Can I..."

She nodded, then shook her head. "No. I'll tell him."

She took a deep breath, but it didn't help her be brave after she answered.

"Zander…" Her voice broke into a dozen pieces as she interrupted his greeting. "Eric's missing."

CHAPTER TWENTY-ONE

ZANDER LANDED at the Kitchener airport five-and-a-half painful hours later. Radio-silence had never been more torturous. He'd stayed on the phone with Faith until he boarded the plane and they pulled away from the gate.

Dean had promised to get good news to him through the airline if he could, so when he landed and had heard nothing, he was in beast mode and not in a mood to deal with a rental car company dick-around or anything else. As he sprinted down the hallway toward the arrivals door he read through the text messages spilling in. Update after update that said the same thing. No news.

And a message from each of his siblings, letting him know that their mother was waiting for him on the other side of the sliding doors in the arrival lounge.

Her face pinched in worry as she waved him down. She handed him the keys to her compact SUV as soon as he reached her. "Everyone else is searching," she said, but he already knew that. His brothers, Dani...everyone would be looking for Eric. "I know you were going to get a rental, but this was something I could do, and I thought it best you weren't alone for the drive."

"It's fine, thank you," he said roughly. He appreciated the gesture, but nothing changed the fact that he wasn't there and he couldn't get over that feeling of uselessness.

He let his mother hug him, but he was moving them toward the exit at the same time. No time for comfort. No time for words.

"I'm parked in the priority pickup up row." Her words whipped from her mouth as she spun, following him.

His pulse thudded with unhappy restraint as he tried not to run—his mother wouldn't be able to keep up. "Any update beyond no update?"

Sometimes text messages were slow to filter in, and he was desperate for good news.

"Nothing yet."

"Who's with Faith?"

"Still Dean, I think. He doesn't plan to leave her side until you arrive."

He dialled Tom.

His brother answered on the first ring, out of breath. "You landed?"

Zander grunted an answer and hit the unlock button on the key fob. He gestured for his mother to get in. He threw his bag in the backseat and turned on the car as he started talking. "It's been dark for an hour, Tom. How many teams have shown up?"

"Anyone who knows what they're doing is here, and we've got a hundred volunteers out as well. We'll find him." Tom gave him an update on the search. Volunteers had been combing the fields and forest behind the school, and as more people joined the search, they were moving down the highway, on either side. "I'm nearly at Greta's. That's where we've set up a command post."

"Faith's still at home?"

"Yeah. Better that she's not at the nerve centre."

In case of bad news. "We're hitting the road. Ma's got my phone. I want updates every half hour. I'll be there as soon as humanly possible."

"Drive safe."

That was a relative concept for Zander at the moment. Be mindful of the safety of others? Always. His mother was a passenger. Other vehicles and pedestrians didn't know he was racing for his life here.

But he knew back roads where speed limits didn't matter. He knew which highways were less populous than others.

He knew how to get to the tip of the peninsula faster than anyone else, and he was going to push himself to the limit to make that happen.

His mother let him drive in silence for a while. A half hour, at least, because Tom called with a terse, no-news update.

After she disconnected the call, she reached for something at her feet and quietly handed over a chocolate cookie.

And hot tears pricked the back of his eyelids. He grit his teeth. "Why cookies?" She always made them. Always had. She was a dragon lady in so many ways, but she'd always made them cookies when other mothers might have insisted on healthier snacks instead.

She didn't answer right away, and when she did, her voice was uncharacteristically thoughtful. Anne Minelli was tough as nails and could do—did do—anything she set her mind to. She never set her mind to being soft and gentle.

"Because life is hard." The last word wobbled off her tongue. Harder than ever today. But he was strong enough to hear it. "And the cookies always made you boys happy." She took a deep, steadying breath. "Sometimes you would get so lost in your imaginary adventures. Dani would happily sit with me in the kitchen, but the only time I'd see your faces was when I'd pull something sweet out of the oven."

Something started to pulse in Zander's mind. He frowned into the darkness. What had just triggered that? "What did you say?"

"Sometimes you boys would be so lost in your adventures—"

His spy base.

"Call Tom back." He told her the password to his phone and tried hard not to grab it from her hands.

"What is it?" she asked as she moved her fingers over the screen.

The dialling was faint at first, then she hit the speaker phone button and it was loud. Jarring. *Answer, damn it.*

"Zander?" Tom's voice filled the interior of the car.

"There's a path somewhere between the playground and Faith's house. I don't know which direction. Can you send me a picture of the search grid?"

"Hang on. Pull over, man."

Zander jammed his foot against the gas and sped up instead.

— —

FAITH PERCHED on the edge of her couch. Someone had wrapped a blanket around her because she'd been shivering. Someone else had offered her a sedative and gotten a growly refusal for their effort.

Every few minutes, she replayed the call from the school in her head. Snapshots flashed in front of her eyes. Stumbling to the car, leaving the front door flapping open behind her.

Dean showing up while she was at the school, holding her to his chest while she sobbed into his uniform.

Zander calling. She desperately wanted to talk to him again, but he was driving and the last thing he needed to hear while speeding through the night was her being hysterical.

He'd sent proxies to take care of her, anyway. His best friend was now on the other side of her living room, listening to yet another phone call. He had two phones on him, and his police radio. She kept listening to the crackle, hoping to decipher something, but he kept the volume low enough that she couldn't make out the words.

Dean glanced up, and when he saw her eyes on him, he hung up the phone and moved toward her.

"Who was that?" she asked hoarsely.

"I was just listening in to the command centre. Tom had me on speaker phone." He dropped to his knees in front of her. "We're going to find him. He's wearing warm winter clothes, and he packed food. He's a smart kid. Focus on that."

That damn heavy backpack. She should have opened it up and asked him about it. She replayed their morning. How distracted she'd been. How weak her goodbye was.

Did he know she loved him and missed him? Where had he gone and *why?*

Dean patted her knee and stood up.

She looked out the window at the darkness. She should be out there, looking. Maybe if Dean took a call again, she could excuse herself to the bathroom and sneak out.

A phone rang. Through the muzziness in her head it sounded far away, but Dean was lifting his hand to his ear. "What is it?" His eyebrows shot up. "Right. I'll ask her."

She was already on her feet. "Ask me what?"

"Did you and Eric go for a hike a few weeks ago? On a day that you met Dani in the park?"

She shook her head woodenly. That was the day she'd made up with Zander. They'd come straight home from the playground.

"Tom, she's saying they didn't." He listened for a minute, his jaw flexed, then looked her way again. "He doesn't see any marked trails between here and the park, but they're taking a team into the woods now."

That sounded terrifying. "Why there?"

He gave her a long, steady look. "Zander thinks Eric's spy base might be in there. Get your coat on. Remember how I said you needed to be brave and strong and wait until it was time? Now it's time."

Time does funny things when you're in the middle of a trauma. Faith remembered that from the night Greg died. Speed up. Slow down. Freeze on a moment and then zoom past others like they were nothing, just fragments in the wind. She was zipping up her jacket, then she was in Dean's cruiser. Mittens and hat were on, but she didn't remember grabbing them.

They didn't go far, just around the corner.

An awful, ugly, heaviness settled in her gut. She started

to cry as he pulled to a stop behind a Fire and Rescue SUV. In the brush at the side of the road, she could see flashlights moving.

"There's an unmarked path here," Dean said quietly as he closed her door behind her. "Have you ever been down it? Tom says it snakes in a bunch of directions."

She started to shake her head, but maybe...

With a gasp, she took off running through the snow-covered grass. Scrabbly twigs slapped at her face as she ran into the brush, and she couldn't really see anything, but she knew where she was going.

"Faith!" Dean yelled louder, right behind her, and then his hand was on her arm, twisting her around. "Stop."

"Let go of me!" Her lungs were burning and her words tore out of her chest. "I know where he is."

"Good. But you can't see anything and you might hurt yourself. Take my flashlight."

He pressed the large metal torch into her hand and she turned again, still fast, still uncaring about cuts and scrapes, but slower enough that she could breathe. How far was it? The other searchers had gone in the other direction. They didn't know that she'd come here with Eric when he was....three? Maybe even two. God, it had been a while. And the brush didn't look the same at all in the winter. Time had changed it, too. But she wasn't looking for a familiar scene. She was looping the memory in her head.

Eric ducking around a tree, pretending to know where he was leading her. "This way, Mommy, this way."

It had been their one and only hike in this direction. It wasn't even a real path. But up ahead, hopefully not too far, there was a rocky outcrop, a shallow cave. If there was any justice in the world, if Fate had any decency, inside it would be her son.

— —

ZANDER MADE it to Wiarton in less than two hours, and when the shadow of a police cruiser pulled onto the highway behind their car, he swore under his breath. No way was he stopping, but it would be incredibly awkward to deal with one of his brother's co-workers charging him with half the Highway Traffic Act if he didn't. He turned to his mother to tell her to call Rafe, but before the words were formed, the lights lit up behind him.

But instead of pulling him over, the cruiser sped up, pulling alongside. Zander didn't recognize the uniform inside, but the hand signal was clear. *Follow me.*

"Get an update from Rafe," he said woodenly, not wanting to dwell on why he was getting an escort up the peninsula. But he needed to know before he got there. Needed to be strong.

His mother nodded, and this time she didn't put the call on speaker phone. Zander listened to her side of the conversation as he watched his speedometer climb. The cop in front of him was going over a buck twenty. One thirty. Dark shadows and drifts of snow flitted by on either side of the car.

"Rafaelo, it's your mother."

"We're in Wiarton."

"Yes."

"I understand."

"Right."

Zander knuckled the steering wheel. He couldn't take the suspense. "Mother?"

She hesitated. "They haven't found him yet."

Fuck. He slammed his hand against the dash as his mother hung up the phone.

"They've just taken Faith into the woods, the area you suggested to Tom. Rafe says Tom's team had a ten-minute head start on her, so hopefully we'll hear something soon."

The kilometres ticked by still too slowly, even though they were going nearly twice the speed limit, and as they streaked past the exit for Pine Harbour, his phone lit up again.

— —

THREE SHARP WHISTLES pierced the air and stabbed Faith in the chest. She stopped still, spinning around. "Where did that come from?"

She remembered from her climbing days—that was a distress signal. And it was close by.

Dean curved his gloved hand around her arm and turned her. As they spun around, the whistle sounded again. She'd been a bit off course, she could see that now. The rise of the land was there, and at the top of it was another flashlight.

"Eric," she called out, scrambling up through the brush faster now.

"We have him," someone shouted, and it sounded like Zander so it must be Tom. "He's breathing. And awake."

Thank you, she silently said to the universe.

It didn't slow her down any, knowing that he was alive. Her feet slipped and Dean helped her up, propelling her forward at the same time.

At the top of the hill, where the rocks rose up from the ground and made a shelter, she found Eric wrapped in a foil blanket and Tom Minelli quietly talking to him. Someone else she didn't recognize was standing nearby, a human lamp as his headlamp clearly illuminated the two people on the ground.

Faith fell to her knees and pulled Eric into her lap. "Oh God, you're okay."

"I'm sorry, Mom."

She swallowed the sob that begged for release and shook her head. "You're okay. That's all that matters."

The blanket crinkled as she tried to get up, but her arms were shaking too much. Her legs, too.

"Hang on a minute," Tom said, and she blinked over at him. "He's okay. We've looked him over, and that's one good quality coat you bought him. He's warm enough for you both to catch your breath and have a hug before we head back to the road."

"I need to call Zander," she hiccuped. The sob might be stifled but the tears rolled down her face, not giving two fucks if she wanted to hold it together or not. Her body was done being stoic.

"He'll be here soon," Dean said, joining their little group on the ground.

"Not soon. I need to call him *now*." She glared at both men. "Now."

Tom nodded and pulled out his phone. He dialled Zander and then held the phone between them.

Zander's mom answered. "Tom, we're ten minutes away. Where should we go?"

"Ma, can you put Zander on the phone?"

"What is it, Tom?" Anne's voice was careful, but concerned. In that instant, Faith had a sudden rush of kinship for her. She recognized that mama bear tone. They might parent completely differently, but once a mother, always a mother.

"Anne, it's Faith. We've found Eric and he's okay. Can you put Zander on?" Faith's breath puffed in the space between their bodies and she shifted, suddenly realizing the ground was wet and cold beneath her. "Come on, baby, we're standing up now."

"Faith?" Zander's voice rang strong. "Do you have him?"

"Hi Zander," Eric said.

"Oh, bud." Zander sighed. "I'm going to give you the biggest hug in like five minutes."

"Okay." Her son gave her a sad smile. "Zander, I think I'm in trouble."

"Don't worry. We're just glad you're okay. I'm just passing Greta's now. Did you go to your spy base?"

"Yeah."

"Okay, you start walking back to the road with your mom and I'll find you."

Faith handed the phone back to Tom and took Eric's hand. The forest that she'd run through blindly just a few minutes earlier now looked dark and foreboding.

"I'll take the lead," Tom said quietly.

Faith nodded, and Dean fell into step on the other side of Eric, reaching ahead of her son to block the twigs from snapping into his face.

They were nearly at the road when Zander called out

for them. He shoved his way through the brush like a raging bull, only stopping once he'd swung Eric into his arms and pulled Faith close.

He stared at Eric, his chest rising and falling heavily even through his coat. He shook his head in obvious wonder, and in the light bouncing off Tom's headlamp, his eyes were bright. "You're okay?"

Eric nodded and touched Zander's face with his gloved hand.

"Thank God." Zander kissed Faith's forehead. "Come on. Let's go home."

CHAPTER TWENTY-TWO

THERE WAS no question about it—Zander hadn't flown back out west to stay. He braced himself for a battle, but as soon as he sat down in Captain Diwali's office the following Tuesday, his commanding officer quietly slid a piece of paper across the table.

"I'll miss you, Minelli."

Zander read the transfer posting. He'd serve the rest of his contract attached to the reserve unit in Wiarton. "Thanks for this, sir. It means a lot."

"About time you found a wife and kid."

"One thing at a time," he laughed. Not because he wasn't there. No, this was real and he was all in. But there was a time and a place for making that official, and he wouldn't rush *that*. He wanted it to be perfect for Faith, too.

And for the next little while, everything would be about Eric. Faith was going to try and fail at not being hyper-vigilant. Zander was going to be stoic and stable and only check on the kid in the middle of the night when everyone else was sleeping and wouldn't know about his fear.

No way was he going to propose until they were all well and truly comfortable with their new family dynamic, when planning a wedding wouldn't distract from parenting and living and really listening to what everyone in their family was saying.

That weighed heavily on both of them, that Eric had been talking about his spy base non-stop and they'd written it off as nonsensical fantasy.

Zander felt awful about talking so much about his own training exercise, the fun parts of it, and not enough about the safety precautions. Rule number one in the Davidson house now: tell a grown up you are planning to take off on an adventure.

The next step for Zander and Faith, before he could ask her to marry him, was showing her that he understood her to her core—adventurous spirit, responsible mother, and all the special parts of her in between.

That night he went back to his apartment in base housing and started packing. By the end of the week, his truck was full and a small shipment had been picked up by movers. Without a single glance back at CFB Wainwright, he headed for home.

CHAPTER TWENTY-THREE

WHEN ZANDER SENT Faith a text message asking if she could get away from her desk for the day on an unseasonably warm December day, she was confused. He'd left for work two hours earlier without a whisper of any such plan. It was a bit early for a nooner, but sure, she could be flexible. She grinned and texted back, **Definitely. What do you want me to be wearing?**

She'd expected his answer to be one of his t-shirts, maybe, or nothing at all.

Warm layers and sturdy boots if you have them, runners if you don't was not the answer she wanted.

On the other hand, an entire day together? Even if she had to go out in the cold—not her forte—it sounded fun. They'd gone from long-distance dating to living together in the blink of an eye. The last three weeks had been a topsy-turvy period of adjustment, with Eric acting out and sometimes Faith acting out. Miriam and Zander were the calm, steady ones. Miriam even more so after she announced she was going to Florida in January with Bill, who apparently had a condominium in Clearwater.

It sounded lovely.

Faith hated the idea that her mother would be so far away. She also loved the idea of having the house just for the three of them.

It was the best and worst of times, and none of it was being spent alone with Zander, until everyone else went to sleep.

She grinned. Okay, maybe she didn't need a nooner. They had nearly-midnighters every single night. Often twice.

Poor Zander. She'd been insatiable since he'd moved home and he had to wake up early to make the commute to the armouries in Wiarton. Not that he ever complained —she was still processing the day that Eric had disappeared for far too long, and Zander was more than happy to help her drive her thoughts from her head every night. She pressed her hand to the love bite he'd left on her neck, where the tendon meets the shoulder. No, he didn't complain in the least.

He pulled up and hopped out, back in civvies. Jeans, a tight cable-knit sweater, and a buttoned-down plaid shirt sticking out from beneath that.

"You look kind of dressed up," she said as he opened the door.

He gave her a look of amusement.

"Well, you know, for you. For us." She'd just put on jeans and a hoodie over a long-sleeved cotton t-shirt. "Where are we going?"

"It's a surprise." He swayed closer, then pulled himself back as he glanced over her shoulder.

She laughed and shook her head. "Mom's out getting evergreen boughs to decorate the window sills."

"Oh, thank Christ." He swept her into his arms, his

hands going straight for her denim-covered butt as he hauled her hard against him.

His mouth crashed into hers, and she opened for him readily. She shared his hunger, and with his new job, they never got alone time in the daytime. There was something illicit about grinding against each other in the foyer.

But he had a surprise for her and she couldn't wait to find out what it was. She pulled away. "So is what I'm wearing okay?"

He gave her a heated look that made her toes curl.

"Should we go upstairs and—"

"No," he ground out. "I mean yes, later. I want to peel you out of every scrap of fabric. Later. Now...what you're wearing is perfect. Let's go before I change my mind."

He headed down the highway, almost as far as Pine Harbour, turning right into one of the provincial parks. He flashed a pass at the guard at the gate, but once they were inside the park perimeter, he turned away from the signed road that lead to the campsites, and headed down a bumpy, rutted lane Faith had never noticed on her previous visits to the park.

He grinned over at her as she barely contained her curiosity.

"Hey, I didn't say anything," she protested, returning his smile. Whatever they were doing, it felt fun. She hadn't had enough of that in her life, and that he brought it back so effortlessly made her chest all warm and muzzy feeling.

He just reached across the cab and looped his fingers through hers. A gentle squeeze was his only response.

The lane opened up into a parking lot, on the far side of which was a brown log cabin, much like all the other park buildings.

Hopping out, Zander grabbed a large duffle bag from

the bed of the truck, then jogged around to her side as she climbed out. "This is the training centre for the Search and Rescue teams. I thought you might like something they have here."

Hand in hand, they walked around the cabin. She gasped when they got to the other side and she found a climbing tower. It was quiet now, but she could almost hear the phantom slide of rope and the standard calls of climbers.

On belay. Belay on. Hold. Roping down. Her limbs all felt hot and her mouth was dry. "Climbing?"

He was quiet beside her for a moment, maybe letting her process it, then he squeezed her hand. "You trust me?"

"With everything," she whispered, leaning into him. She brushed her lips against his jaw, then gasped as he slid his hands between her legs—and quickly reached around her hip with the other and tugged, pulling a length of rope taut against her sex for a moment before sliding it carefully around one thigh.

Looking down, Faith's heart rate sped up. "A sling harness?"

"You'll be fine." His voiced purred as he looped the rope around her thighs, waist and hips, fashioning a perfectly fitted harness that had the neat side effect of turning her into a pile of goo.

"I know." Her voice shook, but not from fear. She inhaled roughly as he tested the tautness of the rope, sliding his hand between the loops and her body.

He tugged again, tightening it a bit further, then tied it off. His knuckles rubbed against her waist as he moved around her body and she swayed against him.

"Thank you," she whispered, and he stopped behind her, his breath warm against her hair. He swept her ponytail out of the way and kissed the back of her neck. Shivers raced up and down her spine.

Settling his hands on her waist, he brought his lips to her ear. "Look up," he said quietly. "See that? Anything is possible. You want to rappel? We'll find a tower for you to bound down."

She laughed. "Bounding is dangerous."

He mock-growled in her ear. "Just when I think you couldn't get any hotter, you go and spout rappelling safety at me." He kissed her neck before continuing. "This isn't a test of anything, babe. It's just fun. Do whatever you want. Or don't. Climb up there and chuck the rope at my head if you want. Okay?"

She nodded. She definitely wanted to do more than that. Every last nerve in her body was twitching at the memory of leaning out over the open air and stepping into nothingness.

"I asked Tom to help us," he continued, turning her so they were facing each other again. "Do you want him up top, or on the ground?"

If she could clone Zander and put him in both places, that would be her first choice. But since she had to pick... "I want you on the ground, guiding me. I can step off no problem."

"How long has it been?"

"Since before Eric was born. Six years, maybe?"

"Like riding a bike."

She wasn't so sure about that, but she was game to try.

Behind them, a cabin door slapped shut, and they turned to greet Tom.

He winked at her and Zander growled. She pinked up. "Thank you for helping me," she murmured.

"My pleasure," he said, his eyes twinkling.

"Don't flirt with my girlfriend."

"That's going to be hard," Tom said, stressing the last word like a teenage boy. "Considering I have to check her harness and get her hooked up to the ropes."

Zander pulled her close. "On second thought, maybe I should be up top with you."

She rolled her eyes. "And then I get to give my celebratory kiss to Tom at the end?"

He gave her a tap on the ass. "Good point. Up you go."

At the top of the climbing tower, Tom did all the work, and as soon as they were out of Zander's sight, he dropped the teasing flirting. Instead, he was the consummate professional, casually asking about her climbing history as he surreptitiously assessed her ability. When he was satisfied, he hooked her harness to the ropes with a rappelling device and tossed the ropes down to Zander.

"Minelli on belay," Zander called from below. He'd wrapped the trailing ends of the rope around his back and was grinning up at her.

Letting out a shaky breath she leaned back into the L-shaped position that she did in fact remember, muscle-memory kicking in, and with her heart in her throat, she took her first step down the wall with her brake-hand firmly in place.

Her head swam with nerves. She took another deep breath and closed her eyes. Legs straight. Full-sole contact at all times. Three, two, one... She extended her brake hand to the side, letting herself walk down the wall, descending a few feet. Then she brought her arm in, braking to a stop again.

"Okay?" Zander called up, and she nodded.

"Just testing it out!" She wouldn't stop again, and wouldn't hold the rope close to her side, because she didn't want to burn out her sling harness. Not after Zander did such a perfect rigging job to begin with—and because she was, above all else, safety conscious.

And she could still do this.

Her heart sang and she looked behind her, seeing where she was going. There was nothing worse than getting yelled at for almost running into something, or someone, because you weren't paying attention.

When she swung her braking arm wide again, she let herself race down the tower, and the ground was coming up fast, but then Zander must have run back a bit, braking the ropes for her, because she slowed right up. Her feet bounced on the ground, then she put her hands in the air and somehow managed to run backwards, right off the ropes. Oh yeah, she remembered all of this.

She whooped and jumped into Zander's arms, kissing his face all over. She nibbled on his jaw and sucked on his lower lip, and when Tom spoke behind them, she laughed and buried her face in Zander's neck.

"Definitely good that I stayed on the ground," he said in her ear.

"We going again?" Tom asked.

What kind of question was that?

"Hell yes," Faith said, her voice breathless and her heart pounding. She grabbed Zander's hand and looked deep into his eyes. "Thank you."

The love she saw shining back at her made her want to cry and laugh and jump in the air.

She was the luckiest woman in the entire world.

CHAPTER TWENTY-FOUR

CHRISTMAS with the Minellis was interesting. They all went to Mass on Christmas Eve, for one thing.

Faith had to give Eric a quick primer on faith and being respectful of other people's beliefs before they went, but he loved it and she found herself promising they'd come back.

And unlike every other Minelli get together, it wasn't loud. It was like there was a twenty-four moratorium on sibling teasing and mother-button-pushing.

Some of that might have been about the brand new baby in the midst. Olivia had given birth to a beautiful baby girl, Sophia Grace, at the end of November. Faith had gotten in a sweet snuggle before Mass, and so had Zander and Eric. They were all in love with her dusting of dark brown hair and her tiny cupid's bow mouth.

Faith tried hard not to listen to her ovaries when Zander stood up and started rocking Sophie when she fussed.

It was hard.

She distracted herself with wine and reminded herself

that pregnant women didn't get *that*. *But they get babies*, her ovaries protested.

After Mass, they drove home to Tobermory. Another new tradition was that Zander wanted each of them to open one present before they all tucked into bed. She'd fretted over what to get him for weeks—Christmas morning was no problem, because she could give him a bunch of presents that all connected into an awesome theme. But one gift? That was special and meaningful?

She wracked her brain for ideas. He had changed her life so much, breathed new life into her heart and soul. She wanted to give him something that promised she'd give back that positive energy ten-fold.

When she stumbled on the perfect idea, it came with its own set of complicating factors.

How to give it to him, for example.

Miriam started a kettle for hot chocolate as Eric bounced up and down the hallway, trying like mad to usher everyone into the living room. But Zander's special present wasn't under the tree—it was outside.

"Babe, can you get some wood from the back deck for the stove?" It was a shallow ruse, because the few times they used the wood stove, it quickly got so warm in the kitchen that Faith opened the windows.

Zander didn't notice. He grabbed his boots and out he went.

The silence stretched on for a few seconds, then he reappeared in the doorway, holding his brand new kayak.

"Merry Christmas," she said softly.

"I'm bringing it inside," he threatened, his eyes twinkling.

"Of course." She laughed as Eric tried to climb into it before it was even settled on the carpet in front of the tree.

Zander grabbed three presents from under the tree and handed them out before kissing Faith gently on the lips.

"Thank you," he said, cupping her cheek. Their gazes locked. She'd tried to say so much with the kayak. *Be adventurous. Look, two seats. First of many steps.* The look in his eyes said he understood. "Now it's your turn."

She wiped away a surprise tear and gestured at her mother and Eric. "You guys go first."

Zander had gotten them both books—a cookbook for Miriam, signed by the celebrity chef author, and *The Dangerous Book for Boys* for Eric, which made Faith whimper a worried Mom-sound, but Zander made Eric repeat the inscription after him.

FOR ERIC, **who has a wonderful, adventurous spirit— and who will never forget to remember to ask permission and stay safe. Love, Zander**

"REMEMBER, bud. There's a lot of fun to be had in life. And we only get to do it if Mommy's content and happy, right?"

"Right."

Zander pulled Eric into his lap and opened the book. "Here, read about slingshots while your mom opens her present."

Faith ran her fingers over the gift. It was something hard and flat inside the wrapping paper.

Inside she found a black leather case, and when she lifted the lid, she gasped at the sight of a silver charm bracelet. One charm hung from it—a silver quill that dangled delicately as she picked it up.

"Oh, Zander, it's gorgeous."

He kissed her cheek, then her mouth again. "I'm testing the jewellery waters," he whispered as she slipped it on her wrist.

"Good test," she whispered back.

Miriam made them all hot chocolate then, and they put out a tray for Santa and the reindeer in front of the cold wood stove. "Wouldn't want to burn Santa's toes anyway," Faith pointed out.

Once their mugs were empty, they all went to bed. Miriam to her room, Eric to his, and finally Faith and Zander to their room.

It was still the same as it had been when it was just her room. Other than an increased number of black t-shirts in the laundry basket and a second dresser squeezed along the far wall, he hadn't changed anything. But in six short weeks—or four long months, if she counted from the week they'd met—he'd imprinted himself everywhere.

She turned the lock as Zander started to strip out of his clothes. They had this routine now—she'd lock the door when they came to bed, and he'd make sure it was unlocked before they fell asleep. He always left the door cracked open for Eric to crawl in with them, which he rarely did, but it made Faith feel better knowing that option was there.

Silently she followed Zander's lead, getting all the way naked. She didn't bother with lingerie. After she hung up her bracelet in a place of honour on her jewellery tree, she crawled onto the bed and into Zander's arms.

He set a slow, exploratory pace, touching her all over but avoiding all the spots that would get her really revved up. She reached for his erection and he firmly removed her hand from the vicinity. "Let me just…" He ducked his head and drew the tip of one breast into his mouth.

She groaned at the tug, deep inside her.

"Yes." He grinned up at her. "Let me just make you do that a few times before you touch me tonight."

Cupping her breasts, he plumped them together and went back and forth until she was restless.

He slid his hands down her sides, shaping her waist and lifting her up to meet his wonderful, questing mouth that seemed intent on loving every inch of her tonight. He even rubbed his finger over her c-section scar as he settled between her legs. She squirmed, suddenly uncomfortable with his inspection, but his touch was gentle. Loving.

She still pulled away. A reflex that he calmly ignored as he chased her, gripping her hips firmly and pressing his lips to her lower belly. "Don't hide from me."

"I'm not hiding."

"There isn't an inch of your body that I don't love, woman."

"I know."

"Then what is it?"

She sighed. They never talked about Greg, and right before sex probably wasn't a good time to bring him up. "A conversation for another time, probably."

"There is nothing you can say that will make me want you less." He nuzzled the soft skin below her navel. "I might tell you that you're silly, though."

"On this point, I most definitely am." She ran her fingers through his dark hair and tried to refocus. "Thank you for my bracelet, again. It's beautiful."

"Like you."

"Stop." She laughed as he nipped at her hip, then returned to her scar. So they weren't avoiding it, after all.

"This is how you had Eric?"

She squirmed and nodded.

"Were you awake when he was born?"

Another nod.

"Tell me about it."

"Another time."

He nipped her skin again. "Now."

She sighed. Zander always got his way. And it was a wonderful memory. "It was pretty amazing, that moment when the doctor lifted him up over the surgical draping and my baby gave his first yell. He was all red and super mad."

"No kidding. He'd just been ripped from his beautiful mom."

"Enough talk about my kid," she whispered, but she didn't mean it. She loved that Eric was always a part of their conversations, that Zander loved her child as much as he loved her. "What's brought on all the questions, anyway?"

He traced his thumb lightly over the knotted tissue one more time before crawling up her body and turning them together on the bed. His arms pinned hers together, holding her right in front of his face. His very serious face. "Would you want more?"

"Babies?"

"Don't sound so shocked."

"You want babies?"

"Hell yeah. At least one. I've got the big kid. But I missed out on the sleeping baby on my chest while I watch football stage. I hear that's pretty good."

"It probably is."

He frowned at her, and she realized she'd said too much. Shit. There was a reason they never talked about her marriage. "Didn't he…"

She sighed. "He loved us in his own way. But he wasn't the type of guy to hold a baby for very long. He got up in the middle of the night and changed diapers, no problem. He was a good father. He researched first baby foods and mashed sweet potato."

Zander rolled onto his back and tucked her into his side. "Rafe was telling me tonight he's scared he's going to break little Sophie."

His endless capacity to see the best in people astounded her. "Yeah, maybe there was some of that."

"Is he the reason you're skittish about the scar?"

In for a penny… "We never reconnected after Eric was born. He'd seen me cut open, and it didn't heal perfectly, and…I was changed. Irrevocably." Zander took a deep breath and she pressed her hand against his chest. Turning so she could see his face, she gave him a soft smile. "You don't need to tell me…It's in the past. I need to let it go."

"You do."

"I know it's not an issue between us. You're so, so good to me in that regard."

"Then why are we talking about it?" He kissed her, like a stubborn bull with just one thing on his mind—if bulls were also annoyingly good at psychoanalysis and unfazed by discussions of first husbands.

"Because you see inside me."

"And why does that continue to surprise you, beautiful?"

"Okay, point taken."

"Do you trust me, Faith?" His mouth feathered against her jaw.

"With everything I am."

His breath warned her neck and that spot behind her

ear. His lips slicked over her skin, his tongue too, and suddenly talking seemed unnecessary.

"Zander..." she breathed.

"Sometimes I talk too much, too," he murmured as he tasted her collarbone. "Clearly I need to show you."

For the second time that night, his hands blazed the path that his mouth followed. First her breasts, then her belly, and finally he hooked one of her knees over his shoulder and pressed the other one wide.

She'd never get enough of the quietly erotic view of Zander's dark head between her legs.

Of the wet, determined swipe of his tongue along the seam of her sex, and the groan he always made when he discovered she was slick with want.

The feeling of complete worship as he licked her up and down, delving deeper once she started rocking.

No, she'd never get enough of Zander loving her. Tingly, precious heat skittered over her skin as he circled her clit with his tongue, coaxing it into a hard, swollen nub.

"Feel good?" His breath puffed against her skin— warm, moist, and shockingly intimate, even for the act, and she shuddered.

"So good," she whispered.

Flick.

"Ahhh," she cried out.

"Quiet." *Flick. Flick, flick, flick.*

She bucked against his face, wanting more contact than that torturous flutter of his tongue, but the begging roll of her hips only got her a quiet laugh as he twisted his face and pressed his mouth against the softness at the top of her thigh.

"Please?"

"Stay still."

"That's impossible!"

"Nothing's impossible." He said it so confidently, she believed him.

Taking a deep breath, she exhaled and closed her eyes. *Flick.* He paused. Maybe he was looking at her. She exhaled again. *Flick. Lick.* Okay, staying still got a reward. She could do it after all.

He squeezed the back of her thighs and tilted her bottom up, opening her even more as his questing tongue explored her folds. Deep inside, her arousal started to coil tight, twisting a bit more with each nerve-pulsing swipe. He hummed as he covered more of her with his mouth, an open-mouthed kiss to her entire sex that made her quiver and shake. It was all so good, so intense, and as he wound her up, she stopped being able to differentiate what he was doing. It was just feelings now.

Amazing, spiralling feelings.

Love and lust.

Primal possession.

Greed.

She laughed helplessly as he sucked on her clit and he pulled away with a growl.

"What's so funny?"

"I'm so greedy," she whispered. "I'll never get enough of you."

He slid a finger inside her, then another. She rocked hard against his palm and he added a third. "Good."

"I want you inside me."

"Then come for me, beautiful. Come for me and I'll be inside you before you come down from heaven." He lowered his head and swirled his tongue around her clit, once, twice, three times, matching the stroke of his fingers.

She slid one hand into his hair and pressed the other against the mattress, bracing herself as a tsunami of sensation unfurled from within. Her legs pulled up tight, then flopped wide, and even as the dark spots were clearing from the corners of her vision, Zander was all she could see—right above her.

Right inside her.

He wrapped his arms around her torso and lifted her boneless body off the bed, binding her to him as he took her hard and fast, spilling himself deep inside her.

Merry Christmas, her lust-drunk brain murmured as she held him close.

One of his hands tangled in her hair and he pressed his lips to her neck. Merry Christmas indeed.

CHAPTER TWENTY-FIVE

JANUARY BROUGHT a change of pace for everyone. Miriam was visiting her friend in Florida. Eric started skating lessons. Zander and Dean started their business plans in earnest, with both of them planning to be at it full-time by the fall.

And Faith was on deadline again. She'd warned him about it, but the last time she'd been finishing a book, he'd just left her and they were only talking once a day or so. Somehow he'd missed the fact that she literally holed herself up in her office every waking second that she wasn't being Mom.

He'd woken up at six that morning to a cold bed. He went downstairs and made coffee. He poured himself a cup and left it on the counter, because he'd be back in a minute to make breakfast. Back upstairs, he knocked on her office door.

"Mmmm."

He pushed the door open. She had a "Faith only" rule for her office that he respected most of the time, but when she hadn't slept much and he was bringing coffee, it was a pretty safe violation to make.

He quietly set the cup on the coaster to the left of her keyboard, then stood behind her chair until she sighed and looked up. "Sorry, did I wake you?"

He shook his head as he stroked his hands over her neck and shoulders, loosening up the tension there for a minute before he left her alone again. "Nope. Just woke up and wanted coffee. Thought I'd make you some too."

"Thank you." She tipped her face up to give him an absent-minded kiss. "Might finish today."

Miriam had warned him that she'd say that at least five or six days in a row before it was actually true. But then again, Faith's mother had scampered off to Florida after the Christmas holidays, leaving Zander to truly discover the craziness that was Writer Faith at her apex all on his own.

Not that he minded at all. She was unbelievably cute when she wandered into bed, all bleary-eyed and bonelessly exhausted. And that was balanced out by her S.O.S. text messages when she needed choreography help on the action scenes, which he never tired of helping with.

Same with the sex scenes.

Living with a writer had some definite perks.

When Eric woke up, Zander gave him a cup of milk and two small bowls, sugar and cinnamon.

"Thought today might be a good day to make that pie for your mom that we talked about," Zander said. "You mix those together while I cut the apples, okay?"

"There's dough, right? Can I roll that?"

"Sure thing, bud."

They worked well together, and Eric didn't complain too much when Zander reminded him that a good baker always did his dishes while the pie was in the oven. While that was baking, he cooked a dozen hard-boiled eggs and sautéed some mushrooms, garlic and green pepper.

The smells must have finally wafted under her office door, because just as the pie was coming out of the oven, he heard her pad into their bedroom and turn on the shower. Ten minutes later she strolled in wearing today's version of her writing uniform, yoga pants and a goofy t-shirt. This one had a picture of a T-Rex drinking from an oversized wine glass. **Wine-o-saur**. Cute.

"What on Earth are you guys making?"

"Pie," Eric proudly announced. "For you."

Faith's eyebrows shot up and she gave Zander an appraising look that made him flex his shoulders. "You baked this?"

"With some help from Eric, I did indeed. My mother taught us all how to bake. I've worn an apron and wielded a wooden spoon since before I could talk."

"Wow, I'm impressed." She narrowed her eyes. "And I'm wondering why we've always gone to Greta's for pie if you can make it?"

He pulled her close and kissed her nose. She knew why he liked taking her to Greta's. "I love you."

She grinned at him. "And I love apple pie."

"Argh," he cried, grabbing his chest before he winked at her. "That's why I made it for you. Love my pie, love me."

"Of course." She looped her arms around his neck. "I love you with all my heart. It's just that pie has this extra-special place in my heart."

"Oh yeah?" His pulse grew heavy. He knew this feeling. Anticipation. Fear that the anticipation might not be met.

But she'd proven to him over and over again that he had no reason to fear her commitment to him. Her loyalty.

Her love.

Even when she was terrified herself, she found a way to fight for them, and she always would. That's why he baked her this pie—to say, *we've had each other from the very first moment we met.*

And that's why he'd gone ring shopping.

His entire body warmed, a heady excitement flooding his limbs as his heart swelled in his chest.

"How long until pie?" Eric asked, totally uninterested in the fact his mom was being wooed.

"It has to cool," Zander said. "Let your mom have her breakfast first, and then we can have celebratory pie after that, deal?"

Eric gave him a thumbs up. "Deal. Can I go play?"

Zander and Faith nodded at the same time, which made her laugh.

She kissed his jaw once they were alone. "I meant what I said about the pie. I met the man of my dreams over a slice of pie. He taught me about katanas and sawed-off shotguns. He makes my kid breakfast and plays the big-bad enforcer on not eating sugar until at least second breakfast and preferably elevensies. And most impor-tantly, he taught me that life was for living."

He caught her lips with his own, kissing her until she was breathless. "And not for living alone anymore, right?"

She grinned. "Right."

"I've been thinking..." He cleared his throat. "I didn't say it quite right last time."

"What?"

"I love you."

"Oh, I like it anyway you say it." She winked at him

and he picked her up and swung her around. He needed a bit of space to do this right.

Setting her in the middle of the kitchen, he took a deep breath and looked her right in the eye. "I-way ove-lay ou-yay."

There. That pink-cheeked, lips-parted, talk-dirty-geek-to-me look. That's what he wanted. Her gaze softened to a sexy doe-eyed look that made him want to sweep her off to bed and keep whispering things in Pig Latin, and they'd get to that once her book was done and their kid was asleep for the night, but the next thing needed to be said here.

On bended knee.

She gasped and pressed one hand to her chest as he lowered himself to the floor. "Zander," she whispered. "You're crazy."

"Razy-cay or-fay ou-yay," he murmured back, taking her other hand. "O-say ou-yay ould-shay arry-may e-may."

"What?" Her brow pulled together as she tried to follow what he was saying. Maybe there was a limit to proposing in code.

"I'm crazy for you," he repeated, his voice unexpectedly full of emotions. Rough like sandpaper and catching on every third syllable. "So you should marry me."

"I got that." She pressed her lips together. "Really?"

Shit, was she going to say no?

"Yes, really." He pulled the ring out of his pocket and took her hand in his, holding the ring between the palms. Letting her feel it before she saw it. Settling her into the idea of becoming his wife. "Are you surprised?"

Her smile was tremulous, but wide. Shaky but bright. She shook her head. "No. And yes. I thought maybe...in the summer. But this is good. You should keep going with this." She grinned harder now, and her eyelashes glistened. Girls and their tears.

He bowed his head and pressed his lips to her hand, resting on top of his. "Last week I took Eric to Greta's. That day when I picked him up from school and we came back with muffins? We sat and had some apple pie then."

"That's why he wasn't hungry for dinner," she whispered.

"It was worth it, I promise."

"Okay," she breathed.

"We talked about you and me, and me and him, and you and him. We talked about a lot of things, and we agreed that we're already a family, but it would be real nice if that was official. If some time maybe in the spring or summer, we could put on clothes that aren't sweatpants and invite our friends and family to watch us make some promises to each other."

"Like what?" The tears were falling freely now. He'd anticipated this, because his Faith was a crier. She was tough as nails, but there wasn't a bone in her body that didn't feel, big time. He grabbed the tissue box from the counter and passed it over before continuing.

"I promise to love you forever. To take care of our family and protect it to the best of my ability. To bring you coffee in the morning and rub your feet late at night."

"Those sound good."

He kissed her hand again. "I'll do those things anyway, you know. But I would be honoured—no, that's not strong enough. It would make me the proudest man on the planet to marry you, Faith Davidson. To wrap you in my arms and kiss you in front of the world, and say, this is my wife.

She's the other half of my soul and the mother of my children."

"Children?"

"Eric said something about brothers. It wasn't super clear, he had a mouthful of pie."

"Oh, wow." She bit her lip and sniffled again.

"Is that oh, wow, yes, or oh, wow, you'll need to try harder to convince me?"

She laughed and tugged her hand free, curving her fingers around his hand, revealing the ring in the centre of his palm. He was pretty proud of it. One big-ass diamond in the middle, surrounded by a circle of tiny diamonds, one of which had been replaced with an opal, Eric's birth month gemstone. "That's an oh, wow, yes, you beautiful man."

He hopped to his feet and slid the ring onto her left hand before picking her up and sitting her on the kitchen counter. "My fiancée. I like the sound of that."

"If I finish this book today, maybe we could find a sitter for Eric tonight and go out for dinner to celebrate." She kissed the corner of his mouth and wrapped her legs around his waist. He liked the way she thought, but he knew better.

"Babe, you're not finishing that book until at least Monday, according to the Rules of Miriam."

"Rules?"

"She says you will say that a book is almost done at least five days in a row before it's actually done."

Faith groaned and dropped her head to his shoulder. "Crap. That does sound like me. Love me anyway?"

There was no anyway about it. He cupped her face and hovered his mouth over hers. "Love you because of that, my genius bride. Never doubt that for a second."

EPILOGUE

WHEN CANADA DAY DAWNED, hot and muggy already because summer had decided to come early to the peninsula, Faith woke up in a rare state—alone in bed.

Zander had left a note, however. **Gone kayaking before it gets too hot. You're cute when you refuse to wake up.**

She hadn't even noticed he'd left. A familiar nervous wiggle teased in her gut, but she just pressed a hand there and told herself to get over it. Kayaking was pretty benign as far as water sports went, and Zander would be wearing a life jacket. She closed her eyes and had a weak laugh at her own expense. Man, she was a spoilsport.

Getting out of bed, she yawned, then peered out the window. No sign of him in the harbour, and his truck was in the drive, so he hadn't gone very far. Maybe he'd paddled around the tip of the peninsula to the Georgian Bay side.

She'd put on coffee and get breakfast ready for when he returned.

As she opened her bedroom door, Eric called out. "Morning, Mom."

She stopped in his doorway. He'd had a growth spurt over the spring and now looked big for five-and-a-half. "When did you grow up?"

He grinned at her and rolled onto his side, his Transformers pyjamas riding up his skinny middle. Not that grown up, maybe. "While I was sleeping."

"Happy Canada Day. Want strawberries for breakfast?"

"Yeah!" He leapt out of bed with an enthusiasm he must have learned from Zander, because he didn't get it from her. Or maybe it was genetic. Greg had been a morning person.

She reached and pulled him in for a hug as he tried to sprint past her. "Hang on, mister."

"What?" He hugged her back, hurriedly.

"You just looked like your dad a lot there." She leaned over and kissed his head. "He'd be so proud of you."

This time his smile was gentler. They didn't talk about Greg enough. Eric didn't remember him, and Zander was the only father her son would ever know. But he knew that she got a little sad every time they talked about it, and even though he was only five, he was pretty in tune with her feelings—more so than ever after his disappearing adventure.

"Okay, strawberries."

"And whipped cream," Eric suggested, eyes gleaming.

"Nope. Yogurt."

"Boo."

"Zander's favourite."

"Yay!"

She laughed. This part was easy, at least.

In the kitchen, she washed and sliced strawberries

they'd picked the day before. They went into a bowl on the counter. Another bowl held a nut and seed granola that Zander loved, and beside that she put the tub of plain yogurt. A red and white breakfast for their national holiday. Fitting for her now retired soldier, who after the summer holidays was starting a new career as a private security consultant.

A fancy word for bodyguard, she teased him, but in the next breath she always told him how proud she was.

A quick double knock at the front door was the only warning they got before her mother sailed in. "Morning, everyone!"

"Hi, Mom."

Miriam had moved out in June, to a small house that backed onto the golf course just outside of town. At some point when Faith hadn't been paying attention, her quiet, hippie mother had taken up the yuppiest of all the yuppy sports and apparently loved it.

They didn't talk about how her moving to her own house allowed them both to have more...active...social lives. There were some conversations mothers and daughters didn't need to have in detail.

"Grandma!" Eric ran to the front hall and dragged her back to the kitchen. "We're having strawberries for breakfast."

"Very appropriate. Listen, sweet pea, I was wondering if you wanted to come with me to the Teddy Bear Picnic at the park before you go to the barbeque in Pine Harbour?"

Faith looked up in surprise. "Aren't you coming with us this afternoon?"

Miriam blushed. "Bill asked me to watch the fireworks here with him."

Ah. Faith grinned. "Got it."

"Grandma, come upstairs and help me choose which bear to take," Eric said, tugging again on her arm.

Faith opened her mouth to remind him of his manners, but the duo was already skipping away.

A gentle thump against the side of the house told her Zander was back. She slid the screen door open and happily took in an eyeful. He was wearing board shorts and nothing else. They rode low on his hips and clung to his thighs, and she was suddenly very thankful for the Teddy Bear picnic.

"Good morning," she murmured, smiling as he glanced up and met her interested stare with a heated one of his own.

He grinned and prowled toward her, pulling her tight against him even as she mock-shrieked about him being all wet.

"Getting you wet is my daily mission, babe."

"My mom is here."

He groaned. "Okay."

"And she's taking Eric out in a bit."

And the grin was back.

"You know, that smile is killer."

He winked at her. "Took you long enough to notice."

"What does that mean?"

"Nothing." He kissed her cheek. "Coffee on?"

"Yep."

She watched him, little glances here and there as they ate breakfast. Counted her blessings as he stretched out on the couch and read a book with Eric before her son—their son—headed out with a stuffed animal friend for a holiday picnic.

And when she finally climbed into Zander's lap, she decided it was her turn to make a proposition.

"I have a secret," she whispered as he palmed her ass.

"Are you pregnant?" he asked, nuzzling her neck.

"Not yet." They'd only been trying for a few months. "But it's kind of related."

"Yeah?" He wasn't listening. He had his hands up her shirt and had his hands full of her breasts. She almost gave up the conversation when his thumbs rolled over her nipples.

She forced herself to concentrate. "I want to get married."

"We are getting married."

"Next week."

His thumbs skittered off her nipples, sending a last jolt of desire down her spine as he sat up a little straighter and dropped his hands to her hips. "Wait, back up. I'm paying attention now."

"I know we've put a couple of deposits down..."

He shook his head. "The way my siblings are dropping like flies, I'm sure Tom will be able to use our wedding date if we need him to." His keen brown gaze, suddenly serious, searched her face. "You want to get married soon?"

She nodded. "I went to see the lawyer yesterday, about a literary trust for Eric, and I mentioned that you want to formally adopt him. He said it would be easier once we're married."

"Ah." He brought one hand up to her face, brushing her cheek with his knuckles before settling his palm at the nape of her neck. "I don't want you to sacrifice the wedding you want just for that."

She shook her head. "It wouldn't be any kind of sacrifice. What I want is to be your wife. I want you to be Eric's father, officially. I want that…tomorrow. No more waiting."

"Thank God." Now he leaned in and kissed her lips. "Yes, let's do that. Tomorrow."

"Should we tell anyone? Your mother—"

"—Is getting another grandkid out of the deal."

"My mother?"

"Won't mind a bit…and we'll work on getting her another grandkid, too." He winked at her as she coloured. "Faith, I'm going to be thirty-eight this year. I'm two decades past the point of needing my parents around for major life decisions. We don't need to tell anyone, we can even keep the big fancy wedding date if you want to have the party again, but I don't want to wait another day to make it official that you two are my family. My world. I want to adopt Eric. I want to call you my wife. I want to be your rock, no doubt about it."

She wrapped her arms around his neck. "You already are."

— —

FIVE HOURS LATER, Zander watched Faith saunter away from him at the Pine Harbour Canada Day Barbeque. She'd just given him a hug and whispered another idea in his ear for celebrating their impending elopement.

She was enjoying this way too much.

So was he.

Maybe he could convince her to wear those cut-off jean shorts to the courthouse.

The next set of arms to wrap around his neck belonged to the other love of his life—his kid. He swung his head out of the way just in time as Eric's heavy little noggin came careening in to ask for something. "Can I have ice cream?"

He laughed. "Did your mom say no?"

Hesitation gave all the answer they both needed. "Maybe."

Zander set his beer on the ground. He reached over his head and hauled the boisterous five-year-old onto his lap. The camp chair he was sitting on creaked in protest, but he braced his feet on the ground. He tickled Eric until the boy shrieked that he was sorry, then he pulled him in close for a hug. "Don't play me, bud."

"Sorry."

"There's watermelon?"

"Okay."

"Let's go get some together."

As soon as Zander stood up, Eric wiggled his legs and reached for the ground and was off, sprinting toward the food tables. He followed slowly, watching his boy run. Maybe they should start doing some trail running in the fall, start prepping him for cross-country. He had a natural athleticism that Zander wanted to foster, but only in ways that Faith would be okay with—nothing too dangerous.

He did a slow circle, looking for her, once they got their fruit. He found her talking to Olivia Minelli—and in Faith's arms was Olivia's seven-month-old daughter, Sophia. The baby kept grabbing at the loose strands of Faith's hair, tumbling out of her ponytail as usual, and Faith just leaned in, pressing absent-minded kisses to the baby's forehead, letting the kid play all she wanted.

Eric bumped into his leg, and Zander dropped his

hand to the boy's shoulder. Hopefully soon she'd have a baby of their own, a little brother or sister for Eric, in her arms.

"Zander?" He glanced over his shoulder and found Hope Creswell smiling at him. "Could I have a minute?"

He pointed Eric toward his mom and nodded at Hope. "Of course."

"It's a professional inquiry, and I know it's a holiday, but…"

"Nah, it's fine. Shoot."

She gave him a nervous smile. "It's a bit of a long story, but the short version is I need a security team that I know I can trust. It's not for me, exactly, but I've got a little problem."

"Okay." He shrugged. "We're not officially open for business yet, but I can certainly help you out. What's the issue?"

"Not what. Who." She screwed up her face, then let out a frustrated sigh. "My best friend in the entire world is hiding at my house right now. She showed up three days ago and swore me to secrecy, so I'm letting her hang there, because that's what best friends do. She's like a sister to me."

"Sounds about right. Got any idea why she's hiding?"

She shook her head. "No. But her manager called me, looking for her. She's got a show in Washington, D.C. in three days, and I don't think she plans to be there."

Three days after Canada Day was Independence Day in the United States. "A show?"

"She's a singer."

"Who happens to be performing in the nation's capital city on July 4th?"

"Yeah." She gave him an innocent, no-big-deal look.

"Hope…" He sank his teeth into his upper lip. He was going to need to work on this angle of the business, for sure. "Are you asking me to help force a superstar onto a plane and get her ass to a nationally televised concert?"

She smiled brightly, like she was relieved that he got it. "As a matter of fact, I am."

And so it begins. He took a deep breath and searched the crowd for Dean. He found *his* best friend sitting in the bed of a pick-up truck, talking to Rafe. "Well, I'm otherwise engaged tomorrow, but I think I've got the man for the job."

THE END

ACKNOWLEDGEMENTS

aka The People Who Make Up My Village

As all my books have been lately, I have to start by thanking my fellow writers in Chatzy, because not only did I plough through the first draft of this book in chat, but then I revised it significantly there as well. They got a *lot* of Zander and Faith. And especially the parts about Faith as a writer—she isn't me, but she is an amalgam of the beautiful women that I have the joy to write with day in, day out. This book isn't particularly autobiographical, I promise, except for maybe the online debates when Faith should have been writing. I recognize myself in that!

And since we're talking about borrowed identities: to the lovely residents of the Bruce Peninsula, especially the very real town of Tobermory, I apologize for any liberties I took in manipulating the geography of your beautiful region to suit my story's purposes.

Thanks also to:

The Wardham Ambassadors, my Facebook reader group, who helped by naming Rafe and Olivia's daughter, pointing out a better name for Zander's book, and just by asking for this book as soon as Ryan's released. Really, thank you for that—writers never tire of hearing that you want more of their work.

Kristi Yanta, who did the first editorial pass on this book and thanks to her, the last quarter of this book is different and better. She saw Faith and Zander so clearly and pushed me to dig deeper where it counted. I'm so lucky to have her trusted eyes be the first to see Pine Harbour books.

Shelly Small and Dana Waganer for tightening my prose and catching the tiny mistakes.

Lynn, Elizabeth, Jaycee, Jessica, Marlene, Bev and a few other ARC readers who caught little inconsistencies here and there—I appreciate that you took the time to send me a note!

Lori, Pine Harbour's biggest fan, for keeping track of the cast of secondary characters better than I can, and helping me with all of the admin tasks so I can focus on writing.

Lee Brice for all of his ballads, but particularly "I Don't Dance" and "Stealing Innocence".

And finally to my family, who are the most understanding and supportive crew a girl could ever want.

Thank you all.

Zoe

ABOUT THE AUTHOR

Zoe York lives in London, Ontario with her young family. She's currently chugging Americanos, wiping sticky fingers, and dreaming of heroes in and out of uniform.

www.zoeyork.com

Made in the USA
Coppell, TX
29 July 2023

19728963R00184